Sons of Heaven

Sons of Heaven

A Novel

Terrence Cheng

To order additional copies of this book, contact:
Xlibris Corporation
1-888-795-4274
www.Xlibris.com
Orders@Xlibris.com
39094

Dedicated to my parents, and to the memory of my grandparents, for their courage, faith, and love.

Praise for SONS OF HEAVEN

"This remarkably structured and textured debut epic seeks to attach a face to the mysterious man who, by stepping in front of the rolling army tanks, became the most recognizable symbol of the massacres. Cheng succeeds in his endeavor . . . a multifaceted and sophisticated portrait of the Chinese people is rendered. This is a rare find."

—*Publishers Weekly* (starred review)

[A] superb first novel . . . *Sons of Heaven* succeeds . . . because its focus is relentlessly personal, and moral."

—*San Francisco Chronicle*

"Filled with carefully measured doses of history, romance, and adventure . . . Stylistically and thematically daring."

—*Miami Herald*

"Terrence Cheng enters history in such a profound and provocative way—his retelling of the events in and around Tiananmen Square is subversive, lyrical, and full of control. Cheng is a painter and a cinematographer and a wordsmith all at once."

—Colum McCann, author of *Dancer*

"[T]his brave, insightful and gifted writer . . . seeks to compassionately understand these fictional (and actual but fictionalized) characters' backgrounds, motivations and uncertainties to help readers grasp the moment from divergent perspectives."

—*Eugene Weekly*

"Compelling . . . powerful . . . a first-class thriller set on the stage of world history that is hard to put down."

—*Pittsburgh Post-Gazette*

"Cinematic . . . powerful."

—*Atlanta Journal-Constitution*

"Who cannot think of those days in June 1989 without recalling the image of an unknown protester facing off against a tank . . . thanks to Terrence Cheng's *Sons of Heaven*, we shall have an enduring reminder."

—*Denver Post*

"An irresistible peek . . . into the human face of modern China."

—*USA Today*

"The writing here is terse and often beautiful . . . this clash between polemic-heavy brothers glows with truth."

—*Los Angeles Times*

"[An] imaginative and minutely researched chronicle of the Tiananmen Square Massacre."

—*New York Magazine*

"Cheng paints a tragic picture of what happens when brothers are caught at opposite ends of the spectrum in a place where clear-cut loyalties are not a choice but a requirement. Packed with emotion and desperation, Cheng's novel speaks for a man who needed a voice."

—*Booklist*

"There is much grace, drama, and insight to be enjoyed; Cheng is particularly effective in depicting the perilous state of mind experienced by risk taking. A ripping good story about a headline event of great power and resonance."

—*Library Journal*

"A vivid and imaginative fictional recounting of the events of Tiananmen Square in June 1989 . . . a compelling read . . . in a brisk style with plenty of local color."

—*Kirkus Reviews*

"Cheng deftly brings to life an icon: the young revolutionary who stared down Red Army tanks in Tiananmen Square. *Sons of Heaven* delves into the heart of this brave individual (who has never been identified by Chinese authorities) but also surprises us by supposing and exposing the mind of another revolutionary, the leader Deng Xiaoping, whose decision to turn guns on his own people marked a tragic end to China's pro-democracy movement. This balanced and daring recreation of events leading to the June 4th massacre illuminates its quintessentially human element, the personal that lies at the heart of the political."

—Pang-Mei Natasha Chang, author of *Bound Feet and Western Dress*

"The whole world held its breath for the man who defied the column of tanks during the Tiananmen Square revolt, wondering who he was, how he had the nerve to do what he did. Terrence Cheng's *Sons of Heaven* finds that mysterious man for us in a wonderfully accessible, first novel, ringing with history. From a shocked Deng Xiaoping to the ordinary people swept up in those powerful events, Cheng's characters stand before us with compassionate, rich clarity."

—John Balaban, author of *Spring Essence: The Poetry of Ho Xuan Huong*

"What is particularly distinctive about *Sons of Heaven* is a style that is clear, decisive [and] straight ahead. Cheng uses this style to keep in tight focus the seething power of the situation he describes and examines. The tension between what is happening in the tortured life of China and the life of the individuals who are that China and the style of the telling is delicious. *Sons of Heaven* will be fittingly admired because it manages to engage the human predicament at many profoundly complex levels even as it reads like an adventure story."

—Barry Targan, author of *The Ark of the Marindor*

"This first novel horrifies, refines, instructs, in all the most meaningful ways. Terrence Cheng treats modern Chinese history with the delicacy and authority of someone who has masterfully re-imagined life inside two of the great civil strifes that tore into the largest population center of the twentieth century. From the brutality of political strife—in a narrative that embraces both the 1966 uprising under Mao Zedong, and the frenzied days of Tiananmen Square in June 1989—to the tender familial rifts and bonds between opposing brothers, *Sons of Heaven* weaves between terror and tenderness. Cheng's unflinching narrative, told in multiple voices, and laced with the dreams of Deng Xiaoping, delivers the despair and hope of modern China to the center of our lives."

—Susan Bergman, author of *Anonymity*

"*Sons of Heaven* is a sweeping panorama of recent Chinese history that in detail and breadth of compassion evokes the great nineteenth century fictional narratives. Imagine *Bonfire of the Vanities* being about Beijing and the bewildering days when China seemed about to explode; think of Paris and Balzac's camera eye seeking out the dramas of the great city and creating breathing beings behind what otherwise becomes stale historical documentation. *Sons of Heaven* is a performance of rare storytelling and intellectual perception and is the next thing to being there as China changed forever."

—Lester Goran, author of *Tales from the Irish Club*

Author's Note

It was only when my grandparents started to die that I began to think about China and my family's story; before I lost them history never concerned me. First it was my grandfather on my mother's side; he was ninety-three. As a young man he had fought the Japanese on the Mainland during World War II as a member of the Kuomingtang. My mother used to tell me about my grandfather's scars, which was why he never took off his shirt. She was right: I had never seen him without something covering his back. It's a miracle he even survived, my mother said.

A few years later my grandmother died, my mother's mother, at the age of eighty-seven. She had been a member of the Kuomingtang in Taiwan, as she was in Beijing before Mao and the Communists came to power. My grandparents and my mother fled Beijing for Taiwan, along with Chiang Kai-Shek and the Kuomingtang, in 1949. My mother was six months old. She has never been back to Beijing. She will not say it, but it's because she believes in ghosts.

By the time I graduated from college and went to grad school, all my grandparents were dead and I had time to think about what they went through, time to hear the stories told by my parents about their struggle and the sacrifices that had been made by three generations of our family to get us to this point: here, in America, New York. It did not make perfect sense to me but names like Chiang Kai-Shek, Mao Zedong, and Deng Xiaoping were somehow mixed through my own family's history.

It was around the time my grandfather was dying that the student protests in Tiananmen Square were going on. Summer 1989, I remember watching on television the flames in the streets and limp bloody bodies being carried away. Soldiers marching through the darkness, shooting. Crying young men and women, pleading. This was not a movie. All the faces Chinese. But the image that continues to haunt me is of a young man, who, in broad daylight, walked in front of a line of tanks and stopped. The tanks, I thought, would run him over, but they didn't. They tried to go around him but he kept jumping in the way. He just would not move until people from the side of the street came and dragged him away. No one knew who he was, or what happened to him. To this day, no one does.

He amazed me: his power, his pride, and his fear. Even from a distance and only being able to see his back, I knew he was afraid. He was afraid and he was angry and he was proud and willing to die for his beliefs. What could make a man do what he had done? What had pushed him to the point, what kind of emotions make you so stupid and so brave and able to transcend in such a miraculous yet mortal way? The whole world was fascinated, but as the years went by that image and the cries over the Tiananmen Massacre (as it is known in the West; it is the Tiananmen 'Incident' in China) dissipated.

But the young man and those tanks never left me, the wonder about how and what and why.

Chinese history is a minefield so fully exploded you can barely make out that it has been detonated. Only if you look closely enough can you see the shapes of the craters, the depth of the scars. I wrote this book because Deng Xiaoping haunted me: his personal struggle and character, what influenced his decisions those fateful days before and after Tiananmen. How history was inextricably his life. The world blamed Deng for Tiananmen, but what was the whole story? The real story? The man and the tanks haunted me because he had no history. So I would attempt to create one for him. And at the same time understand my own family's history; all of it as one.

This book is not a political book, nor is it meant to be. It is about two brothers, two families, the braided history of peasants and soldiers, politicians, gods. It is about boys growing up learning to be men, and the spirit that grants us the will to survive.

I traveled to Beijing in 1999. I smelled the air, walked the streets, and ate the food. It was the place of my grandparents' birth, my parents' birth, and they loved it, as I did now. I visited the house my grandparents used to own, the house where my mother was born. I saw as much as I could possibly see. Everywhere I looked for ghosts. I found none, but could feel them.

I would be honored if I could believe that in these pages all the ghosts might live at least for a moment. Until they find a new voice, a new place, and decide it is time to move on.

PROLOGUE

June 3, 1989

They had been waiting for many days now and an itch had built up in the men. He could feel it, smell it even, a stench like a sickness. Maybe it was the stink of the outhouses coming from a neighboring village, the carcass of a runaway dog or donkey rotting in the bush. But no, these things he would have been accustomed to, would not have bothered him.

It rained like the heavens were testing them. The water hammered down on them an entire day and night, the tents of the makeshift camp leaking among the armored personnel carriers and tanks and trucks. Rivers of mud and no one knew what to say, no one wanted to move. Water like a silver wall, trapping them. Still the days were very hot. They did not know what to do. After morning drills they smoked and played cards and dominoes and slept.

Lu stepped out of his tent and looked up at the rain, he, like the others, in a nervous state of rest. Cigarette smoke filtered through the openings of the other tents, but there was no music, no radios allowed, no joking or laughing could be heard. Beyond the hills and into the swell of mountains and countryside the sky was gray and black. Thunderclaps ripped and crackled but no lightning was visible through the dense quilt of clouds. They waited for word, for the exact specifications of the mission.

When he thought he could no longer feel it, a slight electric twitch tingled inside the lower bones of his left leg. He touched the ridge on the right side of his face, the scar he believed was tingling too.

He was twenty-seven years old and had been in the army for nine years, longer than any of the other men in his platoon, maybe his entire division, including Platoon Leader Ji. Still, he was just an infantryman, a common soldier. Except for the captains and colonels, he was by far the oldest. Maybe this would be the opportunity he had been waiting for, to wipe out all the demerits that had held him back and made him a joke—though a feared one—among the other men. The soldier that could not rise because he was too quick with his fists, his mouth. He was a hard man dedicated to serving his country and people. He deserved more than this.

The peasants in the provinces were always glad to see them, the soldiers, arbiters of justice and strength. But this would not be a mission to rebuild peasant villages and dams after a great flood. Live bullets were lodged in his rifle and for the first time in his career he believed he would use them the way they were meant to be used. Combat, Platoon Leader Ji had told them. There would be no cheering crowd, and maybe that was what he felt now, the metallic taste of battle rage pent up. Maybe it was the unknowing because he could not prepare properly.

Soldiers, he thought. We have to be prepared.

Now they camped in the countryside northwest of Beijing, just beyond the Fragrant Hills, where Mao Zedong used to spend summers lying in the cool palaces and the hot springs, swimming in the lakes. It was the place where Generalissimo Chiang Kai-shek used to live during the warm months, but after the revolution it became Mao's; now it was just a tourist spot, a reminder of how the old leaders spent their leisure time. In these things Lu did not have much interest. Soldiers were fighters, and this was pedestrian entertainment, if not rightist, counterrevolutionary. He wondered if it was wise to camp so close to a place so pregnable. He thought to say something to Platoon Leader Ji, then thought better of it. Do not raise questions out of line.

The rain lessened. In the coming dark of evening he stepped over the puddles around the tents and looked for civilians, wondered if anyone might have spotted them. They had lain covert and undetected almost a week now. If they were spotted, what consequence would it have on their mission? What was their mission?

It was rumored among the men that the mission had been declared by Comrade Deng Xiaoping himself. This could be their chance to become heroes, earn their places in history. The moment he had been destined for since he first truly understood who Mao Zedong was; what it meant to be a Red Guard and to read and carry Mao's *Little Red Book;* what it took to be a soldier in the People's Liberation Army. The moment he had been waiting for his entire life.

*   *   *

He was napping when Platoon Leader Ji burst into the tent shouting, "Get ready, we're moving out!" Lu was up and the men moved fast, how quick they were to tear down the minicamp, sweep up, and move out. The division assembled in the mud, stood in fine order breathing the heavy air. Their commander stepped out before them. He shouted as he read lines from a piece of paper.

"We have been ordered by the Central Committee and the Central Military Commission to enter Beijing and quell a riot that has nearly devoured the city. The beloved heart of Beijing, Tiananmen Square, has been overtaken by hooligans and conspirators who look to overthrow the Chinese Communist Party and destroy any semblance of order and peace. It has been decided by the Central Committee, after trying to negotiate and reason with these thugs, that it is only by use of the military that order can be restored. We are directed to use any means necessary to retake Tiananmen Square.

"I repeat," the commander said, "recover the square at any cost. This is a dangerous and important mission we have been given sole responsibility for. We cannot fail."

Lu watched the commander standing before the troops. He was an older man, close to fifty, thick-faced and with a bullish neck. His eyes were steady and hard, his voice strong and clear. Lu felt a faint fluttering in his chest, nerves crackling up and down his back and legs. All around them twilight bled into darkness. The soldiers chanted, "IF I CAN WAKE UP THE PEOPLE WITH MY BLOOD, THEN I AM WILLING TO LET MY BLOOD RUN DRY. IF BY GIVING MY LIFE THE PEOPLE WILL AWAKE, THEN HAPPILY I GO TO MY DEATH."

A moment of silence as the voices drifted off into the damp heat of the mountains.

*   *   *

The platoon rumbled toward the city and Lu was glad to be wedged deep inside the cluster of men and rifles and gear in the truck. He was sweating. So humid, no wind, he thought the skies might crack and rain would pour forth once again. He did not want to look outside, did not want to see the scenery or people they might pass. He tried to focus, could hear the tanks and armored personnel carriers in front of and behind them. The gentle rumble of their engines and treads created a rhythm he found soothing, sucked the thoughts out of his mind.

He had not been back to Beijing to visit his grandparents in more than two years. His brother had still been away at college then, living in America, though Lu knew he was back now. A few times he could have taken leave to visit them all, but he didn't.

When Lu was a boy he imagined his first live battle. It would be against the Russians on the northern border, or maybe the Japanese would invade again. A massive raid of Tibet or India, or even the United States. But they were entering Beijing, his childhood home. Lu tried not to think. He heard the commander's voice: "Do not be tricked . . . recover the square at any cost." They would not be wearing different colored uniforms, waving a foreigner's flag, carrying weapons and wearing helmets unlike theirs. They would not be brown or pale skinned, have round eyes and hair of yellow or brown or red.

But they were enemies, conspirators nonetheless.

He felt guilty for having not written a letter to his grandparents in many months, though he had received many from his grandmother, telling him about his little brother's return to Beijing: how his little brother had gotten much bigger and stronger eating so well over there, exercising and living a healthy life. But he was being difficult now, and his grandmother was not sure why. Different from in the letters she used to send Lu, that detailed his little brother's exciting life in America: the classes he was taking, the friends he was meeting. His little brother, the overseas star, could do no wrong. Now he was "being difficult."

They rode for over two hours in a hard silence, except for the roar of the column moving over the roads. What might people along the streets think if they saw this procession of trucks and tanks rumbling toward the city? What did they know? Through the back of the truck the light of the evening disappeared. He slowly touched his finger to his face, a habit he had developed since the accident as a child, but he stopped before anyone noticed, did not want to draw attention to himself. Someone began to whistle and was ordered to stop. All of them wound up like new machines, unoiled, creaky and tight.

Platoon Leader Ji said, "Remember what the commander told us. Stay focused."

Off the highway and over a bridge, then the column slowed, chugged to a near halt. As they entered the city Platoon Leader Ji hopped out of the truck and gathered with the other platoon leaders. Then he came back to the truck and called out five men, Lu one of them. They walked alongside the truck as the column continued. Before them Lu could see the hulking mass of the city, his old home, the way the buildings blurred behind the misty haze of summer and the pulsing lights of the high-rise buildings, the emanating heat of cars and bodies and the congestion of so much life. The road they moved on now had been cordoned off, their path unobstructed. With no cars or bicycles in the street, he felt out of place, their march toward Tiananmen dark and distended.

Two big buses, noses touching, a wall of empty metal blocking the road; rebel roadblocks, and they were still two or three miles from the heart of the city. The trucks pulled aside. A tank rumbled through and smashed into the point of the buses touching nose to nose, and broke them open like a joint. Two, three more smashing turns and the tank was through and the buses were cleared. They moved quickly now, as if the sound of metal crunching and the grind of the tank engine and breaking glass had invigorated them, heated up their blood.

The streets were empty, as if the city had been evacuated, the silence huge around them. Lu could not remember ever walking through any part of Beijing and not having some kind of noise in his ear, the physical hum and presence. The biggest, most populated city in the world, and even the fireflies seemed to have disappeared. The air was cloying; he wiped his face with his sleeve. Then there were bodies far ahead, a small cluster at first, hiding behind a parked car. They came out and saw the tanks and trucks and soldiers, and for an instant they stood awestruck, wondering. Then they ran and Lu raised his rifle and Platoon Leader Ji pushed the muzzle back down.

"Wait," said the platoon leader. "Wait for the enemy."

Lu stared back blankly, then nodded.

More trucks and cars blocked the roads, burned out by riot and fire, garbage and waste strewn about. The tanks bashed through the roadblocks and they trudged on as if nothing had been there at all. It was past eight o'clock and Lu could feel in his gut a hunger and pain like cramping, a visceral buzz in his brain. He was sweating from marching alongside the truck, they all were, their steps hard and clopping. A line of garbage cans and boxes had been set afire, and over this thin wall of defense the soldiers stepped and the vehicles overran. Around him stood the tall buildings and storefronts, the darkened windows of shops that sold sweets or fixed bicycles and had no signs, that only neighborhood and common patrons would know to enter. He could hear now the sounds of people though he could see none, feel and sense their beings as if aligned together in some inextricable fate.

"Wait," said Platoon Leader Ji. "Wait for the enemy."

The heat made Lu dizzy. His stomach tightened and wrenched. His left leg was hurting again, pulsing. A rock clanged off one of the trucks and they did not know where it came from. Then he saw a small band of young men down the road, close enough so Lu could see that two of them were wearing glasses and the others were short and wiry and wearing white shirts, rags tied around their faces. Bottles and stones landed harmlessly before them and Lu heard the shouts, "THE PEOPLE'S ARMY DOES NOT ATTACK THE PEOPLE!" Lu raised his rifle and fired, watched as two men in the distance fell. They lay in the street for a split second before a cluster formed around them and carried them off limp-limbed and dragging, vanishing into the darkness and back alleys. No one chased them.

His first hits, he had never shot a man before. He thought he would feel different, like something inside him would change, but at that point he felt no different at all. He kept marching, felt his legs and boots stomping slowly forward step by step, rifle raised level with his shoulder.

"I said wait!" the platoon leader shouted, but Lu would not look at him. Men were piling out of the trucks and marching now, and Lu saw in their faces the tension and tightness. He heard men's and women's voices coming out of the darkness like ghosts calling warnings from the afterlife: "YOU ARE THE PEOPLE'S ARMY! YOU'RE SUPPOSED TO PROTECT THE PEOPLE! GO BACK! YOU'RE NOT NEEDED HERE! DON'T TURN ON THE PEOPLE!" He thought of the commander's words, told himself these were the enemy's tricks.

A wall of garbage barrels burned and the soldiers kicked them over and rolled on. A rain of rocks came from overhead. They saw dozens of teens in the street in front of them, tagged by their glowing white headbands, shimmers of moon and firelight, the pale glare of their faces. Two soldiers were hit by rocks, one in the neck, another in the face, bleeding from his eye. Then Lu heard a blast of machine-gun fire going off to his right and watched the bodies go down as if this were a movie, like he was in a dream, playing a game. The voices did not stop and the Molotovs came now in a hail. Another soldier showered with glass, fuel splashed over his chest and arms, he looked like a scarecrow burning. They threw him down and smothered him. The soldier screamed, but he was drowned out by the guns now, the roar of the tanks. Lu held his rifle up to his shoulder and aimed and fired.

He heard Platoon Leader Ji's voice in his head, Wait, wait for the enemy. Wait. The guns, each shot like a bomb in his ears.

They moved forward. Some enemy bodies had not been dragged away. He saw a young man in a large pool of black, lying in the street at an odd angle. The back of the man's head was gone and a stream of blood still trickled, brains and gray pieces of skull in a tiny heap next to his ear. Another nearby curled like a fetus, chin tucked snugly against his sternum, hands clutched over his midsection, not tight enough to hold in the stomach and intestines, which had spurted out and lay oozing in the streets. A woman kneeled alongside the road, wiping one hand with the other where her fingers used to be. Lu aimed, squeezed off one round, and the woman hit the ground motionless. They stepped over the bodies and the trails of blood, stray shoes and crimson shirts scattered and random.

They had made it past the military museum and were moving east down Chang'an Avenue toward Tiananmen Square. He wondered if the tanks would really fire: would they blast holes into the facades of Beijing? Where were his grandparents now? Were they home? Were they in one of these local stores, caught in the midst of the chaos, off guard? And where was his little brother? What was he doing? Were they listening to the bullets and chants and screaming deaths? He looked down one of the side roads and thought he could find his way home if he had to, but he did not want to think about this. The mission . . . these rebels . . . stay focused. He looked around him at the dark and empty buildings, felt like he was being watched, an alien city.

Another soldier down, hands to his face, fresh blood seeping through his fingers. Lu heard rustling along the side of the street. He fired and listened to the bodies hitting the earth. They all kept firing. More roadblocks, cars and buses and metal rails for the bicycle lanes meshed in jagged angles like a child's toy fort across the wide street. Beyond the roadblock Lu could see the first lights of Tiananmen, the glimmering square heart of the city. Molotovs popped and made flaming slashes on the concrete. They opened fire, hell-crackle bursting from their hands. The men and boys throwing rocks, bottles, sticks, and gas bombs, all so clear in Lu's eyes, as if things had slowed down for him. The noise was not so great and the machine gun in his arms was steady, as if it fired through some greater will of control. He did not hear the people's screams. He told himself, Focus, be alert . . . focus on the enemy. His breathing was smooth though he could feel his heart smashing away inside his chest. Sweat poured out from underneath his helmet and into his eyes. He had come to a state of believing.

The line moved forward. The soldier next to him said, "Are you okay? Are you hit?"

Lu said, "No, I'm fine."

The soldier said, "You're limping," then they kept on marching. They took random shots at the people running to retrieve the bodies, like hunting rabbits in the woods. They stepped over the bodies that had not been dragged away, blood speckling their boots and legs. They did not bother to clear the path of the rebel dead. Tanks and APCs rolled through. No one looked down.

On the avenue Lu saw the streetlights ablaze and the dim glow of the square straight ahead. They moved even more slowly now, as if anticipating, inviting attack. Men to his side and behind him clapped new clips into their rifles. Then from the darkness he saw the shape of an old woman hobbling into the street. At first he thought her a spirit floating, silver white hair bright in the evening. She spoke to them in a dialect none of the soldiers could understand. She wore a thin shawl and shuffled on sandaled feet. The soldiers watched as she wobbled out in front of them. The tanks kept moving and the soldiers kept marching. Lu stared at the old woman and did not know what to do. He thought she looked like his grandmother but maybe she did not and he was simply imagining things. In the dark the old woman looked so clean.

She stopped, stood before them as they approached. Thirty yards, twenty yards, the old woman rambling, chattering nonstop. She closed her eyes, raised a crooked finger above her head. Then she seemed to crumble, her body collapsing in sections: buckling knees, then her waist, then flat on her back in the center of the road.

She had not been touched or shot but she lay dead still. Platoon Leader Ji told Lu to move her. He went forward and looked down at the old woman who wept with her arms straight at her sides, staring up into the night. She was not a ghost, he could see the wrinkles and age etched in her face. She sobbed and howled like a little girl. Behind him he heard the other soldiers barking, "Move her! Throw her on the side!" He stared at the old woman like a miracle or curse, dazed.

She said, "It's wrong . . . you're killing your own people."

She said, "You have to stop. Please."

She said, "Your face. What happened to your face?"

Her voice was raspy but gentle, she spoke a hard and broken *putonghua*, a street dialect with a peasant's accent, a practiced version she used only in cases of emergency.

They were shouting behind him and he felt a boiling inside him as if his blood had burned afoul. He kneeled and scooped the woman up in his arms, she was light, bird's bones inside her. As he ran with her she wept and screamed and told him he was already dead. He laid her down on the sidewalk and ran back to join the column. A new crowd had materialized and they came at the tanks and soldiers like a horde released, wild, enraged. The soldiers blasted away, dragon-tear and spitfire. Lu watched them grab at their arms and shoulders, hands and legs, as if they could hold in the blood and the pieces of their flesh; they grabbed at their heads and ducked and dodged, as if they could catch the bullets like magic in the night. A young woman's head, he was close enough to see it explode. The bodies lay fallen and gray.

He fell back from the front and doubled over, felt the rush coming from his gut, the splatter on his boots and in the street. He struggled to breathe. It took only a few moments to empty himself, but the wait felt much longer. When he stood straight again he thought he could not march because his left leg hurt so badly now, like fire pins threaded through the core of his bones. Even the scar on his face sizzled, flecks of acid on his skin. He collected himself. Dots of light sparked from rifle barrels, the random calls of people issued all around. He thought he could hear the mumble and murmur of the loudspeakers coming from Tiananmen. But loudest was still the tanks, the movement of machinery, the roar and rumble and crush of the treads over the broken streets.

He wiped the spit and vomit from his lips, the tears from his eyes. He aimed and saw nothing and pulled the trigger and fired. He did this over and over again. He marched and the pain in his face and leg went away. He wondered who would collect these bodies, the dead and wounded lay myriad and countless in the streets. He aimed at nothing and shot at everything. Who would take care of the old woman? Would they have run her down if he had not carried her to the side? It did not matter. Don't be tricked, wait for the enemy. He took a deep breath and raised his rifle to his shoulder, eyes leveled through the sights, as they marched and shot and smashed their way into the heart of Tiananmen Square.

PART I

I may be honoured as the Son of Heaven but I have no freedom.

—YANG JIAN, THE EMPEROR WENDI,
FOUNDER OF THE SUI DYNASTY (581-618)

1

Dissident

Grandfather believed in warriors, and dragons. When Lu and I were children—Lu still young enough to tolerate bedtime stories, and I too small not to believe them—Grandfather told us of warriors from China's great dynasties, the Song and Han, the Tang and Ming, and the battles they fought riding horseback and on foot, using weapons of the earth and steel. They were called warlords and they fought for land, for power, the honor of kings, the sanctity of their promises. They battled barbarians who swept down in wild thundering hordes from the north, trying to devour the great land of the Yellow River by sheer savage force.

This is what Grandfather told us and what we grew up to believe.

In the annals of Chinese lore the dragon symbolizes the emperor, who has had bestowed upon him the mandate of heaven, chosen by the gods to lead the people to prosperity and grand light. This is not so much a goal but the sole purpose of his existence. He has the wisdom and knowledge to teach and lead, and yet harbors the potential to unleash a cold fury upon those who countermand his judgments. The dragon emperor is always right, and if challenged he must answer with an inscrutable and unmatched ferocity; he cannot tolerate impunity, lest his total control be doubted and the mandate of heaven be shaken from his crown. If the dragon emperor's temper is revealed and punishment is exacted, it is always the victim who has wronged and never the emperor, for a son of the heavens makes no such mistakes.

*   *   *

My parents were peasants, farmers from Shandong province in eastern China, south of Beijing, as were my grandparents, and their families before them. This is where my brother and I were born.

Normally the younger generation migrates to the cities to sample the ways of the new. An old friend of our family, a midranking government cadre, promised my parents and grandparents a secure place to live, simple work in a textile and machine factory, low-ranking Party membership. We would live in relative comfort and feel the new modernization taking place, what was supposed to become the true face of revolutionary China.

My mother was twenty-five, my father barely thirty. I was one year old and Lu had just turned six.

But my parents would not go. They wanted to continue farming, to finish the work they had started and come to completion with the land. They were in no rush to embrace the future.

"You take the boys," my father said. "We'll go in the fall, after the harvest."

"Don't be stupid," Grandfather said. "This is your chance. This is it."

My mother said, "You're the old ones, remember?" My mother looked at my father, then said to my grandparents, "Look at what we've lived through already. What could hold us back now?"

This is how Grandfather told the story. Later my mother apologized for her disrespectful tone. She was a temperamental girl and had grown into a fiery woman, Grandfather always said.

I've seen pictures of my mother and father, grainy black-and-white photos, lost visions of history. My mother is short and round-faced, her eyebrows thinly drawn like a hand-painted doll. She is a complete head shorter than my father, who is gangly in a dark tunic and cap, scarecrow shadows in the pockets of his face. Mother wears a tunic as well. They do not hold hands. In the picture they smile with strain, their faces haggard, raked with lines.

I recall being a small boy and seeing these photos for the first time. Lu had stormed off to our room and thrown himself on our bed, huffing and puffing. I didn't understand then, I was only three or four, but I know his feelings now. There are still nights when I lie awake trying to remember the feel of my mother's hands on my back, comforting me in sickness or telling me stories in those gray moments before sleep. Or the rough scratch of my father's stubble on my skin, the calluses on his hands. But I cannot. As far back as I can remember it has always been my grandparents. But Lu remembers because he is older.

My grandparents took a train to Beijing with my brother and me wrapped in blankets. Lu has no recollection of this trip. When we were small I would ask him, and either he had truly forgotten or he simply refused to tell. News of my parents' deaths would not reach us for months, only when the last embers of fire that had disintegrated our small wooden home had gone cold, our parents' bodies lost in charred wreckage. A fluke, an incredible mishap. They had lived through the famine of the Great Leap Forward, bodies piled in ditches like mounds of firewood, dead from starvation. They'd eaten only handfuls of rice, the husks of grain, sipped muddy water from community wells with hundreds of miserable and dedicated others. They hoisted plows with their own legs and backs and shoulders because they could not afford an ox or horse or mule; had spent weeks, months at a time waist deep in soy and wheat fields, skin saturated and crusted with mud and rotten earth; countless nights maintaining shifts to keep the furnaces burning during the drive to make iron. All that hardship survived, only to die from the flicker of a last meal's fire.

There was no funeral. My grandparents—my mother's parents—never went to retrieve the bodies. The year was 1968, two years after Mao Zedong had announced the launch of the Great Proletarian Cultural Revolution. *Dongluan* (chaos) was rampant like a plague. Bands of Red Guards patrolled the cities and the countryside in search of the Four Olds: old thought, old culture, old customs, old habits. Thousands died, some say millions: artists, writers, teachers, landlords. In our own Shandong province, in the hills of Qufu, Red Guards destroyed the relics of Confucius. He had been labeled by Mao as "history's greatest reactionary." Tablets, statues, and columns were smashed with sledgehammers, ancient shrines that had been protected by Confucian descendants for more than two thousand years. What would stop the Red Guards from taking the life of a common old man or woman for using an ancient proverb or wearing a certain type of clothing or shoe?

My grandparents dared not leave the confines of our home, and we were just children. There was nothing any of us could do. And even with these apprehensions we could not avoid Grandfather's incident, his eyesight taken, could not avoid the dementia that would afflict Grandmother ever after. As if all our precautions had only further stricken our fate.

Things Lu and I regret to this day. I know there is unrest still in his heart, though it has been years since we have spoken like brothers, much less friends.

* * *

In March of 1989 I was unemployed. I'd returned to Beijing from Cornell in January with a degree in mathematics. Before I'd even stepped on a plane or taken my first step on Cornell's campus, I'd had it all planned out: in three years, I was going to graduate and come back prepared for a number of different occupations—finance, accounting, even economics. Or I should say, *we* had had a plan: my family, Xiao-An's family. I was the one who had initiated it all, but thinking back now I can't help but feel I'd been baited.

Xiao-An's father was a supervisor at the district employment bureau, part of the Ministry of Labor and Social Security; her mother was a manager at a women's clothing factory. These were respectable and well-earning jobs that allowed them to lead secure lives. The problem was that their daughter was ugly. She had short arms and stubby legs, a thick straight torso. Her face was too round, moonlike. She had purple acne scars dotting her big pale cheeks, down to her chin. Her mother had encouraged her to grow her hair long to give her a prettier, more feminine look, but her hair was naturally dry and strawlike, and Xiao-An was too short for it to have a real flowing effect.

From the beginning I felt her father was happy to have me in her life, even though my family was poor. We had been introduced by a matchmaker that Xiao-An's father had hired, that Grandmother had met at the market. When I met the matchmaker—Grandmother dragged her back to the *hutong* from the market—I was out front, fixing my bicycle. The lady was dressed in a dark pantsuit, had gold hoop earrings and many bracelets clanking on her wrists. She reeked of perfume, like a modern-day businesswoman and fortune-teller morphed into one. I could not define her age; she wore so much makeup, she could have been thirty, or sixty.

"Give me your hands," she said. They were dirty, but I held them out to her anyway. I watched her rub them, grease sliding onto her own white skin. Then she grabbed my face, looked in my eyes. "There's someone I want you to meet," she said, and told me what the situation was: a wealthy couple's daughter. I laughed and turned back to my bicycle.

The matchmaker told us how she had brought more than a dozen young respectable men to the house to meet Xiao-An, but half of them saw her and did not return, and the other half Xiao-An said she did not like, without further explanation. The matchmaker said, "This is the chance of a lifetime for someone like you."

My grandparents were excited. I had always spent so much time studying—knowing that everything I did led up to the college entrance exams, a decent future—that I'd never had a girlfriend, nor had I been encouraged to go out and find one. But this had to be pursued, Grandmother said. "Your parents are watching over us still, especially your mother. I can feel it." She told me how my mother and father's marriage had also been arranged by a matchmaker, though not a modern one like we had met. "Back then a family like theirs would never consider people like us, but that doesn't matter. The point is, I didn't think much of your father when I first met him," Grandmother told me. "But your mother liked him. It was the right thing. He was a good man, the only one tough enough to handle your mother."

Grandmother's superstitions aside, I met Xiao-An one week later in her house with her parents sitting around us. I wore a clean, pressed pair of gray pants and a white collared shirt. Xiao-An's hair was tied up in a bun on top of her head, makeup caked on her face to hide her acne scars. She wore a pretty beige dress with a high collar and lace trim, but still her body looked blocky and thick. I stared at her for a moment, then tried to hide the surprise on my face. I could feel her nervousness. Her mother brought out tea and almond cookies, then her parents left us alone to talk. I asked her what she liked best in school and she said, "Lunch." I agreed. For a moment we laughed loudly, and I saw her mother and father peeking around the corner, elated. I told her I was going to major in math when I went to college the next year, but she had yet to decide what she wanted to pursue. She told me she liked movies very much, and I told her I liked to read stories and novels.

"Reading makes me feel like I'm doing schoolwork," she said.

"Watching movies makes me wish I was in the movie and not here."

"What's the difference? You're reading about a different place, different people. Just like movies, except it's not as much work."

"I don't think you understand," I said, ready to debate, if not argue. But I could feel her parents around the corner, invisible, listening. "We'll discuss it some other time," I said. "These cookies are very good."

When I went back a second time a few days later, her parents treated me like I was a prince, made of gold.

One year later, Xiao-An and I both first-year students at Qinghua University, her father told me how the best new jobs were going to young people who had studied abroad. They came back with Western degrees and were instantly regarded as at a higher level than those who had spent their lives going through the Chinese system.

"Look at me," Xiao-An's father said. "I didn't go to college. I couldn't because of the Cultural Revolution, all the schools were shut down. My job now, I know it's as far as I'm going to get, maybe for the rest of my life. If I'm lucky I'll be promoted to director of the district bureau. But we will never have the chances that you and Xiao-An have."

Her father chain-smoked and always seemed to be frowning. But I liked him because he was never defensive about me being with Xiao-An. During the time we had been together Xiao-An and I had only kissed, really, a little touching. We spent our time studying, going to the movies, holding hands. After the first few dates, I paid less attention to how she looked, and eventually I stopped thinking of her as ugly. I liked her company—she was not the most exciting girl, but she was very nice to me and we could talk, debate. I thought about dating other girls in my classes, but word had gotten around that Xiao-An and I were a pair. No one made fun of us, probably because everyone knew her father worked for the employment bureau. My grandparents were happy that I was with her. But we knew—she and I, as well as our families—that things would never go much further unless we were married.

When her father told me about the new government scholarships to go abroad, I said, "I want to go." My English was adequate, and my board scores were very good. The Cultural Revolution was long dead and intellectual development was no longer frowned upon. Deng Xiaoping had opened the doors for students to learn and come back, to make China a smarter, better place. My second chance of a lifetime in less than two years.

Xiao-An's father said, "Do you know exactly what you're saying?"

"Of course I do." I told him I needed to take this chance if I was going to make something of myself. "If I'm going . . . to marry Xiao-An someday, I want to

provide well for her. Not just properly, but well. I'm not going to be poor forever."
I couldn't believe my own words—marry Xiao-An? Of course, from the beginning,
everyone had been thinking it. She was not pretty, but she was a good girl, decent,
not stupid. Her family was well-off, and my being with her made everyone seem
so happy, especially my grandparents. I thought I could learn to love her. It was
unspoken, but merging my family into Xiao-An's would mean security that my
grandparents and I couldn't even begin to understand. Was this possibly more
important than personal love?

Her father said, "Xiao-An's grades are not bad, but they're not good enough.
Even if they were, she has no interest in going abroad. Trust me, I've asked her.
We know people in the State Education Commission. They can help us, but she
doesn't want to go. If she were a boy, I'd have none of these problems. I could
force a son to go. I wouldn't have to worry about him getting married. But that's
not the case, is it?" He looked at me, then lit a cigarette. "Xiao-An is not a beauty
queen, I know this. But she really likes you. She's smart, kindhearted, and sweet,
and will make a good wife. She's not like some of these young women today, so
opportunistic and ambitious, out for only themselves. They have no respect, no
sense of tradition or honor.

"I know you'll do well. As our son-in-law, you would be bringing honor to the
whole family." It was one of the few times I remembered him smiling.

I took a special round of exams. I did very well and was chosen to go away.
But no doubt it was Xiao-An's family's backing that helped put everything through,
especially for a school like Cornell. I was proud of myself for having gotten in
and through one year at a school like Qinghua. But Cornell was one of the best
schools in *America*. At our own university among the students we heard stories
about how different education was in the United States, how freedom of thought
and speech were not just bylines of the Constitution; they were rights, exercised
especially by intellectuals, defended by American laws and democracy. Besides
math, I could learn world history and literature, politics, science, sociology, all
free of dictated norms, free of fear, no need to regurgitate how the Party translated
life. People were not afraid to speak the truth; the people needed and lived on
the truth. Who knew how much I could learn and grow? How different things
would be, how much I could change. I would make myself worldly, invaluable. It
sounded like a fairy tale.

But it wasn't, thanks to Xiao-An's father. Their family's political history was
clean. They had been Party members for years and were in a circle of midranking
families. Even though they knew about Grandfather's incident, their support gave
me the chance: a poor, peasant boy with good grades but suspect political blood,
out to make a new name and legacy for himself and his family.

Our families decided that Xiao-An and I should get engaged when I returned,
after I had secured a solid job and had a little saved up to do things right. They
would have a big party in our honor. I signed a contract that said I would come

back after graduation and do my best to put my skills to work for the people. But even as I signed, with Xiao-An's father and my grandparents watching me, I knew their wishes and my duty to them would be greater than any paper bond. I had no idea that my life would change forever in every imaginable way.

*   *   *

The scholarship paid for everything, except minor living expenses, so I got a part-time job at the student fitness center. The manager was a big black man with a mustache, a huge ball-like stomach, and gigantic arms. During my interview I tried to hide the fact that I was looking him up and down, the darkness of his skin, the whiteness of his teeth and eyes. I'd be working the front desk, checking passes and I.D. cards, helping to clean up the weight room. The pay was five dollars an hour.

For the most part I stayed behind the front desk and never answered the phone. When my shift ended I'd go to the weight room and dabble with curls and presses, see what felt right. Mostly I did push-ups and sit-ups. I saw boys and girls flirting openly in their tight sweaty clothes. Casual, careless even. They did not have to be wary of who might be watching or listening. I didn't understand. I was learning.

I worked ten to fifteen hours a week. Each paycheck was fifty or sixty dollars, worth close to five hundred Chinese dollars. I sent some back to my grandparents, and the rest I put toward my meal plan and saved. I felt rich.

That's where I met Elsie. I had noticed many pretty girls on campus, but her skin was so white, her eyes blue and shining, her long blond hair tied back in a ponytail. She always wore a plain T-shirt, shorts, and sneakers, not skimpy tight outfits like some of the other girls. She came in three or four times a week. She would smile at me, sometimes stop to chat, which no one else did. She told me her name, I told her mine. She would ask me what exercises she should do for her stomach, her legs. I'd get nervous and tell her to talk to a trainer.

About a month after first meeting her, I was at the fitness center in the middle of a game of basketball, guarding a boy much taller and stronger than me. He was bumping and knocking me around, saying things under his breath that I didn't understand. I saw Elsie on the side, watching. The boy turned his shoulder and elbowed me in the jaw. I fell. He stood over me. I had a brief flash, that instant moment of rage when you decide whether you are going to fight or cry, the same thing that used to happen when I was a child fighting with Lu.

I sprang up and tackled him around the waist. I was not sure if I was hitting him or getting hit, then everyone pulled us apart. I walked away. Elsie was in front of me, her hands reaching out, barely touching my shoulders. She was looking at the corner of my right eye. She pulled me toward the water fountain, doused her workout towel, and brushed it over my face.

"Just a scratch," she said. "It's not bad, though. You're pretty brave. You're half that guy's size."

"He hit me," I said.

"Yeah, I saw." She was still holding the towel spotted pink with my blood. "Maybe you should go to the infirmary, just to be safe."

"Okay," I said. I didn't thank her. I could feel spots on my face and at the back of my head pulsing. I found my keys on the gym floor and left.

Later that week Elsie invited me to a bar in town. I went by myself and met her. She seemed to know the whole crowd and introduced me. Everyone was friendly and shook my hand, though none of them could pronounce my name.

"Call me Xiao-Di at home," I explained. "Little brother."

They bought me drinks and I smoked Elsie's cigarettes. I felt completely cool, relaxed and happy, but I didn't understand why she had invited me. We were not talking about much. The bar was very loud. After an hour I said, "I going home now." She said, "Wait. How's your head?"

"Not hurt. No problem."

"You haven't had any more fights lately, have you?"

"No hit me, I no tackle you." We both laughed. "Lift weight much easier. Weight not hit back."

I stayed and drank more. Later, by the bar, Elsie held my hand. We left when the bar closed, the night winds cold, close to the mountains. I had my arm around Elsie's shoulders and she was holding me up much more than I was holding her. We stumbled back to her room, up the stairs and through the door. She kissed me and I was not so much stunned as scared. She had a thin face, compared to Xiao-An's moonlike visage. Her body was firm and round and strong, her hair thick, full soft lips. We grabbed at each other and she pressed me against the wall. The only other girl I'd ever kissed or touched was Xiao-An, my grandparents' chosen, and she did not feel or kiss or move like this girl. Elsie put her hands on my face, then pushed me down on the couch. My head was spinning. I could feel myself grinning.

"You very strong," I said. Then, "What . . . what you doing?"

"I'm getting naked, stupid."

"Wait . . . you wait. No naked . . ."

We stopped kissing, my face still in her hands.

"What's the matter? You like me. I know you like me."

I looked up and saw the shadows of night, thick gold hair blurring her face. I said, "No . . . sex before . . . never."

"Never?"

"Never."

She was sitting on top of me. She lit a cigarette, handed it to me, and when I inhaled and smelled I knew it was not a cigarette. I did not care. I smoked and felt my head go numb from front to back, like my brain had been put on ice. All the warnings and stories my grandparents had told Lu and me through the years about drugs and opium and the "sick man of Asia" dissipated as Elsie knelt before me and undid my pants and slid me slowly into her mouth.

*   *   *

After our first night together I was afraid this would be a fling, that I would see her again at the fitness center and she would act like nothing had happened, or worse, that I'd done something wrong. But the next morning we had breakfast together, and that night we ate dinner and studied. We kept spending time together and things did not go bad. Then I was afraid that we might be ridiculed, but around campus I saw black boys and white girls, Asian girls and white boys, white girls and Indian boys, all kinds mixed. They held hands and kissed out in the open. To be different was acceptable, if not normal. We were all free to be and feel how we pleased.

We would make love inside the smooth alabaster walls and ceilings of our dorm rooms, heavenly cubes stuffed with warm thick blankets and pillows, soft spacious beds, trinkets (in her room) from her childhood, from home. We would lie naked, talking, in all that comfort, telling each other stories about our families, our lives. I was a poor boy from Beijing, here with a plan to make the family proud. She was from California. Both of her parents were doctors. They had lots of money. She said she had dated many boys since high school, but never someone Chinese.

"Why you like me?" I asked

She smiled, turned her head away, then said, "You're different. Not just the way you look. I mean, I love the way you look. Your face is so . . . big! But your eyes and nose and chin, they're so small. You have petite features."

"Peh-tit?"

"Never mind. You're different is what I'm saying. In a good way. My parents are always trying to get me to date their friends' sons, premed or prelaw—white, Catholic, trust funds. Telling me how pretty I am, how much they love me. They never fight with me. Like you, you're not always giving me what you think I want. You're not afraid to fight."

"You not always right."

"I am, but that's not the point. The point is you don't *think* I'm always right and you're not afraid to say it. Those people back home, they're all about money, cocktail parties, the country club, new cars. Everyone's talking, but no one's listening. They believe they're cultured, but can you be cultured if the only colored people you know are the housekeeper and gardener? They think they're better than everyone, but the worst part is they won't admit it.

"But you know about real things. You're fair, and smart, and nice. A little temper, but that's okay. You mean the things you say. I can feel it."

At the end of my first semester I wrote Xiao-An to tell her that I'd met someone else, that we needed to move on. I wrote my grandparents, and presumed

Xiao-An told her father. Grandmother called me, screaming, "You're going to ruin everything! They can take away your scholarship, and what are you going to do when you come back? You're throwing it all away!"

But even then I had begun thinking that I might not go back after all. I was free, happy. My scholarship was not taken away. I couldn't afford to go back to Beijing, so I worked summers and winters at the fitness center. Elsie would call once a week until she returned. As each season passed I compared Elsie to Xiao-An. Next to Elsie everything I had ever done with Xiao-An felt scripted, like we were reluctant characters in a play.

I told Elsie about Xiao-An and the situation with her father, that I had broken it off for her. She was quiet for several moments, then she said, "Thank you." She did not seem happy or upset. I thought it was a strange thing to say.

Thinking back, maybe I should not have been surprised when Elsie told me there was no going forward for us. It was October, senior year, our final semester. We were graduating in December, late because we had minor credits to make up. She said things were changing.

"Everything you know is over there, and everything I know is here. It would be so hard to make it work." Her father had arranged a job for her working with a movie producer in Los Angeles. "It's a great chance. I can't pass it up."

"I want to stay. With you. If you want."

"No," she said. "You don't understand. It's not about what I want. I just can't. I don't know how to explain it." She kept talking about going back to California, her father, the job. I said I knew all about great chances. She told me that during the summer she had dated a boy back in Los Angeles. An old friend of the family, he was studying to be a doctor at UCLA. His name was James.

"It was nothing serious, but . . . My parents, they would never understand if we were together. It just wouldn't work. You don't know what they would do to me, what they're like." She cried, which made me want to console her, but I was numb.

"You lie to me."

"No," she said, "I didn't. Please don't hate me."

That night I wrote Xiao-An a letter; it had been over two years since my last. I said I was sorry and that I was definitely coming back to Beijing. I had been stupid and selfish and wanted to work things out. I wrote my grandparents and told them the same, that they had been right about dating an American girl, that they were not trustworthy and were selfish and had no moral values. Last, I wrote Xiao-An's father telling him that I'd been a fool. I knew that I'd offended his daughter and their family, but it had been a stupid, immature mistake. I wanted to come home and make things right, as we had originally planned.

I received a letter from Grandmother telling me that she was glad I'd come back to my senses. That it wasn't too late to fix things up with Xiao-An. But I never heard back from Xiao-An or her father.

Our final weeks together Elsie and I went to class, ate, did the usual things. We acted like nothing had happened. We made love each time with a sure sense of desperation, as if it might be our last chance. As graduation neared we grew tense. We avoided the inevitable conversation. I realized that in almost three years I had never met her parents, had never been invited back to her home to see what the other side of her life was like. I had never seen the flaw in this, but now it made sense.

The last time I saw her was in her room. It was empty, had been packed and picked up to be shipped back to California. Her parents were waiting by their rental car to go to the airport. Light, dusty snow was falling. Her father was tall and handsome, a square jaw and big nose, wide shoulders. Her mother was svelte in her long coat, blond hair and blue eyes like her daughter. There was a young man standing with them in khakis and a brown jacket. He was tall, looked bigger and older than me, sandy hair buzzed close to his head. Her father called up to her window, "Elsie, I've got a surprise!"

She looked out the window. When she turned back she wouldn't meet my eyes. She walked around the room once more, seeing if she had forgotten anything. I didn't say anything. I didn't know what to say. We had already exchanged phone numbers, addresses. She hugged me and I could feel her tears on my neck. She had my face in her hands, as she had the first time we ever made love. She looked up, was struggling to smile. We kissed. Her father called to her again, then beeped the car horn.

"I don't love him," she said. "God, I don't know if this . . . how am I supposed to know?" I couldn't look at her anymore. I started crying and told her she should go. She left and I did not follow her out. I stood in the empty room and looked out the window. Her father reached out to hug her but she walked by him. Her mother got in the front seat, her father got in the driver's side. The young man hugged Elsie and dipped his head to kiss her on the mouth. I saw her body tense up, her neck stiffen and jerk back. They got in the backseat. She did not look up, look back. They drove away. I looked around the empty room as if seeing it for the first time.

*　　*　　*

Two weeks after returning to Beijing, I went to see Xiao-An. It was January. I didn't tell my grandparents. I rode my old bicycle to her house in the university district. I had been away so long that I almost expected the roads leading to Xiao-An's to have changed, but they hadn't. The sense of déjà-vu, the same streets and buildings, the taste of the air, sounds of the city, almost made me think things would be okay. When I knocked on the door her father opened it. He looked as if he had aged ten years since I'd last seen him: his face more wrinkled, gray slashed through his hair. Before I could say anything he said, "Xiao-An isn't home. Even if she was, you would not be allowed to speak to her." The wind was blowing, it was very cold. On the doorstep he told me that she was recently engaged to a young public security officer.

"Did you really think you were that wonderful, that special? Did you think a few letters would worm your way back into our lives? Xiao-An loved you, so we accepted you. And you threw her away like she's the peasant? You will never find a job in Beijing, I promise you. Private sector, public sector, it doesn't matter. I'm going to tell everyone I know about what you did to my daughter, my family. Maybe you are not so smart after all.

"You disgraced my daughter, my family," he said. "If you come back here again, I will do everything I can to make sure your family rots in hell."

*   *   *

I never told these stories to my grandparents. They wouldn't have understood the way I would have wanted them to. I came home to nothing: no job, no girlfriend, no future. Each morning I woke feeling like a bomb was going to blast open my chest.

Of course Grandmother noticed I had spent very little time interviewing for jobs. The two interviews I did go on—the first to be an accountant at a city factory, the other to be a financial assistant at a hotel—did not go well. Both interviewers (men in their forties or fifties, both with glasses, both with fat bodies, cold stares, and sallow skin) asked if I knew Xiao-An and her father. To the factory manager I said I did. He looked at my application, then nervously back at me, and told me nothing was available. To the hotel manager, a week later, I said I did not know Xiao-An. Still I was not called back.

"What's going on?" Grandmother asked. "Did you talk to Xiao-An's father again? It shouldn't take this long."

"I talked to him," I said. "He's busy. He says they are working on it."

"I hope they hurry," Grandmother said, "or you'll be ready to retire before you even begin."

"Why do you have to wait for the ugly girl's father to get you a job?" Grandfather said. "Can't you find your own job, with your fancy American education?"

"What do you know about work? You haven't lifted a finger in years."

"Watch your mouth!" Grandmother said.

Grandfather, sitting in his chair in the corner, laughed and shook his head. He raised his glass toward me and said, "Prove yourself from the inside, instead of trying to go over the wall." His voice had no inflection and I could not tell if he was drunk.

"What wall? What are you talking about?"

"The wall, you know. The wall . . ." Then he said, "What the hell are you looking at? Stop staring at me!" He sipped his drink and his head tipped back to rest.

I went to my room and did a few sets of push-ups, then sit-ups, trying to maintain the muscle I'd worked so hard to build while at Cornell, muscle I could feel shriveling up each day I'd been back in Beijing. After that I leafed through my photo album, snapshots I'd taken of Elsie sitting on a picnic blanket or the rails of a fence, in the background a wide green field of grass or hills glazed yellow by the sun. Behind her were endless paths lined with students reading on benches, groups talking under the shade of a tree. The pictures trapping smiles and frozen hands waving. Gold summer or blue winter and always the fat white clouds in the sky. The world I used to belong to. I'd been going through this routine every day since I'd returned, but it was making things harder instead of relieving the pain.

A part of me could not believe that I was no longer there, though I had been back in Beijing since January. I'd wake up and think that it was a dream, that I would turn and Elsie would be there, asleep, snoring with the slightest whistling sound. I wanted to feel her warmth next to me, the soft heat of her skin, smell her hair. I wanted to go to the dining hall where I would pile sausage and ham and toast on a plate, drink down glass after glass of milk and orange juice. I wanted her to be with me so we could talk or fight about trivial things, just to hear her voice, her anger or her laugh. But each morning I stared up at the cracked ceiling of my old room, felt the bed's sharp broken coils digging through the straw and rags, scratching into my back. I could hear Grandmother and Grandfather, up at dawn, pots and cups and glasses clinking, their voices dueling.

Grandmother came into my room, stood next to me with her arms crossed.

"You've been brooding ever since you came back," she said. "What's the matter? You can't keep wallowing."

"I'm not wallowing. I'm thinking."

"Right. You're thinking about America, and that girl, everything that's behind you. What good does it do?"

"You don't know," I said. Grandmother took a seat beside me. We sat in silence for a few moments. She took my hand and said, "Go visit Xiao-An. You'll feel better."

"She's busy. And we're . . . not getting along that well."

"I thought you two were working things out? Things are not going to get better if you don't talk. Look at your grandfather and me, how do you think we've stayed together all this time?"

"I don't know. Who else would have either of you?"

"Stop it! I'm serious. I'll bake some *mantou* for you to bring over. You can talk to her father, too."

"If you want to see them so badly, then you go over there." I immediately regretted this, afraid that she would. She was silent for a moment, then she said, "I'll bake the *mantou*. You let me know when you're ready to go." She sighed, straightened her back, stood, and left the room.

I felt bad about fighting with Grandmother. She was right—I'd been snapping at her and Grandfather over small, stupid things every day since I'd come home. But how could they really understand what I was going through? They had never left China, had never seen the things I had or had the same hopes. They didn't know what had really happened and I still didn't know how to tell them.

When I wasn't home feeling angry and confused, I spent time with my best friend, Wong. We went to the new nightclubs and restaurants that had sprouted through Beijing. Wong was twenty-one, an art student graduating from Beijing Normal University that spring. I'd known him my entire life. We had fought the neighborhood bullies together, and I had protected him from Lu when Big Brother could find no one else to antagonize. Wong and I used to steal fruit and candy from street peddlers, harass girls on walks home from school. We played hide-and-seek and made up games that required no props or balls or toys of any kind. Because we didn't have any. We had the *hutong*, our neighborhood, and our imaginations.

Now he came to my house as if we were still kids, asking permission to play. Grandmother gave him a kiss on the cheek, a pat on the top of his head.

"You're here so often, and you never bring me any gifts," she said, half-joking. "No respect. You should be ashamed of yourself."

Grandfather said, "Why would he buy you gifts? He's buying gifts for all the girls he's chasing!" He raised his glass in our direction.

I grabbed my jacket and satchel, a habit I'd picked up at Cornell, always having a jacket and a bag. From my *hutong* we walked out past the cluster of small homes mashed together in the confines of medium-high gray stone walls, past the communal bathroom we shared with the rest of the families. Inside were rows of sinkholes with no partitions. Dried turds and toilet paper often littered the floor, half-dry puddles of piss. The stink was relentless. The tiny room inside our home where we ran water and bathed was a small blessing. I stopped and looked back.

"What's the matter?"

"Nothing," I said.

"You miss your big American dormitory?"

"Yes, I do." I gave him a stare, but Wong ignored me.

"Give it time. Soon it will feel like you never left."

"That's what I'm afraid of."

We navigated the side streets, nameless unpaved roads, and the feeling was still there: that at night, in complete darkness, I would be able to find my way regardless of sight. We had walked these paths so often they were ingrained in our senses. They had changed some since I'd left, rebuilt for passing vehicles, but still there were rows of food stands and street vendors selling everything from plucked chickens and sliced pork cutlets, fresh turnips, cabbages, and leeks, to imitation Calvin Klein and Hugo Boss shirts, fake Italian shoes and belts, and remote control cars and action figures and other Japanese-made toys. Taxis squeezed by, nearly hitting the stands, the children, but never doing so. Sounds of birds in cages, chirping and singing. There were children naked and pissing in the gutters, running barefoot over garbage and gravel, unfazed. Here and there I saw

American or European tourists, white Western faces, pale-skinned and adorned with sunglasses and hats, either lost or on a mission to find "authentic" Beijing. Since childhood I could spot the tourists from afar because I was used to seeing and being around only Chinese. But after three years abroad, I had grown used to being surrounded *by* them—not just white, but black, Indian, other Asians, mixes of all kinds—and now my eye could target their faces even faster, sharper, as if it had been trained.

The vendors shouted at us to come look at their wares. I was wearing a gray Cornell T-shirt and Nike sneakers I had bought at an outlet sale before coming home. I saw the vendors and shopkeepers assessing me, smiling. They had never called out to me before when I was a filthy peasant boy. Did they think I was a tourist now? I ignored them. Wong laughed.

"No one in Beijing wears gel in their hair. You think you're a movie star?"

"Shut up."

"Here, I'll buy you something to eat. It will make you less cranky."

We walked up to a food stand. The old woman smiled at us and started scooping two cups of *si-fan*, soupy rice with bits of corn and vegetables. She sprinkled on some dried shredded pork. "You need to eat more," she said to Wong, "so you can look like your friend—bigger and stronger!" I had grown up eating from the food stands, with Wong, with Lu, whenever we scratched up some extra money: dried salted strips of pork, sliced pickled cucumbers. Sometimes, if we were lucky, a small bowl of oxtail soup. But now I looked at the old woman and the cups in her rag-wrapped hands, dirt beneath her fingernails, hard yellow stains on her smiling teeth, mottled spots on her fingers and face. I shook my head, turned away. Wong followed.

"What's the matter?"

"I'm not hungry."

"Seriously, I don't care how big you got over there. If you keep this up I'm going to whip you."

"I'm thirsty," I said. "Let's get a drink."

Near Wangfujing Road we drank beer in an empty bar. I felt better in there. It was cool, air-conditioned, empty and clean. We chatted about my grandparents and his mother, about his upcoming graduation. Was it possible that we would both be college graduates and be unemployed?

"Did you talk to Xiao-An's father again?"

"No."

"Did you tell your grandparents what happened?"

"No! And don't you dare . . . don't even insinuate."

"I won't. But I can't believe he threatened you like that. At least you don't have to marry that girl."

"She was a nice girl," I said.

"But she was ugly. And you didn't love her. You never did. Admit it, you were trying to marry into the family. Which is fine, it happens all the time. I would probably do the same if I had the opportunity. But things will work out for the best this way. Trust me." We were quiet for a few moments, then he said, "Maybe if you wait a few weeks, he'll calm down. Things will work out."

"She's engaged already, to a public security officer." I took a sip of my beer, lit a cigarette. "I'm so stupid. I really screwed up this time." I thought of how this was going to affect my grandparents because sooner or later I had to tell them. They had such high hopes, for me, for themselves. I could feel their anticipation in every word they uttered. If I had just stuck to the plan, things would have been okay. But maybe that was the problem, having such plans. Once they are in place, forces go out of their way to destroy them.

Wong said, "There are plenty of jobs out there. You have to look in the private sector."

"I tried," I said. "Two interviews. They both knew Xiao-An's dad somehow. He probably knows every factory and business manager in the city."

"What did you do? You didn't rape or kill anyone. These people are just jealous, old-fashioned. What would they do if they fell in love with a gorgeous white girl in America? Most of them would never have come back." He took a sip, then said, "It's not like you defiled one of Deng Xiaoping's daughters. That would be a real problem."

I didn't necessarily agree with his logic, but I appreciated his support. It was one of the things I liked best about Wong, his upbeat sarcasm, which was why we had been such great friends for so long. He had a tiny diamond stamped through the lobe of his left ear, and his moppy hair now hung in his face. All this in contrast to the glasses that gave him the look of some derelict scholar. Since coming back I noticed that he always wore jeans and a T-shirt with a rip somewhere on it—sleeve or back, frayed on the ends like he was trying to look poor. He liked to run his hand through his hair in rock-star fashion. I told him all this and he laughed and shook his head.

"I watch too much television," he said.

"You don't have a television."

I asked what had happened to all our friends. Some, like my brother, had gone off and joined the People's Liberation Army. Others were working in factories, attending college, or had gotten married to their high school sweethearts and were living in small apartments on the outskirts of the city. I shook my head; all the stories sounded the same. We listened to a jukebox filled with Madonna, Bruce Springsteen, American superstars, most of whom I'd first heard while listening to the radio at Cornell's campus fitness center or in Elsie's tape collection, which she had in a big black case underneath her bed.

"Do you like this place?" I asked.

"On weekends, it's the most popular bar around. But every week there's something new opening up. A McDonald's down the street, and now a Kentucky Fried Chicken. Did you eat that stuff?"

"All the time."

"That's how you got so big, eating all that meat and lifting weights with the Americans. Maybe I should try eating just McDonald's for a while." He poked at my stomach. I was nothing like the monster basketball and football players I used to see wandering around campus and through the fitness center, but compared to Wong, I really noticed it—my arms and chest, legs and stomach thicker, tighter, and more defined. Wong was still a string bean, the way we had all been growing up.

"Look at your face," he said. "Your chin and cheeks are all sharp now, no more baby fat. You know the old wives' tale, square faces are untrustworthy. Look at me, big round face. Trustworthy."

I said, "What are you going to do after graduation?"

Wong finished his beer, shook his head. "Who knows. I'm an artist. Maybe I'll paint portraits for the Party. You know, like the one of Mao Zedong hanging on Tiananmen Gate. I'm sure Deng Xiaoping would pay a high commission for one of his own."

After the bar we walked down Wangfujing Road past all the new stores that had risen. A new city, one of color and fortune. Like an old house torn down and rebuilt, is it still your home? Or is it something different, a mutation of the original that will never really change? People were looking at me as we walked, like the food stand woman and street vendors had. Was it just because of my T-shirt and sneakers, the gel in my hair? Because I'd put on some weight? Or was it something else? Did I walk differently? What made me stand out now the way I had never before? All these people, being surrounded again by only Chinese . . . I did feel funny, the way I had when I'd first gotten to America and saw the rainbow mix of skin, the sizes and shapes of the bodies and features, heard the varied tones and accents, strange tilts in the voices. It had taken me my first semester to feel really comfortable inside the jumble; maybe now I was looking at all these people—my people—oddly, thus they were looking at me.

I tried to imagine some freeness to the air but could not feel it because there was no open space. It had been happening since the first day I came back, the crowd and buzz of the *hutong*, the giant swarming city. This was my home. But it was a shock, because I had changed. The memories in flashes were discordant, like connecting streams from parallel universes. I saw it now—they all looked so tired, the men, the women, as if in their quiet private lives they faced pressures and circumstances too hard and too deep to ever reveal. Like invisible weights strapped to their backs, I could see it in my grandparents, and in strangers; I could sense it even in Wong, the way his sarcasm often betrayed him. Only the small children in their bright clothes and hats and shiny shoes, cared for and hopeful, seemed to float above it all. Everyone else looked sad and pained without knowing it—the old men and women squatting and smoking, shopkeepers, people walking and talking. Something in the way they carried their shoulders, their heads and faces, like gravity was greater for them, always pulling them down.

I had grown up here—had it always been this way? It must have. But I saw it now. No one knew because they all looked the same. They had never seen anything else. That's why I was staring. That's why they were staring back.

"What's going on with the white girl?"

"Nothing," I said.

"Do you still talk to her?"

"No. She . . . we broke up, remember? I told you this."

"Let me see that picture."

I said, "I don't have it," though it was tucked away in my wallet.

We turned into a small record store. The music was very loud and there were dozens of schoolkids milling about, bumping into us. All the stores were small, it seemed, compared to America, where stores were really warehouses, whether it was food or records, clothing or cars. The racks here were mostly filled with Chinese tapes and records, hits by Cui Jian and Hou Dejian. There was a big section for American imports. I recognized the icons: Michael Jackson, Jimi Hendrix, U2, Run-D.M.C. I smiled as I looked for other singers and groups Elsie had introduced me to, records to which we would make love. I found none. They were either too obscure to have made it over here or simply had not been allowed in.

"You didn't have to come back," Wong said. "There's no way they could have found you."

"What are you talking about? My grandmother was writing me letters telling me that she couldn't breathe, that Grandfather's heart was going bad. What was I going to do, abandon them?"

"But they're fine now."

"They're old," I said. "You never know. Plus, I . . . I was going to try and fix things with Xiao-An. And her father. I figured if I came back . . ."

Wong shook his head. "Do you know how many students go abroad and just disappear? I was willing to bet you were going to be one of them. Your grandparents would have been fine. And Lu is already a soldier, what could they do to him?"

"Just shut up for a while, okay?"

He was not looking at me or for any record in particular. "Don't get me wrong," he said, "I'm glad you're back. I'm glad you got to go. But I always wondered what you were doing, how different it was. I'd read your letters and wish I'd been able to go with you." He looked at me. "Was it really that good? Was it worth it?"

I paused, turned toward him. "It was, Wong. It was the best. But I had to . . . I was going to work it out with Xiao-An. My grandparents . . . it's really important to them. Me coming back, Xiao-An, everything. I couldn't just leave." Then I said, "I just thought . . . things would be different, that they might have changed just a little. But they haven't. Nothing has."

"Except you." He sighed, then slapped me on the shoulder. "Don't worry, I understand. You could have stayed and been with a beautiful gold-haired goddess. Instead, you're stuck with me."

*   *   *

My grandparents were in their eighties, living on social security. They had survived the war with Japan in the 1930s, then the civil war between Chiang Kai-shek's Nationalist Kuomintang and Mao Zedong's Communist Red Army. After that, the numerous trials set into motion by Mao Zedong, who promised to give the people better lives—the Hundred Flowers Movement, the Great Leap Forward, the Cultural Revolution—all witch hunts, blind persecutions.

All this my grandparents survived.

Grandfather was tall for a Chinese man, though you couldn't tell because he spent most of his time sitting. He had silver hair and always a saggy smile, as if he knew a joke too dirty to tell. But there were times when he'd had too much to drink, when the smile became a scowl and he would sit in the corner and brood, his eyes closed, facing the wall. I could feel the heat emanating from his body, his mind, as if he were waging a silent battle with the gods on why his life had taken the turns it had.

"Who do you think you are?" he'd shout. "If I could see you, I'd . . . hey, don't talk behind my back! Get over here! Talk to me!" Sometimes he'd let loose with a string of curses, calling us pigs and whores and other filthy names. We'd ignore him and it would die down. There was no use trying to stop him when we knew he'd eventually stop on his own.

Grandmother was short and chubby. Her skin was flecked with age spots, her knuckles swollen and fingers bent by arthritis, her back and shoulders arched and tilting forward. She had endured years of labor, first in the fields, then in the factories—both my grandparents had—but she never complained. It was only after Grandfather lost his sight that her mind began to waver, as if she, too, needed an affliction to stay on even ground. When they both fell into their trances and began to speak—to the spirits that haunted them, or those they begged for mercy—it was like they never crossed paths, never interfered with each other's experiences. Lu and I would sit in our room, drawing or making up fantastic stories for each other, but with one ear we were always listening to the conversations taking place between our grandparents' netherworlds, waiting for them to grow tired and stop, though they never found their answers.

Our house was tucked away inside a narrow *hutong* near the core of the city. Cars could not get by. Even rickshaws and bicycles had problems navigating because the road was broken up with stones and debris. We were used to it. It was a part of our home and no one ever had the need or means to repair it. There were fifteen families of various sizes in our *hutong*, jammed into this looping street like a wide-bent horseshoe, all our homes touching through the walls we shared, the roofs that leaked if a break occurred a few doors down.

The house was more of a corridor, three small rooms snugly fit in a row like aligned boxes; all the houses were like this. Our main room was the kitchen. In it was a small splintered table and gray iron stove that Grandmother cooked on and heated the rooms with simultaneously, whether it was cold or not. There was a small refrigerator, a few wood chairs, Grandfather's big chair in the corner. Next was my room, which I had shared with Lu ever since I could remember. The walls had several thin cracks from the roof to the floor that we had tried to paste and seal since we were boys. Now all that was left of our work was some chipped residue, faint stains.

My grandparents slept in the smallest room, which contained two small beds, with a framed painting of a green, red, and gold dragon, the paper old and yellow, and a calendar the only decor. Their walls were cracked too, and on the ceiling were perpetual spots of mold that we scrubbed and cleaned, but it never fully went away. The floors, which had once been hard-packed earth, were now concrete and covered with thin brown rugs. But water, Grandmother told me, still seeped in during the hard rains. Our windows were not broken, but the rotted wood frames and thin glass did not hold out the cold in the winter. The communal bathroom we still shared with all the other families in our *hutong* reeked painfully to me now, though it had never bothered me when I was a boy. The shower room in our house was like a closet or stall.

When Grandmother was doing housework, she would tell me how lucky we all were. "Your grandfather, they could have killed him. And we have you and Lu, though he doesn't write as much. The army keeps him busy. They're not allowed to read the newspapers or watch television, did you know that? All those letters you wrote us from America, the stories about funny movies and shows. And that girl, Lu doesn't understand any of it. I told him the last time he was home visiting, but he wouldn't even let us finish. He said it would interfere with his ability to work.

"When your parents died . . . We only had your mother, and even keeping her was a miracle. Then they took your grandfather's eyes. I ask myself why they chose us to suffer, but then I think my only daughter gave us not one grandson, but two: one a soldier of the people, another educated in America. Going to be married to a nice girl, a good secure family. What more could we ask for?"

"Why do you like Xiao-An so much?" I asked. It was April now and I'd listened to the same speech one too many times. This was my chance. I would tell her that it was over between Xiao-An and her family and me, that we were once again on our own.

"What do you mean?"

"You always talk about her father, her family. But do you like her? Do you think she's a good person?"

"Of course I do."

"That's what I'm asking. What do you like about *her*?"

Grandmother turned away.

"When you get old like us, maybe you'll understand. Security, young people take for granted. We might not be rich, but we always had food, we never had to scrape to keep you children alive. You didn't see what people used to do to each other. Fathers killing their own sons for stealing rice or food coupons, families selling their children for a meal. You don't know how lucky you are."

When I was not listening to Grandmother's lectures or worrying about finding a job, I wrote letters to Elsie. A part of me kept saying that she had lied to me, cheated on me, that I should forget about her completely, move on with my life. But I couldn't. I'd gotten so used to spending all my time with her that the writing felt like talking, therapy; I could trick myself into believing she was sitting across the room, tucked away beneath blankets, or around the corner in a chair. I told her how hard it was being back, feeling like I didn't belong. All these people, the looks on their faces, to them I was now the foreigner. The air was too thick, layered with dust and smoke. When I went out into the street I felt confined in some invisible cage. Everyone was coming right at me, trying to knock me down. In the *hutong* I was even more cloistered by what my grandparents wanted me to consider such joyous luck.

I told her that Xiao-An was newly engaged, and that her father was screwing me in ways I didn't and would probably never know. I wanted to blame her, say, "It's your fault," but I knew that wasn't true, and even if it was, I didn't have the courage to say it like that. In the letters I said I was angry with her for making the decision for us, for letting me believe that there had been a chance for a future when there never was. I told her how confused and scared I was, how I wanted to lash out, but I was not sure how.

I let her know that I did not hate her, that I missed her terribly and still loved her, that I always would. I said I was going to go back someday, so we could pick up where we had left off. I'd been thinking about it since returning, but how would I get back? Could I escape illegally, pay off a snakehead and ride in the bowels of some tanker or fishing boat, land on the coast of New York or California? Where would I go from there? Where would I get the money? And could I leave my grandparents for a second time, forever?

I'd let the pages pile up and every few days I'd edit them down, compose only the most important sections in my neatest handwriting, cut out what I felt was too bitter, too venomous, and ship it off. Even the editing reminded me of her—how she used to read all my papers and assignments, go over the grammatical errors, explain the correct usage using workbooks. She helped me sound out my mistakes, would stare with such focus and concern as I mimicked the shape of her mouth, the curls and twists of her tongue.

"It's a good thing you're a math major," she'd say. "Your English is terrible!"

When I didn't get any letters in return, I thought it was because I had angered her. Or maybe she was too busy with the boy from UCLA, the one who was going to be a doctor. I didn't want to think about that. Maybe she was just busy going through the same things I was: looking for a job, leaving the old life, building the next phase. She would write when she could. But weeks passed and I received no letters. I was certain I'd given her the right address. We had practiced writing it in both English and Chinese. Me teaching her, I watched her trace the scrawl of my characters.

I sent more than a dozen letters and still received nothing. After that I told myself that it was better this way. Ultimately she had lied to me, not the other way around. I had nothing to feel guilty about. Even if things had ended well between us, I could not go back right now, and she was not coming to Beijing. What would we do? Listen to Grandfather berate America and any way that was not Chinese? Listen to Grandmother's daily incessant rants? Where would she sleep? On the cold cement floor? Next to the burning stove? In my room, on that wretched bed where Lu and I had slept together all our lives? My grandparents would never allow it. Even now, sleeping alone on that broken bed without Lu's body to crowd me seemed like a luxury.

I was so caught up in my own woes that I had not thought much about Lu since returning, had made no attempt yet to get in touch with him. Big Brother was a soldier now, in the thirty-eighth group of the People's Liberation Army. I wasn't sure of his rank. There were pictures of Lu on our walls, snapshots and larger. He is in his olive uniform wearing silky white gloves, his face thin, sharp, and clean-shaven. In the pictures he marches in form, he salutes, he chants and sings with his division. Most of the pictures are taken from a distance so you cannot see the scar, but in one portrait in particular, the scar jumps out, as if it has been drawn in afterward. It happened so long ago, and we'd grown up with it, so that I'd almost forgotten about it. It takes a picture to remind me.

It was mid-April now. I was trying to find more job opportunities, more interviews. I dreaded the idea of running into another one of Xiao-An's father's associates.

During one of her lectures, Grandmother said my anguish stemmed from becoming "too American."

"I knew it would happen," Grandfather said from his chair. "How could it not? You send a boy to a different country and let him grow up there."

"He did not grow up there. He grew up here. We raised him, remember?" Then Grandmother said, "It's that white girl you were with. She filled you up with all those funny ideas. I hear it in your voice, see it when you walk around. You think you're better than everyone else."

"Maybe I am."

Grandfather, though he could not see, had turned his face in my direction. I was sitting at the table; there was silence. Tears filled Grandmother's eyes. I didn't look up for several moments. I didn't want to see the expression on her face.

She said, "What did they teach him over there? And what kind of girl . . ."

"Shut up," Grandfather said. "Everyone shut up! My head is killing me!"

The aroma of cooking filled our tiny house—scallions and mushrooms, sliced ginger, the tangy smell of sizzling sesame seed oil and soy. Every house in our *hutong* was redolent with the same, nearly identical smell. I went to the door to let in a breeze. I heard children playing and laughing in the narrow walkway, the sound of a bouncing ball, children arguing, fighting. Just like when we were kids, Lu and Wong and I, those eternal sounds. It was only April and the days were warm already, but cooled considerably by night. Smells changed in the dark. I wanted to breathe the fresh scent of trees and green spring leaves in upstate New York. See the students scrambling for open spaces in the libraries and study halls at all hours to prepare for final examinations. I had always preferred to stay in my room, or Elsie's, where no one bothered us and where we had a view of gray mountains, could feel the occasional hot breeze blowing through the windows threatening another coming summer. I wanted to feel again all that wide space. But it was the onset of another Beijing summer—the air thick and cloying, choked with dirt and dust and smog. I was halfway across the globe from the world I'd grown so quickly accustomed to and yearned for. Soon would come the daily blaze, the odd pungent stink of Beijing's streets. I came back in shaking my head.

Grandmother said, "Young people don't know how to appreciate."

On the radio an emergency broadcast was coming through. The reporter's voice said, "Former Party General Secretary Hu Yaobang died yesterday of a massive heart attack. A loyal fighter for communism and a great proletarian revolutionary, he will be dearly missed by all for the great achievements and efforts he made on behalf of the Party and the people during his honorable lifetime."

My grandparents stared at each other, then at me. I could hear through the open windows and doors an old woman sobbing, a young man calling out, children crying, confused.

* * *

Growing up we studied and learned the great lessons of the imperial dynasties, of the Long March and the wars against Japan. We were taught the virtues of Sun Yat-sen and Mao Zedong and those who had sacrificed and fought for the independence of our nation. For a time we read Mao's *Little Red Book*. I did not so much read it as I did carry it around in my pocket, trying to emulate Lu, who read it and discussed it with his pack of older friends. Big Brother wore the green cap and red armband and donned the silver and gold Mao pins like medals won in war. But he was much younger than the real Red Guards, all middle school kids, and no one took him seriously.

"You're going to fight the revolution?" Grandfather would ask him, and Lu would answer with lines from "The East Is Red," singing, "The red in the East raises the sun/China gives forth a Mao Zedong." We would all laugh because we knew Big Brother did not really know what he was talking about, he just liked to recite the words. But he looked so passionate and romantic in his fervor, singing bars of "I Love Beijing's Tiananmen": "I love Beijing's Tiananmen/ The sun rises over Tiananmen Gate./Our great leader Chairman Mao Zedong/Will guide us into the future."

Seldom did Lu take off the armband, and he always wore the green cap and his Mao buttons, unless Grandmother made him take it off to clean himself or go to bed. No one stopped him, even though at night we often heard bands of real Red Guards parading through nearby streets, mass stalking, calling out in a vitriolic singsong. They were unpredictable. No one knew who they were looking for and for what reasons, which home they would target next.

Then an old crazy woman from Grandfather's factory accused him of stealing her money and food coupons. The Red Guards came and called him out. We all followed. A group of three or four dozen waited for him, young men and women in olive uniforms. I thought I recognized some of them, middle school kids, neighbors from nearby *hutongs*. Grandfather was charged with stealing from the people and having capitalist, counterrevolutionary tendencies.

"HOW DO YOU PLEAD?" they shouted.

"I've done nothing wrong," Grandfather said.

They kicked Grandfather behind his knees until he bent and went to the ground. We watched the Red Guards pull his arms behind him and scream in his face, "ADMIT YOU'RE A CAPITALIST PIG! ADMIT YOU'RE AN ENEMY OF MAO ZEDONG!" Grandfather denied and wept because he wasn't and Grandmother was held back, her arms twisted behind her. They grabbed Lu and tore the hat from his head, Mao pins clinking against the street as they ripped the armband from his shirt. Trapped by the backs of our necks we watched them cut clumps of hair from Grandfather's head with a pocketknife and dump ink on his head. The ink seeped into his eyes and they rubbed his face into the gravel and dirt.

They took Grandfather away to be reeducated. Lu burned, by himself, his hat and Mao pins and buttons, the red armband he had worn with such pride. He did this while crying and muttering in the street. Grandmother and I watched from afar. She said little to us during those days, waiting for Grandfather to come home. Lu was sure it was because of him, that he had brought this bad luck upon us. I was a little boy and I told him, "No, that's not true," and I believed it.

Weeks later Grandfather returned. Lu hid under the bed for hours. It took us an entire evening to get him out. Grandfather came in with Grandmother at his side holding his arm. His face was ripped up and bruised, the scabs and scars around each eye flaring out like red stars. His head, at the reeducation camp, had been shaved completely bald. He looked starved, skinny, and sick, a stranger, but his voice was the same, heavy and strong. He said, "Come out, Lu. I'm not mad at you. Don't be scared. We can't be scared right now." But we were, we were little kids with a blind and beaten grandfather who had committed no crime at all.

After that, every year when there were public celebrations and events, Grandmother refused to go. Grandfather would still ask us to walk him out to the avenue, so he could feel the presence of the people and listen to the songs and chants because they made him feel alive.

The day after Hu Yaobang's death was announced, Wong was at our house eating dinner. Grandmother had prepared spring dumplings and wheat pancakes, shredded stir-fried pork and eggplant. We huddled around the table. Grandfather ate slowly, as he always did. Wong was shoveling into his mouth. I looked at the food and picked at the small plates, but had no appetite.

"Eat," Grandmother said.

"I'm not hungry."

"What do you mean, you're not hungry? You haven't had an appetite since you came back. Is my cooking not good enough for you anymore?"

"I'm not hungry, that's all. Don't make a big deal out of it."

"Big deal," she said. "You think you're a big deal." Then she left the kitchen.

"The students are very upset," Wong said. "They feel like Hu Yaobang was one of the last people left in the Party who could really help them."

"Help them?" Grandfather said. "He's been out of power for two years!"

"Yes," Wong said, "but just his presence. He cared about the people, not just politics. He had the guts to think differently, that's why Deng Xiaoping put him down. He didn't believe in maintaining the old ways just for the sake of preserving them." Wong turned to me. "We're organizing a march. Will you go?"

Grandmother came back into the kitchen. "He won't," she said.

"It's just a short march, then a rally at Tiananmen. You should go," Wong said.

"Students protesting, I guess it's about time," Grandfather said. "When Zhou Enlai died students came out to protest the Gang of Four. Everyone did, right, Grandma? Over ten years ago, you boys probably don't remember." Grandfather nodded, then stuffed his mouth with a dumpling. "But you can't compare Hu Yaobang to Zhou Enlai. You want a reason to protest against Deng Xiaoping? He's the one who brought back the colleges. Without him, you'd be milling away like some mindless mule in the countryside for the Gang of Four. Deng Xiaoping saved us from that!"

"You're not going," Grandmother said. "Do you hear me? Listen to your grandfather. What do you all have to protest about?"

"The conditions at the school," Wong said. "We fight so hard to get in, but what do we learn? The universities say they've modernized the system to adapt to the future, but they're teaching us outdated propaganda! And they know it. And look at what Deng Xiaoping's reforms have done. Everything is so expensive, and unemployment is going up, not down. Even for students who go away, there's no guaranteed future. You"—Wong pointed at me—"you know."

"Shut up, Wong."

Grandmother said, "Wong, finish up. It's time for you to go."

Wong and I locked eyes. "Thank you," he said to my grandparents. Grandmother quickly took away Wong's empty bowl and chopsticks.

History detailed how demonstrations were a part of our culture, our tradition. When a great leader died, people took to the streets to protest against the existing leadership, as they did for Zhou Enlai. He was a Long March veteran and one of the principal architects of the People's Republic of China, Mao's right-hand man. Grandfather was right, Hu Yaobang never had such stature, but he had been the Party's general secretary, and it made sense that the students would do something, even if it was minor, just for one day.

I did remember the demonstrations that took place in Zhou Enlai's memory; I was nine years old. A river of marchers flooded Chang'an Avenue, the Avenue of Eternal Peace, which leads to Tiananmen Square. I was with Grandmother on the sidewalk and we were crowded off to the side, backs against barriers so the protesters could sweep past. One man had a white rag tied around his head. It read THE PEOPLE WILL SPEAK. A tattered red banner with gold characters flapped in the breeze: LONG LIVE DEMOCRACY.

I didn't know what democracy was. They sang and chanted with their fists high and pumping the air. Some carried wreaths and giant posters that they would tack to the base of the Monument to the People's Heroes in Tiananmen Square. They sang the "Internationale." "No one will give us our deliverance/No god, no czar, no hero/We'll arrive at our freedom only by our own hand." They walked with locked arms creating a human barrier. I saw police and soldiers scattered throughout the bystanders, but they were only observing. I grasped Grandmother's hand, afraid, unknowing. I watched and listened as the flow of bodies made their way to the square where they would air their grievances for all to see.

Afterward my grandparents talked about how unfair it was for Deng Xiaoping to take the fall for the protest. Years later, after Deng had become our nation's leader, we were taught how the Gang of Four had convinced Mao, on his deathbed, that Deng had been his enemy all along. Deng would be vilified as an "unrepentant capitalist roader," and sent down, but it was not the first time he had been deposed by Mao, after surviving the Cultural Revolution in the 1960s. History had proven that Deng Xiaoping, when faced with adversity, would undoubtedly bounce back.

2

Comrade

It was not unusual for Mao to appear in his dreams. They had been together for so long, more than forty years, and at times he considered Mao a friend. Until the end, the final years when dissension was ubiquitous, the Gang of Four running rampant, trying to take total control of the country, and in his dementia no one knew what to expect from the Chairman next. But then, and even now, Deng felt a loyalty to the Chairman, an attachment, as if more always needed to be said and done to prove his loyalty, and beyond that he could not explain.

Toward the end of Mao's reign, while Deng was still in exile he had had dreams of Mao bedridden, his face bloated and shiny, as if made from wax, lips chalky and white, numb, hair gray and oily, combed back so that it did not hang in his face. In those dreams Mao spoke clearly, eloquently, not like a plaster figure frozen in a mausoleum. He sat upright in bed and told Deng to lead on, to take up where he had left off when his mind had been straight and clear. Deng and the mantle of the dragon throne, his destiny. In his dreams Mao apologized, admitted his hubristic flaws.

"I was trying," Mao told him. "I thought I was doing right."

"I know. No one blames you."

"But they do, Deng. I know they do." Then the ghost said, "Little friend, you've always been loyal, never conspired behind my back. Now you take the reins."

Deng told him he would fight to purge the state of enemies and die for the revolutionary cause, a cause that had begun over seven decades ago. Deng believed in the things he said, even though they were spoken in dreams.

Lately, more than twelve years since Mao had died, the dreams brought them together in action on the trails of the Long March, when they were young hard men marching at night to avoid enemy eyes, sleeping on the packed earth as they wended their way through the hills of the countryside, exhorting village peasants to join their new Red Army. They slept and worked in caves, some so small they could feel the closeness of the land around them as they breathed the dirt and felt the coolness or heat of the rocks like another body next to them, giant domelike caves where they gave speeches and recruited new members to fight as a part of this new Communist brotherhood. They preached to the peasants about Karl Marx and socialism, how one day the people would hold the power, and bureaucrats like Chiang Kai-shek, who made himself and his governing powers rich and kept the simple farmer and worker down, would be no more. This is what people wanted to hear, what they envisioned as the future, and they believed. On the trails they carried rice and dried meats, killed animals and ate flowers and fruit given to them by villagers. They shot mountain lions and wild boar. From southeastern Jiangxi province, west to the city of Zunyi, then north through the mountains and marshes of central and western China, the Nationalist armies and mercenaries were always on their tails. A spiraling journey through the land, a march into history.

In this dream all the men eat from the same iron rice bowl, as they had been taught by communism to do, the way to uniformity, and victory. Except Mao, who eats from his own bowl, separating himself. Here is a wolf-faced Mao, lean and sharp-eyed, his hair long and wavy framing the sides of his face. He smokes cigarette after cigarette, blowing clouds into the air of the blue night. He says to Deng, "You know, you are blessed. Your size gives you an advantage. People think the bigger the better, but we know strength comes from the heart and mind."

"They underestimate," Deng says. "I'm used to this."

"But no one should ever underestimate you, Deng Xiaoping."

Mao stands with a rifle and blasts a shot into the night, and in the purple drop of evening stars shatter and rocket the sky.

Deng woke up, wondered what it meant. It was early, the dawn silver and bleeding. He felt his heart beating fast but it did not worry him. His wife lay next to him, snoring. He realized he had not the time to analyze silly dreams, for there was work to be done, business to be taken care of.

* * *

At first what happened did not surprise him. Passionate, discontented students (always discontented—where would the world be if not for the unhappy young?) took to the square with wreaths and flowers, posters hailing Hu Yaobang. Smaller crowds than the last demonstrations Deng remembered, when the great Zhou Enlai had passed away, but that was a different time, thirteen years ago, and Beijing was a different place. Back then the people were poor and sick; they no longer believed in the personality cult of Mao. They hated the Gang of Four, their totalitarian and shrewish conniving. It was the students who gave the people their voice, who put themselves in the path of danger. Deng knew it would be the students, now and years and decades after he was gone, who would always take on this responsibility.

The papers did not report on the first student demonstrations. A few days before memorial services for Hu Yaobang, Deng received reports from the Public Security Bureau at his home telling him of the small mass of bicycles and marchers who carried their protest flags and memorial wreaths. All of this was fine. Let the students have the day, air their petty grievances, the harmless swagger of a youthful crowd. Was China not a land built on revolution? It was a tradition the students had inherited. Without revolution you did not achieve change. History had taught the people, exemplified through years of struggle and turmoil. Police strength was increased and spotters were placed in the crowds to observe, but nothing more.

Then came the demands.

The students had organized, the reports said. They were no longer just a casual, harmless mob of youth out for a public display. There were thousands of them. They had a focus, a center and point. They demanded the reassessment of Hu's career, so that his name in the history books would not be shamed. An independent student union demanded to be recognized by the government. They wanted Party leaders to publicly reveal their income and assets. They wanted freedom of the press, more money for education, a stop to official corruption. The report mentioned a giant wall poster hung on the Monument to the People's Heroes in Tiananmen Square. It read, "Those who should live are now dead, and those who should die live on."

They smashed bottles in the square. Xiaoping, "little bottle," was the name he had been given by family and neighbors as a child. In years past, when he'd just taken control of the government after Mao's passing, they had waved bottles in the air to celebrate their new leader. Now they smashed them on the stone steps of the Great Hall. This kind of behavior was unacceptable. Something had to be done.

*　　*　　*

He called his driver and told him to pick him up in a half hour. They were going to the square.

"Sir, are you sure?" the driver asked.

"Why? Is there a problem?"

"No, sir. But the protests . . . the square is very . . ."

"We're not going for a joyride."

When the car arrived the driver asked Deng if anyone else would be joining him, if they should call for a motorcade.

"No motorcade. We're just going to Tiananmen."

"Yes, sir. Will Comrades Yang or Zhao be joining you?"

"No. What is your problem today? Just get in the car and drive."

From his house to the square was only a short ride by car, ten minutes at most, unless halted by Beijing's unforgiving traffic. The constant cramming of bodies and bicycles and cars and trucks that could leave entire city blocks immobilized by one stalled engine or blown tire. But now they moved quickly through the side streets between Jingshan Park and the Capital Theater. It was oddly quiet. Though he had problems at times seeing through the dark tinted glass, Deng saw the stores and coffee shops and even many of the street vendors were closed. Rickshaws and pedicabs were nowhere to be found, the few random bicyclists zipping through the streets seemed as if they trailed or precluded some greater parade. The emptiness made him uncomfortable.

He remembered when Beijing was the newly inhabited capital after the defeat of Chiang Kai-shek. The streets were scattered and violent, in total and flushed disarray, and Mao had gone on a tear to redesign. The peasants and vagrants were removed, either imprisoned or relocated back to the countryside. Trees were uprooted and buildings torn down only to rebuild those buildings and replant those trees, different and new ones according to the Chairman's plans; they would be called "revolutionary" trees, "revolutionary" buildings. Roads were repaved, widened. There was talk of decimating the Forbidden City, that symbol of oppressive imperial rule, but ultimately they talked the Chairman out of it—it was impossible to move forward if the people did not remember and learn from the past—thus the Forbidden City survived. The Chairman would be mildly placated with the rushed construction of Tiananmen Square, the Great Hall of the People, the Monument to the People's Heroes, and all the surrounding museums. They hung the Chairman's portrait on the Gate of Heavenly Peace, the entrance to the Forbidden City, directly across Chang'an Avenue facing Tiananmen Square. The irony, Deng thought. And even with all this rapid transition, through the years it was still a slow kind of metamorphosis that led to the greatest of change: no more the wild congestion of poor, indigent, and sick families in the streets and on the corners and in alleys, bewilderment in their eyes, selling their children, big and small, for just the slightest grace of food. Where do we go? What do we do?

Deng remembered. It was what drove them to change the world.

At the corner of Chang'an Avenue and Nanheyan Street the car idled into a crowd at the intersection. There were no police in sight. The light was green but the cars were not moving because of the large cluster of people on bicycles and on foot, meeting like a team planning their next strategic play. The driver honked and when they saw the black car and government plates they turned head by head to look at it. They started to shift out of the street, one by one. They were mostly young men, but there were some women in the crowd. College students, Deng thought. Too old to be middle school. They did not know who was inside the car.

"Don't honk again," Deng said.

"If I don't honk, sir, they won't move."

"They will. Just wait."

On Chang'an Avenue they headed toward the square and only when they were blocks away could Deng sense the vibrations in the air, tremors of instability. To his right was the Gate of Heavenly Peace, the giant portrait of the Chairman hanging clear and shining in the sun. To his left the square was roiling.

"Go around. And keep going," Deng said. "Don't stop, no matter what."

The driver turned left. The Great Hall was to Deng's right, but he was looking left toward the crowds. He had not seen the square like this in so long, not even during last year's National Day when the people lined Chang'an Avenue and came to hear him speak, watch him drive down the avenue standing through the opening of his black car, saluting. Now there were mobs of black-haired children—they all looked like children to him. Hundreds and hundreds of packs, like the group at the intersection before, mostly young men. As they had been when he and the other leaders were considered young revolutionaries, rebels. They drove slowly, stopped for walking packs and people on bicycles gravitating toward the square. They circled around the south end of the square where the Chairman's Memorial Hall stood. The crowd was thinner there. When they passed the Memorial Hall Deng saw a young man in a white shirt shouting into a megaphone, though Deng could not hear what he said. They passed him and there was another young man with a megaphone. Then another. They sat on each other's shoulders so their voices could travel farther and Deng could see the strain of screaming on their faces. The signs above them an explosion of color, as if the original revolution had been reborn. Through the tinted glass he could not read the posters and signs and banners, but he knew this was not his revolution.

No one in the square recognized the car circling, the people smiling and gathering on the fringes, to be a part of this mass gathering, witness an event of magnitude unknown. They kept filing in, already the square resembling a bowl of humanity ready to spill.

As he watched he remembered Mao more than thirty years ago assembling his Red Guards in Tiananmen, when the Great Proletarian Cultural Revolution officially began. Teenagers, some no more than twelve or thirteen years old, Mao's generals had collected them from all the provinces of the nation to come hear him speak, give his approval and order to establish a new . . . what? What had he wanted to do? How many people died, how many persecuted unjustly? Himself, all the brothers of the Long March. His own son, Deng Pufang, "suicided," dropped four stories from a dorm room, crippled. The result of calling to arms the masses.

Examining the crowd he thought of his son at home right now, in a wheelchair forever, watching television or reading a book. The days when he could not help his boy because he was himself in exile and knowing the boy was hurt and scared and there was nothing anyone in the family could do but pray that he live, or die, whichever option the gods deemed less painful.

A loud clanking noise and Deng ducked down, swung his head around, expecting to see a culprit, but he saw only the crowd.

"It's nothing, sir," the driver said. "A stray bottle or something."

"Be more careful, will you?" He sat back up. To have debris thrown at an official government car would have been . . . it made Deng boil inside.

From the moving car he saw it in their faces, the fervor, minds whipping. A part of him wanted to hear what these student leaders were saying. Then he thought, No, I will not call them leaders. They are just children, kids. They have done nothing. He remembered the summer of 1966, when Mao had brought together his Red Guards before the release of *dongluan*, the terror and turmoil of chaos, a sea of fanatics crying and screaming, chanting and singing as they waved Mao's *Little Red Book*. They lined Chang'an Avenue and jammed every inch of the square. A part of him still believed that the experience should have steeled him for what came next, shown him the direction of what needed to be done. But no one could have known.

He took one last look and saw young women sitting on the shoulders of their boyfriends, clusters of schoolkids holding hands and laughing in awe of this gathering so great. Many were smiling like they were celebrating New Year's or the Harvest Moon Festival, a concert or some kind of fair. And he felt in that moment a separation, as if viewing a different life, like a ghost would see the land of the living and not know what to make of it.

"Home," he said to the driver as they finished their third lap around. He felt his heart pounding and thought maybe this had been a bad idea. But he had to see things firsthand, for himself, or else he would never be able to take control.

*　*　*

At home he thought he was alone. This was good, he needed quiet time, away from even the family. He had been lacking strength lately, his hands shaking more than usual, the occasional heart flutter, losing his breath in midsentence. He thought of the student demands. Let's see where they go. He knew in the heat and glamour of public outcries things were said and done that often fizzled very quickly. Had he not been a hunted revolutionary as a teenager living and working in France? He had been young once too.

In the screening room, where they held private Party meetings, and where he liked to show movies for himself and the family, he found Pufang. In his wheelchair reading, Pufang looked sad. A middle-aged man, handsome, with his mother's pretty features, a solid build across his chest and shoulders and neck. Even in the chair he looked much larger than his father. He had been living with Deng and Zhuo Lin for years now, and Deng had built wider hallways and an elevator and even installed intercoms in every room so Pufang could communicate throughout the house if need be. He saw his boy like this every day, the useless and emaciated legs that dangled from the seat. A college student then, he had been locked in a closet and beaten repeatedly by Red Guards until his mind became bleary, for being the son of a "capitalist roader." The window on the fourth floor of his dormitory was kicked out, leaving a huge gaping hole. They beat him and kicked him and cursed. They pointed to the hole in the wall and said it was the only way he would escape alive. Somehow he went through: had he deliriously crawled by himself, or was he thrown?

He did not remember, Pufang had said, and Deng was glad for at least this. The incident was never discussed again.

Now Pufang looked up at his father and Deng sat next to him.

"Why read in the dark?"

"It's quiet in here. I have a light on."

"What are you reading?"

"Nothing," his son said, an answer he was accustomed to.

"Do you want to watch a movie with me? *Rambo*?" Deng said in English.

Pufang laughed. It made Deng feel better. "I'll never know why you like that movie, Ba. It's a little weird, if you ask me."

"I'm an old man. Let me have my small pleasures." He patted his son's hand. They laughed together, then they sat quietly. Deng let go of Pufang's hand.

"You've heard about the demonstrations going on in Tiananmen?"

"Of course."

Deng lit a cigarette. He offered one to his son, but Pufang declined. "It's bad," Deng said. He stood and paced behind Pufang, spit in his spittoon. He could feel the boy wanting to talk. "You have something to say, say it."

"They're upset about Hu Yaobang's death. You remember how popular he was."

"I know, but it's not about Hu anymore. It's . . . never mind. I shouldn't be talking about this with you."

Pufang reopened his book. Deng felt the air thicken around them. It was a mistake to bring this up with Pufang, with his humanitarian ideals and unrealistic goals. He had probably walked in on the boy preparing another speech to raise money for the China Welfare Fund for the Handicapped, a mission he had started on his own, without his father's pull and support. Though he had decreased his activity in the past couple years, Deng admired Pufang's verve, but questioned his judgment. He was sure that Pufang would be out there with those students if he was normal and whole, if he was not the son of the nation's leader and confined to the steel chair. He was not much older than the majority of the students, and he had never hidden his independent ideas from Deng. Pufang feigned reading for a moment, then wheeled himself out of the room and down the hall.

Deng returned to his study where he made a few calls. He wanted the latest Public Security Bureau report on what was happening in the square: how many students, what they were doing, what they were saying. As if he had not been there himself, as if he could blot those images from his mind and reform them through the words and perceptions of others. He called senior members of the Central Committee, President Yang Shangkun, then General Secretary Zhao Ziyang, then Premier Li Peng. They were all unavailable, in meetings. All his career—his life—he had learned to deal and live with insurrection. It was easier to extinguish a small fire before it grew into a blaze.

He wanted to know why they were so angry, so dissatisfied. This way of life they despised, didn't they understand how many had fought and died to get to this point? Inflation was high, but the average person's quality of life was so much better. Deng witnessed it himself when he drove through the city and out the window he saw the young men and ladies dressed smartly, walking and riding bicycles, businessmen in suits clustered together crossing streets. People owned their own homes, cars. New businesses from inside China and out. China's first McDonald's, and Kentucky Fried Chicken. Coca-Cola, major clothing manufacturers; the Japanese were putting in millions, even industries from Taiwan. He had constructed these deals to bring in revenue, make the country a richer, better place. He had always said, "It does not matter if it's a black cat or a white cat—if it catches mice, then it's a good cat." There was no series of five-year plans. If he thought a new policy might work, they tried it right away. They were not afraid of experimenting and failing if it meant development; politics did not clothe and feed the people, but action just might.

And still they were not satisfied. They wanted life to be more free, liberated in every facet, like America, the West. He was afraid he had already given them too much freedom, made life too easy. Otherwise they would not constantly be asking for more, they would learn to appreciate. Democracy: they chanted the word and scrawled it across posters, but could they define it? Could they live it? The loudest voices of dissent, they didn't know what it was, wouldn't know where to start. The people needed leadership, whether they chose to believe it or not.

He thought about going swimming but felt the drive around the square and all this anticipation had depleted him. It was midafternoon and he just wanted to rest, keep his mind clear and agile for when reports would be more detailed. He sat and smoked a cigarette and when he was finished he lit another. A part of him wished it was not Hu Yaobang's death that had started all this. Hu had been too liberal: he did not speak or behave like a Marxist, which Deng knew was why he had become so popular with the media, the people. Hu had been in love with the West, and Deng remembered him serving French snails at dinners and introducing to the nation's intellectuals a writer named Camus. He had even carried on an occasional correspondence with Richard Nixon. Too much, Deng thought. But Hu was a good man and had been a good Party general secretary, until he had overstepped his boundaries, allowed too much freedom to the people. His own actions and policies made the government too vulnerable. It was necessary for him to be taken down.

He had received his punishment and played the role of victim admirably, as Deng himself had during the Cultural Revolution. Know your role, have respect and honor, patience. The course of history was unpredictable and often illogical. You had to be prepared to take a fall if you wanted to climb higher. These were virtues he prided himself on, and in the end Hu had done his best to live up to such a creed. He wanted to give Hu a hero's farewell, this was his priority. And in one month Mikhail Gorbachev was coming to China to discuss the Sino-Soviet future, the first peaceful visit by a Russian leader in thirty years.

3

Dissident

Immediately following the announcement of Hu Yaobang's death, there were minor demonstrations in Tiananmen Square. I did not go. But now an official government warning had been issued that the square would be closed off the day of Hu Yaobang's memorial service, one week after his death. Wong and his university friends and I gathered the night before in his cramped gray dorm room, drawing up posters and placards, some scrawling messages on rags to tie around their heads. He had four other roommates, and they all slept on bunk beds held up by gray iron posts. The paint was flaking off the walls, the windows dirty. Compared to my old dorm, this was a prison, which was why many of the students wanted to protest—the squalid conditions, terrible food.

"Who brought the guns?" Wong said. I told him not to be an idiot.

We met up with other groups from around the campus in a quad near the main entrance. A night of stars, the airy feeling of suspense, and I saw it was more than just two handfuls of bodies; there were hundreds now. We marched straight down Xinjiekou Avenue. In the streets on the way to the square we rendezvoused with packs from other universities—Beida and Renmin, others—and made our way in the darkness, each clandestine meeting at a street corner or intersection doubling the size of our march. Who had organized all this? Was there some kind of network of student bodies? Our numbers were growing so fast. It was exciting, too, because I hadn't been through these streets, these neighborhoods, since I'd come back. I was relearning my city, my home.

I locked arms with Wong. "Isn't this fun?" he said.

"Sure," I said.

He gave me a firm shake and said, "I'm glad you're here."

"You know, when this is over, my grandmother is going to kill me."

"I'm not afraid of her," Wong said. "Besides, we've done worse."

We kept our voices low but we could not mask the pounding of so many feet, a steady wave. I thought I could see spying eyes from the black windows of buildings. When we reached the square it was like a flood of buzzing bodies pouring in. I could not tell exactly how many were there, several hundred, maybe a thousand. It was incredible to me that so many had made it through the maze of the city without incident or detection. The square was lit by high lamps, the energy and feel and smell of all these people, the humble murmur of vast voices. No one gave any loud or direct orders but the majority crowded the base of the Monument to the People's Heroes. It had taken over an hour to march to the square. It took some time to get settled, spread out, people lying down, sitting, squatting, tacking their signs and wreaths and banners to the base of the Memorial. Many were still talking and lively, invigorated.

"So now we wait," Wong said. "We made it."

"Great," I said. "Wake me when Deng Xiaoping arrives."

I closed my eyes and woke two hours later, the stone gray bleakness of dawn creeping over the square. Police and soldiers came and found us sitting quietly. There were dozens of trucks and at least one hundred police officers and soldiers. We did not know what to expect. The commanders watched us from a distance like we were beasts escaped from the zoo, their expressions dumbstruck as they huddled together making calls on their radio phones. The police and soldiers moved back, no one quite sure what to make of the situation.

Someone said, "What if they come back?"

"I don't see them leaving—what do you mean, 'come back'?"

"With more . . . you know."

No one replied.

But by midmorning no extra troops had come and those that stayed showed no signs of aggression. They acted as if we were not there, lining the roads that ringed Tiananmen, hoping to deter more people from joining us. But as the day stretched the crowd grew. We could feel it hour by hour, the massed energy, building, compressed. The time of Hu Yaobang's memorial arrived. We saw black government cars driving on Chang'an Avenue past the square, heading toward the rear of the Great Hall.

"They're going through the back door!" someone shouted. "They're afraid to look us in the eye!" The crowd erupted.

Only in broad daylight could I see just how many had accumulated. A sea of black heads and peering eyes, congestion that stretched across the square. People intermittently trickling in off the streets. All this energy, it was impossible to tell exactly how many were like myself, disgruntled and swept up by the fervor, how many aspired to be leaders of some future revolution.

Wong said, "Never had a rally like this at your American college, did you?" He gave me a wink.

Throughout the day students gave speeches on topics ranging from the conditions of their dorms, to human rights and democracy, all framed by the death of Hu Yaobang. One student claimed that his university's food was poisoned, to keep the students slightly ill, brainwashed so they would not complain about all the government's squandering. I thought his conspiracy theory was funny, but some took him seriously. We listened and clapped.

I remembered Elsie first taking me to a rally; it was to help protect the environment, held on one of the great lawns on campus. Hundreds filled the open grass. They brought banners painted in splashing, swirling colors, blankets to sit on. A podium was set up, and one by one, young men and women stepped up to the microphone and gave torrid, angry, emphatic speeches. Or so they seemed as they were delivered. I couldn't understand their accents, all the words. Their voices were loud and fast, booming through the sound system. One girl could not help but shriek every time she tried to make a point. The man following her had long wavy brown hair, his face covered by a heavy beard. He spoke slowly and raised his fist, pumping the air. It was early spring, sunny and breezy. Campus security officers and town police stood on the perimeter, but there were no incidents. When the speakers were done we picked up pamphlets and walked away. All the following demonstrations that Elsie and I attended—supporting animal rights, pro-choice, a heavy-set middle-age woman running for local office—were similar. Occasionally there were arguments or hecklers and someone had to be led away by security, but that was almost expected. There was never any violence. To push it to that level would have been like admitting you were wrong.

Wong was right, the Cornell rallies had never been this big, this exciting. But even then, without fully understanding, I knew that the Americans knew they had the right to gather and express without fear, the power of collective voices; we were living that now like the discovery of some ancient rite.

By midafternoon the sun was high and hot. The number of armed police and public security officers guarding the perimeter thinned. People started streaming out of the square like water rushing out of a great pool. Out the windows of stopped cars and taxis people cheered. They came out of their stores to hand out sodas and juice and free sweets, stopped their casual strolls to flash peace signs or give the thumbs-up, to take part in this odd train of festivities. The stoic, flat sadness that I'd felt clinging to me, the city, the people, was gone. Like the protest had ripped off an old scab, making room for new, fresh skin.

*   *   *

Later that afternoon I walked into the house. Grandmother smacked me hard across the face. She stared, did not back down. For a moment I felt like I was five years old, caught fighting or stealing candy from the neighbor's child.

"What do you think you're doing!"

"Don't ever hit me again."

"What are you going to do, hit me back?"

I went to the sink for water, rubbing my face. I said, "You think I'm still a little boy?" I heard my own voice trembling, felt the sting of Grandmother's hand, something vibrating in my chest. Grandfather was sitting in his chair. I thought he was passed out from drinking or just sleeping. I turned to go to my room when he said, "Where do you think you're going?" He reached for his glass, but there was none by his side. "You learn how to dodge bullets in America? You learn all that at your fancy college? Look at my face, boy. Look at me." He groped the air around his small table once more, then said, "Get me a drink."

Grandmother handed him a glass filled with a few splashes of rice wine. He slurped it loudly.

"You're drunk," I said.

"That's right . . . I'm a blind drunk old man. I don't know anything. You young people . . . think you rule the world!"

I went to my room to be away from them, calm down, though I had no door to close. I fell asleep to Grandfather's mumbling, then both their voices lingering behind me. I woke up near dinnertime, came out and sat at the table next to Grandfather. I tried to explain what had happened, why we were out there, how natural it had all seemed, but no one was listening. Grandmother stood by the sink with her back turned to me. Grandfather was grumbling to himself.

"I called Xiao-An's father," Grandmother said. She stared at me. Her eyes were scratched with pink veins, disbelieving. "He told me everything. You stupid, stupid boy."

"Wait . . . let me explain . . ."

"Do you know how hard it was to find Xiao-An, how fortunate we were? Such a nice girl, a good family! Look at all they did for you! They liked you. They were going to accept us into their family. But no, you had to throw it away with that white girl, that piece of trash! You waste all this opportunity, all the chances you get. Don't you know how fortunate you are? You're so selfish! We couldn't do any of these things for Lu, and did he ever complain once? Look at his face. Never once did he feel sorry for himself. I am so ashamed of you. Your mother is ashamed of you." She said a prayer to herself.

Grandfather said, "If Lu was here, he'd beat you! Lu still has respect." He took a loud gulp and set the glass back down. Grandmother said, "Lu would never do something like this. He's got common sense, he understands being loyal. Your mother, she's screaming in Heaven . . . ."

"Lu's a warrior," Grandfather said. "Not like this one. Stinking intellectual!"

"You're a lousy drunk, you're both crazy! You make me sick!"

It didn't surprise me when it happened, the hard crack high on my face. I was amazed at how fast Grandfather was, like his hand moved of its own volition. I stared into the table, felt myself starting to shake.

"I'll kill you myself! I swear I'll kill you!" Grandfather was swinging at me, but I'd jerked out of reach. He was standing and shouting, wobbly. I went to my room and threw what I could grab in a small bag. Grandmother stormed in and grabbed me. She was crying, shouting, "Why did you do this? We wanted you to get out of this, to move up! Are you trying to destroy the whole family?" I shoved her aside. In the kitchen Grandfather was still standing at the table, his arms stretched in front of him. Grandmother followed me out into the *hutong*. "You're not my grandson! You're worthless! Don't come back!" I heard Grandfather's voice behind her, "He's not worth a rat's shit!"

I marched through the dark streets, headed toward the square.

*   *   *

I used to go to Tiananmen with my grandparents when I was small, Lu and I each holding my grandparents' hands. This was before Grandfather's incident. Even after, there were times when we would walk through the square and he would hold on to us and take slow careful steps with his arms draped through ours.

Grandfather told us it had been built by Mao Zedong as a symbol of his new regime. If Stalin had Red Square, Mao would have Tiananmen. Thousands of volunteers worked day and night for no pay; it was an honor to do the bidding of the Chairman. To the west would stand the Great Hall, to the east the Museum of Chinese History and the Museum of the Chinese Revolution. Rigid columns and sprawling stone steps, the grandeur of institution meant to be immortal. At the south end rose the Monument to the People's Heroes, and directly north, across Chang'an Avenue, was Tiananmen Gate and the Forbidden City. As if the square and this circle of history had been strategically placed to balance, if not rectify, the imperial oppression of old.

"The work never stopped," Grandfather said. "Like they were racing against the end of the world." The square and its surroundings, as Mao had wished, were complete by October 1, 1959, National Day. It was the tenth anniversary of the founding of the People's Republic of China. In 1949 Mao had stood on Tiananmen Gate overlooking the masses lining the avenue and filling the square, and declared that China was no longer a doormat of the East. Like the emperors who had erected great projects in their own honor, Mao now had his. It was only fitting that when Mao died, his mausoleum would be built just south of the Monument to the People's Heroes, the anchor of Tiananmen Square.

Each year state celebrations were held in Tiananmen, like National Day, and New Year's celebrations, as well as state memorials. As was supposed to happen for Hu Yaobang, but did not because of us.

On April 26, four days after Hu Yaobang's memorial, an editorial ran in the *People's Daily*. It was titled "It Is Necessary to Take a Clear-Cut Stand Against Disturbances." It claimed that a small number of agitators were spreading rumors and attacking Party and state leaders, that illegal organizations had been formed on many college campuses, and that the agitators were actually undermining the democracy and legal system that they blatantly flaunted. It also said the agitators' goal was to "sow dissension among the people, plunge the whole country into chaos and sabotage the political situation of stability and unity." Wong and I read this in his room.

"*Dongluan,*" I said.

"Does the government think we're trying to revive the Cultural Revolution?"

Students were outraged, and in the days to follow they gathered from all over Beijing and other cities. The crowds for Hu Yaobang's memorial had been large, but now the square was teeming. We slept out every night, in sleeping bags and under thin blankets, some covered and padded by only newspapers and jackets. We sat piled on one another, back to back, side to side, not a spare bit of space to stretch or move. Smells all around me: sweaty skin and oily hair, cigarettes, garbage, food. No one tried to stop us: no barricades, no soldiers, not even foot police. Had the authorities forgotten? In the past there had always been quick and decisive movement to quell such disturbances, but now there was none.

During the days, students stood on big empty boxes with microphones and voiced their problems, all the things Wong and I had been talking about: how the universities were run-down and the teachers were getting old, how the Communist and socialist rhetoric had become outdated and proved unsophisticated, almost naive. How they studied so many hours each week, were expected to fulfill strict requirements only to take a lousy state job that overworked them and paid so poorly, if they could even get one.

I was a living example, proof that the system didn't work. If the *People's Daily*, the government's mouthpiece, was going to insinuate that we were trying to cause chaos, then we would make it obvious that we were peaceful, civil, organized. We wanted fair treatment and to be heard, not chaos. A leadership group of more than a dozen students came together. They said they had been voted in, but by whom Wong and I were not sure. The leaders proposed three main demands: the renouncement of the April 26 *People's Daily* editorial; for the government to meet with students and begin a dialogue; and for the press to report honestly on what was taking place. They were fair demands, everyone agreed.

There were hundreds of banners flapping and waving above the crowds—PATRIOTISM IS NOT A CRIME; JUSTICE WILL PREVAIL; THE PRESS MUST TELL THE TRUTH. They represented universities and middle schools, and were joined by the flags of factory unions that had chosen to voice their discontent as well. Low wages and long hours, the lack of opportunity to move up. It was greater than a student demonstration now because all the people of the city had joined in—teachers, workers, the common people, *laobaixing*. The square besieged, the pop and crackle of charged voices, among it all vendors sold beverages and ice cream, setting up on the fringes of the square, some walking through peddling their wares. Parents brought their small children and couples held hands as if attending a carnival or bazaar, that feeling of new celebration replacing the downtrodden old.

Cardboard donation boxes for us students were passed around and always came back full. So we could eat and stay out in the square. Indeed, the *laobaixing* was growing a new skin.

At times when it was quiet I thought of Elsie. We knew all the little things about each other. She was an English major, a liberal Democrat who wished elections were every two years instead of four, so she could vote more often. She loved animals, especially dogs. I used to say that if things got bad enough, the Chinese would eat her pets, part of our history, tradition. She didn't find this funny. When I worked out and played ball at the fitness center, she did aerobics and yoga. At every meal I stuffed myself with meat, and grew to like cheese. In the dining hall there was always an entrée with cheese, breakfast, lunch, or dinner, whether it was meat and cheese, pasta and cheese, bread and cheese. Americans loved cheese. Elsie would not even take a bite of hamburger, chicken, or cheese, because it was all made from animals. She loved music, loved to dance, to move her body in her own smooth rhythm. She did not go to church on Sunday mornings as many of her friends did.

"Organized religion is bad," she said. "Mind-controlling."

"Like Communist Party," I said.

She knew that my parents had been farmers and had died when I was a baby, that my grandparents and I were poor. I explained the Great Leap Forward and China's history of famine. I explained how we had lived our lives buying food with tickets and coupons, small money, from stands and kiosks, all of it measured and standardized. Nothing was purchased that was not a necessity. Sometimes I talked about Lu, all the nasty fights we had as children, and even as teens, until he went off to be a soldier. I told her about his Red Guard phase. I didn't tell her about his face. She nodded because she had seen a documentary on the Cultural Revolution. She knew Grandfather was blind, but I never said how he had gotten that way.

We were always battling each other's viewpoints. We loved to argue—neither one of us would back down. But to be around this person who had enveloped my life and become not a tangent, but a part of everything I had lived and seen and done these last three years, that was the most incredible thing. I had never looked for someone like her, thought about it, imagined living a life like this. It had happened and I didn't realize it or have time to cherish it, until it was over.

I lay in the square, eating *mantou* and cold noodles bought by donations, sipping juice and sharing bottles of soda with Wong. He seemed happy, and you could sense that everyone was electrified by what was happening around us—we, the students, the common people, were standing up to the government. But I wondered what all these people were really thinking and feeling. Why? I had my reasons for being out here. The dreams you are promised that never become reality, the threshold where you stop being a youth and become an adult; you begin to recognize the shape of your life and how little control you really have. Or the control you do have that you waste.

I felt guilty about what had happened with my grandparents. I wondered what Xiao-An was doing, what her father was doing, if they suspected or even cared that I was out here. I wondered if Elsie was happy being home, at her job, with her family, and told myself that I could no longer afford the luxury to care.

*   *   *

By the first week of May everyone knew Mikhail Gorbachev's visit was approaching. Visits from foreign ambassadors to Beijing were well documented—from Nikita Khrushchev, to Richard Nixon and Henry Kissinger—and they always included a ceremony in historic Tiananmen Square. But we were still there. And we were not going to leave.

"Do you think they'll try to move us out?" Wong said. "Bring in the police?"

"With all these people?" I said. "Impossible. They'd have to bring in the army."

"Deng is a capitalist at heart. Maybe he'll charge us rent."

"That would be counterrevolutionary," I said. "He would have to send himself to the countryside for reeducation." I passed him my cigarette and he took a long drag then stubbed it out. There had been no response from the government to our demands, no renunciation of the *People's Daily* editorial. But we had noticed something quite incredible: a crowd of several hundred Chinese journalists had joined a march to the square. One of their banners read, NEWSPAPERS SHOULD SPEAK THE TRUTH!

"Maybe the newspapers have gone crazy," Wong said, "like us." It was the closest thing to freedom of the press that we had ever seen. You could feel how it strengthened all the voices giving speeches, exhortations. We were making progress.

Sometimes during middle school, studying for the college entrance exams, I'd go to the square at night and sit on the ground, my legs folded underneath me, in the midst of all that space, that emptiness and awesome quiet. I imagined the ghosts of great emperors watching me from the Forbidden City as I sat with other students spread hundreds of feet apart under the white lights. Surrounded by our world's history, with our work and goals and the pressure built inside. I'd seen pictures of Mao and the one million Red Guards gathered in Tiananmen to launch the Great Proletarian Cultural Revolution. Black-and-white photos filled with billions of gray dots, the heads of that legion grown from every sector of China. And now I saw it was not a lie, that the square and its inhabitants was the greatest open spectacle. Would I have been as moved by Mao's words, in that crowd years ago? The Chairman's visage still hanging over us on Tiananmen Gate, the sky dragon ruling even from the afterlife. What would Mao have said about all of this?

Wong said, "You should give a speech. You're the perfect example. They sent you away, but for what? You learn freedom, but you get none here." I thought he was going to go into Xiao-An and her father, but he didn't. I was glad.

"There are already too many speech-givers out here."

"Who, all those student leaders? I don't know any of them. What they're saying is all hot air. They're starting to sound like die-hard socialists, not freedom fighters."

"Go tell them that," I said. "Why don't you give a speech, if you're so disgusted?"

"You're right," he said, "I should. But I'm a painter, an artist. I can't express with words." We all laughed. I threw a crumpled napkin at his head. He bragged that I used to have a beautiful girlfriend while going to school in America, that she was golden-haired and blue-eyed, looked like a movie star. His friends asked me to tell them stories.

"There's not much to tell," I said. I wasn't sure if I was supposed to feel embarrassed or proud.

"We date Chinese girls who think they're too good for us," Wong said. "We have to live vicariously through you!"

I evaded their questions—Do American girls smell different, taste different? Did they make love better than Chinese girls? What did she like to do in bed? Did she ever say why she fell in love with a Chinese?

"They like to give head," one of them said. "I read it, in a magazine."

"Is that true? American girls are easy?"

"No," I said, too fast. "I mean, who knows." A part of me wanted to tell them stories, revenge for not writing or calling or loving me anymore, for helping me wreck my life. But I held my tongue, shook my head.

"All fantasies," someone else said. "If Chinese girls don't act like that, why would American girls?"

"Haven't you ever seen a porno movie?" Wong said. "Chinese girls do act like that."

We laughed. I took out my wallet and showed them the picture. In it she sits on the ledge of a fountain. The wind was blowing that day, in the picture her hair is caught gently whipping behind her, revealing the slim heart shape of her face. The sun bright, the crystal blue of her eyes, the curls and curves of her body clear in her sundress. I did not ask for the picture back right away, though I was afraid one of them would muddy or stain it forever by saying something lewd or foul. No one did. Wong and his friends passed the picture around. They all kept looking at the picture then back at me.

I took the picture back. Someone returned with several cartons of rice and steamed cabbage. It was incredible that we had been eating so much for free, all on donations from restaurants and vendors, everyday citizens. So many times growing up I'd had to haggle over an inflated price. Now we tore the cartons open and ate for free.

Wong was right, some of the speeches had turned repetitive, if not fictitious, but still it was invigorating to be able to be in this place, with men and women like me, feeling the same things, to express openly, freely. I thought people from different places might see pictures of us and think we were courageous, brave. My grandparents undoubtedly thought we were being stupid, childish, but the people around China, the world, I believed were recognizing.

We wondered aloud why the police or army hadn't come in and muscled us out. Portable bathrooms were set up around the perimeter of the square. Garbage and debris had begun to pile up and stink, so state workers came through in small bands to clean, as if we were expected to continue rallying. Was this reverse psychology?

Maybe it was working because the crowds began to dwindle. Some were returning to classes, others were just tired of sitting in the square day and night. The talk was "We've made our point. Let's go back to classes and continue. There's nothing more we can do." The demonstrations had been going on for over ten days. But the student leaders and most of the people among us did not want to go; I did not want to go. If we left it would be a victory for the government. We would evacuate before Gorbachev arrived, and it would seem to the world that our demonstrations had been nothing but an immature tirade. Having tolerated our protests, China would appear more modern and open. We could not let this happen because it was not true. The independent student union had made demands to meet with government leaders to resolve the standoff, but the government had made very little effort to address the students, except to insinuate in the papers that we were a counterrevolutionary mob. So we stayed.

As the days continued to linger the temperature rose. In Beijing the summer comes fast. Days of grace in April and early May when the wind is level, the sun high, the air dry and cool. Then it turns like a whipping tail: the humidity rockets with the temperature, the air thickens, the winds die, and a gray dusty haze settles.

I'd been away from home for over a week, the days swept up by the frenzy of protests, speeches, the excitement like we were striving toward an unheralded achievement. I was going with Wong back to his dorm to take showers and change clothes when necessary. The campus was nearly empty, everyone was in the square. Still their tiny bathroom, shared not by one entire floor, but by two, was disgusting. The stalls and toilets were coated with muck. Garbage littered the hallways and floors. Even with the absence of the students, no one had come to clean.

I was starting to worry about my grandparents. It was good to get away for a little while, to let things calm down, so we could talk sensibly about how to right all that had gone wrong. But they were old. Who knew what could happen? I told Wong I had to go home and check in.

It was evening, and as I walked away from the square the streets were loaded with young and old, *laobaixing*, the common folk of Beijing. Everyone smiling, electricity in the air like the whole world shared that charged sense of change. A van drove by, a cameraman hanging out the open side, filming. Red-and-gold banners hung from storefront windows and flagpoles: DEMOCRACY FOR CHINA and SUPPORT THE STUDENTS. Had we really sparked all this? It did not feel or even look like the same place—the light in the people's eyes, the smiles on their faces. They looked at me and every young person my age like we were bringing them a gift. I didn't feel so different anymore.

At my front door the smell caught me first. Grandfather was in his corner chair, head lolling to the side. I walked over to him, saw the pink and orange splattered over his chest and on his thighs. The stink rose off of him like a sewage pile. His face looked greasy, as if he had not washed for days. I put my hand to his neck and felt his pulse. He grabbed me and turned his face toward me.

"I . . . I knew you'd come back! Your . . . your grandmother thought you'd run off for good, but . . . I told her we weren't so lucky!"

I pulled away, went to the sink to get a wet towel. "Where's Grandma?"

"Where . . . where's Grandma? You sound like . . . a girl. I thought you were a big tough man . . . a rebel."

Though I'd seen him throw up before, he'd always had the wherewithal to have us help him to the sink, or at least double over and throw up between his legs. I wiped his face with the towel. He tried to bite me and spit like a child. When I tried to pull his shirt over his head he flailed his arms and cursed.

Grandmother came home just then. She was carrying a small bag of groceries. She set the groceries on the table and said, "What are you doing here?"

"He threw up on himself. Why did you leave him alone?"

Grandfather was still barking curses at my back. Grandmother said, "What difference does it make to you? I thought you were busy starting a revolution." She pulled the mop from the closet and started wiping at the dried vomit around Grandfather's chair.

Grandfather was shouting, "Get away from me! All of you, get away!"

"I thought we needed to talk."

Grandmother continued to mop. "About what? There's nothing left to talk about." The mop was dry and did nothing more than shift Grandfather's mess around. She wet it in the sink. Grandfather seemed to have lost all his energy, like a battery had run out. He sat with his head back, silent.

"I had another talk with Xiao-An's father," she said. "I baked *mantou* and *bao-tze*, brought it all over. I tried to convince him that you knew you were wrong, that you had changed. He asked where you were, what you were doing. I was ashamed to tell him. Xiao-An was there. She was in her room, studying, the way normal, decent young people should. Her father doesn't care anymore. Xiao-An is going to marry that officer, and what are we going to do?"

"Her father," I said, "is blackballing me. No one will give me a job." But she wasn't listening. She said, "We can't live your life for you. I'm done meddling."

While she spoke she did not raise her voice. She went to the corner and tugged at Grandfather's pants. I looked at Grandfather sitting half naked in his chair, the loose skin and moles, the withered muscles. Grandmother came back with clean pajamas. I helped Grandfather stand so she could slide the pants on.

In the kitchen I said, "I know . . . and I'm sorry. I'm going to find a job. Trust me. But right now . . . you have to see what's going on out there. We're making a difference—the whole city is changing!"

"A difference? For who? How is this going to help us, Xiao-Di? How is this going to help you?" She stood, went to the refrigerator for vegetables, took them to the counter and started cutting. "Do what you want. I have nothing more to say to you. If you want to come home and live, that's fine. If you want to stay on the streets with Wong, that's fine too. You are your own man, you have to learn your own lessons. Maybe I've done wrong by trying to take care of you too much. Look at Lu, we let him grow up without coddling, and he has turned out fine. I'm sorry—it's my fault. I should have let you be and maybe this never would have happened."

She spoke with her back turned to me, the sound of the knife cutting all the while. I was not angry, I did not know what to say. She would not turn to look at me. I had never seen her this way before. I wanted to hug her, to cry, but I was stiff, frozen.

I went back to the square, did not tell Wong what had happened.

A few days later we signed on for the hunger strike.

*   *   *

We prepared with a giant meal contributed by restaurants and local stores: steamed pork buns, rice, sautéed eggplant, fried eggs, candy, ice cream, sugar cakes. I stuffed myself, we all did, until everything was gone. In the evening we would begin. Most of the strikers wore white headbands, but I did not. They had set aside a large segment of the square where we would lie out. Gorbachev was coming in two days. Already cameramen and reporters—foreign and Chinese—were hawking the fringes of our roped-off zone, ready to pounce like vultures following a wounded herd.

Wong pointed to the side where a handful of students kneeled together scrawling last-minute wills. Some cried as they wrote. A girl wore a plastic crown like the American Statue of Liberty. One of the student leaders, a young woman, stood on a box with a megaphone. She was small and skinny, had bobbed straight hair and a round face, skin tan from lying in the square.

"We, the children, are ready to die! To use our lives to pursue truth! Death is not what we seek, but we are willing to contemplate death, knowing that the eternal broad echoes of our cries and the cause we write with our blood will suffuse throughout the republic!" She raised her arms over her head and waved. She was smiling. The crowd roared with clapping and cheers. Later Wong and I read the handbill that had been posted at numerous colleges in the city, the official hunger strike declaration.

> *In this bright sunny month of May, we have begun a hunger strike. During the glorious days of our youth, we have no choice but to abandon the beauty of life. The nation is in crisis—beset by rampant inflation, illegal dealings by profiteering officials, abuses of power, corrupt officials, the flight of good people to other countries, and*

deterioration of law and order. Compatriots, fellow countrymen who cherish morality, please hear our voices! The country is our country, the people are our people. The government is our government. Who will shout if not us? Who will act if not us? This hunger strike has been forced upon us. Do not feel sorry for us, mothers and fathers, as we suffer from hunger. Do not feel sad, uncles and aunts, when we bid farewell to life. Our only desire is that the Chinese people enjoy better lives. Farewell, countrymen, let us repay our country in the only way left to us.

My grandparents said I did not know struggle. Now I would prove them wrong. Since the beginning of the protests Wong had had a steely air about him, impregnable, that our rights and destiny were somehow preordained. But now I could see the glaze of his eyes, the fear and doubt.

When we all safely reached the hunger strike zone, we chanted, "This is our country! Its people are our people! The government is our government! If we do not speak out, who will?" The banners hanging above us read, I LOVE LIFE, I NEED FOOD, BUT I'D RATHER DIE WITHOUT DEMOCRACY. Another read, WE SACRIFICE OURSELVES TO REJUVENATE THE NATIONAL SPIRIT. With each word I chanted, each minute that passed for the first few hours in the square, I felt the food dissolving inside me.

* * *

The papers reported that Gorbachev was in Beijing. We knew the Russian leader would probably not lay eyes on Tiananmen, that we were striking a blow to the government's pride by making public to the world our pleas. I wondered if any reporters were even covering Gorbachev's arrival and meetings, because they all seemed to be surrounding us and mixing through the square.

The strike was on its second day. The press took the keenest interest in those hunger strikers worst off. A heavy girl who stood to stretch collapsed as if she'd been pierced by a bullet. A nurse and aide rushed over, medical staff waiting on the fringes swooped in and carted her off. Two white camera crews and journalists with microphones tagged just a few steps behind until a hospital aide cut them off. I was sure they would have gone into the ambulance if they were allowed. We heard their cameras clicking, their foreign voices jabbering. They scribbled in their notebooks and stuffed tape recorders in the faces of any student wearing a headband willing to speak.

We killed time by talking and singing songs. Someone had a guitar and there were sing-alongs of old folk tunes we'd known since we were children. We chain-smoked cigarettes. For the most part people just tried to rest, motionless, silent. I had a fuzzy dream about Lu and the day of his accident, when he broke his leg and ripped open his face. We were fighting, he was throwing rocks at Wong and laughing, and I threw one back at him and hit him in the foot. He chased me over one of the low stone walls and I went up the nearest tree. He came up after me; I could hear Wong trailing us somewhere behind. I was halfway up the small tree when Lu grabbed my foot, lost his balance, and fell. I felt his hand slipping off with my shoe.

Wong and I had carried him to the doctor's, where his cheek was heavily stitched and bandaged, his leg tied up with splints. At home Grandmother took the doctor's dressing off. I went with her to the herb store where she bought lily bulb and fresh ginger, extract of mushrooms, lotus, and mustard seed. She crushed and mixed them with hot water and spread the salve on Big Brother's face. She fed him cup after cup of tea boiled with the powder of crushed tiger bones, the raw eggs of snakes. To strengthen his blood, let him heal faster. She did this for weeks until the cut started to scab and the doctor removed the stitches. Grandmother continued to use the salve, but the scar thickened, hardened.

Big Brother's leg had not mended fully yet and we could not afford Grandmother's extravagant remedies on top of the doctor's fees. So I did work around the doctor's house and yard, cleaning and running errands and doing all the odd jobs a six-year-old could handle: taking out garbage, raking the yard, helping the doctor's maid. All that work and yet I never felt guilt for Lu's leg; it was just another thing that had happened. To deal with it, we just did what we had to do.

When we grew older, it was one thing Lu never mentioned, as if it had never happened. Grandmother would talk about it like a miracle, that it could have been so much worse. The branch could have ripped out his eye, the fall could have cracked open his head. We were lucky that the leg had healed properly and Lu had been able to lead a normal life.

By the fourth day of the strike Wong's face was pasty and gray. He looked thinner than I'd ever remembered, like he was shriveling before my eyes. I could see and feel the affects myself: no more did I have any muscle tone or definition in my arms, the slight size I'd gained gone. We were the same again. I could feel my stomach clenching. I was having a little trouble breathing.

"Let's forget this," I said. "Just go to the McDonald's and buy a bag of hamburgers."

"Sure, go pick me up a few. A nice big soda, too."

"I told you, you like to eat too much."

"You're lucky you're the fat one," he said. "You can live off your fat cells."

A young man passed out, hit the floor. The nurses and doctors were in and out with a stretcher. The whirl of the ambulance sirens took off again, reporters chasing. I looked at Wong, his eyes opening and closing in the gray dusk.

I shook him. "I heard Deng Xiaoping is going to come feed us himself. Don't miss it."

"Wake me when he gets here," he said.

At night people wept silently to themselves. Others lay quiet, dead still, as if waiting for some great revival. Talk of ending the strike rose. A meeting had taken place between some student and government leaders to try and quell the situation, but it had gone badly. The meeting was supposed to be televised, but the government didn't broadcast it. They chastised the students like children. We heard this information passed on through the crowd. If we left now, while Gorbachev was still here, with the government having shown us such little respect, what would it say? It would tarnish all we had already sacrificed.

A gray drizzle fell, dripping through the raggedy tents. No one seemed to care. A nurse made her way through the aisles, checking pulses and IVs. She gave us bottles of sugar water, wiped the sweat from our brows, and told us she would be here if we needed her. She signaled to her team when she found someone too weak to carry on. The sight of our fellow strikers being hauled off like the dead became all too regular to shock us anymore.

Each day things got worse, though the number of strikers only increased. Our original few hundred was well into the thousands now. As the sick were rushed off, there was a line ready to fill the martyr's role. We were crowded in like a cage at the zoo, the featured animals with the press cramming around us. I saw a young man dry-heaving in the corner, wanting to vomit and having nothing in him to throw up. Another lay close by, knees tucked up and arms wrapped around his stomach, screaming. One of the student leaders, who sat close to us, seemed to faint every time a camera crew was near. He was going down two or three times a day, always in broad daylight as he was about to make some vitriolic plea. There were rumors of students secretly eating. They were harangued out of the square.

I was dizzy and had had an IV stuck in my arm by a nurse. My body was eating itself away, the burn of acid in my gut and veins. I laughed to myself, how I thought I would keep the muscle and strength I'd built up in the fitness center, how hard I'd tried to change. And here I was, skinny as a chicken, the way I used to be when I was a boy. I would have given anything to have Grandmother prepare for me just two steamed yams and a few strips of salted pork.

Families started to arrive to see their children. A father had made his way through the student guards and walls of press. He found his daughter among the strikers. He knelt by her side and held her hand as he wept openly. She was maybe nineteen, a pretty girl. He said, "Baby, come home, you're killing yourself!" She told him she could not. When he asked her why, she could not say. We could smell it, it was not just the waste and garbage, the rankness of our own bodies. It was the idea that death was a consequence not far from our grasp. I wondered if my own grandparents knew at all what I was doing, if they would be proud, if they cared anymore.

A Chinese reporter caught the father who had come to save his daughter. He asked the father what had happened, what he was feeling now.

"She's so brave," the man said, sobbing, wiping his eyes with the palms of his hands. "All these years we listened and obeyed. We never had the courage to do what she's doing. And she's so young. I love her and I'm proud. She's stronger than I am. But I don't want my baby girl to die."

A route had been established by the medical people, paths swathed through the crowds so that stretchers and ambulances could make easy way.

The morning of the fifth day I woke early, used to not sleeping because my body would not let me. Reporters were scarce. I looked out across the square. Cars ran in a steady flow out on Chang'an Avenue, the gray backdrop of smog and buildings. The eerie peace and hugeness of the square, the sky heavy with thick clouds. The square was a mess by now. Garbage was heaped in huge deep piles on the outskirts, our shelters and tents ragged and torn. The bathrooms were overflowing, the stink horrendous, worse than our shared *hutong* bathroom. We stank as well; since the hunger strike, we had not showered or brushed our teeth, washed our hair, our clothes. Like a city of lost vagrants, we slept and starved. I looked at some of the new banners and posters hanging across the square. One read, XIAOPING, XIAOPING IS OVER EIGHTY. HIS BODY'S ALL THERE BUT HIS HEAD'S GONE BATTY! There was a caricature of Deng with blood dripping from his mouth and a red X over his face, another of Li Peng wearing devil horns, Nazi swastikas painted on his cheeks. Posters like these had just recently appeared, a sign of our hungry bitterness.

Wong looked very bad, so thin that I wanted to force him to quit. He still made the occasional spiteful or dirty joke that made us laugh. We'd formed a bond with those near us whose names we did not know; we shared something stronger than names. We knew this could not go on much longer.

I found a copy of the *People's Daily* and couldn't believe my eyes. I nudged Wong with my foot, but he ignored me. I knelt and shook him gently. His eyes did not flutter. He felt stiff and heavy.

I pinched him and he did not wake up.

I slapped his face and he did not wake up.

Over the sleeping bodies I ran, felt like I was floating, my legs like sticks underneath me, my arms waving. I found a nurse. She and two aides brought a stretcher over to Wong. She put her hands on his neck and face, then they loaded him up and carried him away.

Those who were awake didn't seem to care. They all looked so sad, and I wished I had a mirror so I could see my own face, register the shock or sickness of my own condition. The ambulance drove away, sirens blaring. A breeze made me shiver. I looked at Wong's friends. They stared at me as if I would have answers.

I showed them the newspaper I was trying to show Wong. The front-page headline read, "One Million from All Walks of Life Demonstrate in Support of Hunger-Striking Students." Another article's headline, "Save the Students! Save the Children!"

The press was reporting . . . the truth.

I sat back down and closed my eyes.

Later that morning I saw reporters again flocking to the fringes of where we lay, mostly foreign press crews, some Chinese. I stood and walked over to where they hovered. They turned to me one by one. I could feel the eyes of the strikers watching me from behind. Microphones and tape recorders were thrust in my face—one, two, five, ten. Cameramen were slamming into one another for position. Some of the nurses tried to push the reporters away, but I told them it was okay.

One of them shouted, "Do you speak English?" The rest of the voices were a mixed barrage. "Why are you doing this?"

I took a breath, composed my thoughts, then said, "We . . . prove to government . . . our will strong . . . like them. What we want . . . is fair . . . we are not give up." I had not spoken English in some time, I tried to focus. The questions flew: "What's your name? What school do you go to? Did you study overseas?" And again, "Are you one of the student leaders? Why are you doing this? When are you going to stop?"

I told the reporters my name. The standing and talking was making me tired, but I kept seeing Wong being carted away. He was right, I needed to talk. The press had opened up, was speaking honestly now. I wanted everyone to know.

"I go school America, Ivy League . . . Chinese scholarship. I come back, have no job. Old girlfriend, her father work for employment agency. He tell everyone I am bad person . . . I don't love daughter.

"I work very hard . . . I get good grades. My grandparents poor, no money. I am only hope. But no hope because of old girlfriend father . . . no job. My best friend starve today . . . go hospital. He graduate soon, have no job. This . . . old society. Chinese government say they new . . . open . . . but they not. They do same thing, no chance for people hard work. Too many people. We need change . . . to democracy . . . people work hard, do good. Then people happy. Then we part of world.

"Deng Xiaoping know this . . . all government know this . . . they keep people same, but people change. Time is change. Deng Xiaoping, you like emperor . . . Chinese people work too hard . . . be poor."

I turned away from the reporters. They kept shouting at my back. I ducked into the anonymity of the crowd.

Later that day a meeting took place between student leaders and Party Premier Li Peng. We heard it did not go well. It was televised this time. The leaders returned claiming victory, but some were saying that they had come off too arrogant, brazen. "That's because we weren't offered a real dialogue," the leaders said. "We had the meeting. We actually met with Premier Li Peng—us students! That in itself is a victory."

In the afternoon the skies broke open and the rain came down in walls, great gray sheets of hammering, thundering rain. The winds were ripping and beating our banners and flags, our tents. It did not matter. We stayed on through the night. If we had not, then we would not have been there to witness Party General Secretary Zhao Ziyang and Premier Li Peng coming to the square. It was four or five in the morning and the rain had just begun to subside. Zhao made a path, was followed by Li Peng, shorter, smaller than Zhao, along with diligent reporters and television cameras, an entourage. I saw them from a short distance, they had waded through. Zhao was shaking hands with the students. He was crying. He had a long, haggard face, pulled down by exhaustion, his glasses smeared with rain and tears. His sleek gray-black hair shone white in the television camera light. Li Peng stood off to the side. We crowded toward them in our sleepy haze.

Zhao said, "I'm sorry, fellow students, I do not come to ask you to excuse us . . . . We demonstrated and lay across railroad tracks when we were young, too, and took no thought for the future. But I have to ask you to think carefully about the future. Many issues will be resolved eventually.

"We have come too late," he said. "I beg you to end your hunger strike." He was crying too hard now to keep talking. I looked for Li Peng, but he had disappeared without saying a word to us. Zhao was led away by his aides, still waving to the crowd as they offered him notebooks, umbrellas, T-shirts. They wanted autographs.

The next day was May 19. Gorbachev had boarded a plane and gone back to Moscow. The rumor was that a military crackdown was now impending, that martial law would be declared.

The students announced the end of the hunger strike. Wong was already gone. I went home to my grandparents because I was tired, because I had nowhere else to go.

4

Comrade

He sat waiting. It was all he could do.

Officially he was retired. If he had been present at Gorbachev's arrival it might have overshadowed the younger leaders like General Secretary Zhao and Premier Li Peng. But when it was obvious that the square would not be cleared with warning words, the welcome ceremony was moved to the airport, right off the tarmac, and all official plans were made at the last minute. The students were on a hunger strike now and thousands upon thousands were flooding into the square each day, if not to participate, then simply to watch, to lose themselves in the anonymous crowd so they could feel important, part of the spectacle. Public Security reports said that the foreign press was swarming. They were here to cover Gorbachev and the Sino-Soviet summit. Instead they swam in the square as well. How could he stop them? He couldn't, unless they did something blatant, wrong. And General Secretary Zhao had recently given his own press the jurisdiction to report what they saw in the square, about the demonstrations. Zhao had suggested that it would help diffuse the situation, but so far it had only made things worse.

He wished there was a way he could have instantly cleared the square and all that had taken place in the last few weeks with one flick of the switch, one sweep of the hand, one phone call. Things would have been much different. Maybe then he would have gone to meet Gorbachev right off the plane. He could have held his head high, proud. Shaken the Russian leader's hand with a firm, confident grip. But that was impossible now.

Deng was glad he was not at the reception. It was, he thought, a disgrace.

He pictured the spectacle of Gorbachev's welcome as it should have been: the Soviet and Chinese flags flying high, side by side, the wreaths and flowers arranged beautifully about a great stage, troops and students and honor guards in disciplined order. A long, flowing red carpet. The way a nation of prominence should display itself, with grace and pride. If they had done things his way from the beginning, this debacle in the square would have been over by now. But liberals like General Secretary Zhao had opposed, had hemmed and hawed about dialogue and listening to the people. What was there to listen to? How could a government have a dialogue with its own people when they were supposed to be one and the same? The government worked for the people, the people were part of the government. It didn't make sense.

He and President Yang were military men and knew the old code. They had wanted to declare martial law from the beginning to quell the voices of dissent. Premier Li Peng, he knew, would follow whatever they said. It was a small band of agitators who were the true core of the problems in the square and they had to be dealt with. They had affected so many by now with their spew of invectives that it seemed like the whole city was ready to turn on the Communist Party, if not the whole country. But Zhao was the Party general secretary, younger and full of free and new ideas, a favorite of the students and the people, much the way Hu Yaobang had been. They could not simply quash his opinion without consequence. It would have made them look very bad. But he did not understand Zhao's thinking and was growing tired of the dissension. Something would have to be done soon.

He did not like the way he felt, dizzy, short of breath. The past few weeks he had not been eating right. It was the combination, he thought—the demonstrators, the conflict with General Secretary Zhao, the political wrestling going on between Zhao and Li Peng. Plus Gorbachev's visit. All of it, too much. He was supposed to be retired—why was he still the linchpin of all these decisions? Wasn't that why they recruited smart, younger leaders? He thought of the old relationship with the Russians—Mao and Stalin, Mao and Khrushchev, all the ego and mind games and politicking. It was a gap Mao had left for him to bridge and he thought it would remain unchanged, not because of differing ideologies or policies, but because of ineptitude, incompetence.

What would Mao have done? A part of him felt the childish need to be chastised, as if he had personally gone astray, broken the required mandates. He knew this never would have happened to Mao.

President Yang called.

"Did everything go as planned?"

"Yes," said Yang. "We ran into . . . some mild congestion getting into the city, but otherwise everything was fine."

"How did he react?"

"React?"

"Gorbachev. To the reception."

"He was smiling. He shook all the hands, he even hugged one of the girls bringing him flowers. It was very nice. I'm meeting with him later. I will report what we discuss before your meeting with him tomorrow."

*   *   *

He was going to meet the Russian in the Great Hall of the People, which sat to the west of Tiananmen Square. He dreaded the meeting, the ride. How was he going to play this, like it was nothing? Or should he bring it up and dilute the tension. No, that would not be a good idea. What the Russian had said the night before, Yang told him. "Difficulties." What was the Russian trying to convey? That he thought they were weak, that the Soviet Union was still the foremost Communist power? That they were still in control? Should he bring this up? He would see how things went.

From his home traffic was impossible, even several miles from the square. All the commotion had backed up the city to its fringes. The motorcade was not helping.

"Can't you find a better way?" he said to the driver.

"I'm sorry, sir," the driver said. "It's like this everywhere."

They waded through traffic, all the hordes and packs of bicycles and motorcycles, trucks with students and workers on their flatbeds, waving banners, hoisting signs, and shouting like a wild caravan. He didn't want to look but had to. The motorcade moved quickly through the crowds when the opening was there. They did not want to get stuck in a mob. Finally they made it to the rear entrance of the Great Hall. As he walked up the steps, lined by soldiers, police, and guards, he could feel the students out in front, hear the buzz of indistinguishable voices. Still they were starving themselves, would not stop until . . . what? Until all their demands had been met? Impossible. The square would be littered with corpses if that was the case.

In the meeting hall Gorbachev came forward, thick and bulky in the chest and shoulders, long heavy arms, a huge round head with that brownish purple birthmark. He was much taller than Deng had expected, towering. But everyone is taller than me, he thought. Deng looked up, shook the Russian's hand vigorously, feeling it thick and puffy and soft. They smiled at each other and kept shaking.

The press was allowed to cover the meeting. Camera lights flashed in waves. Deng did not feel nervous. This was the way things were supposed to be going, this achievement. This was part of the plan. They sat and talked about what a momentous occasion this was, how it would help both their countries and people for decades to come. Gorbachev seemed relaxed, sitting back comfortably in his big chair, crossing his legs. Deng made small talk, asked about Gorbachev's itinerary, even though he had already seen it and knew what it was. Gorbachev said they were supposed to visit the Forbidden City the next day.

"Excellent," Deng said.

A small meal was served, warm noodles, sliced beef and vegetables, shark fin soup. Deng watched the Russian eating carefully with chopsticks. He was good. He said to Gorbachev, "You said yesterday in your meeting with President Yang that . . . what was it . . . that you recognized difficulties in creating a new social system. What kind of difficulties were you referring to?"

Deng looked at the translator and the translator spoke quickly. Gorbachev also looked at the translator, then back at Deng. "Nothing specific," he said. "But how can there not be difficulties, with the challenges we face, the kinds of lives we want our people to live?" He dabbed at the corner of his mouth with his napkin. "I hope . . . you do not misinterpret my meaning or intent, Comrade Deng."

Deng smiled. "Of course not."

When the meeting was over Gorbachev told Deng he looked forward to meeting with General Secretary Zhao later that night.

"Good," Deng said. "I'm sure everything will be fine."

Together they exited to applause.

* * *

That night he dreamed himself in the middle of it all, a short chubby man among the screaming, roiling masses, bands and clusters of youth in green caps and red scarves. Howls coming from their mouths, the hundreds of thousands that crowded the square looking north toward the Gate of Heavenly Peace, Tiananmen Gate. Mao stood on the gate, the entrance to the Forbidden City, awash in elaborate red tile and jade green settings, surrounded by the flora of past and glorious victories, his figure monstrous and looming, a giant larger than life. The immense portrait of Mao hanging just below, so lifelike and vivid, some eerie dream-cast shadow. Long arms and barrel chest, he told the ocean of Red Guards how proud he was of them all, how they would take the shape of the nation in their young hands and remold it, shape it to fit the needs of their future.

"You cannot be constrained! Take the revolution and forge your destinies! Let your handprints stain the world!"

Deng heard himself saying, "No, no, no."

His voice was thin and small and no one could hear him. He could barely see out around him, the walls of flesh and rage, a sickness, palpable and physical. His fear of being trapped inside them all, their brute and natural urges, cut off from the avenues of operation he had grown accustomed to: rules and regulations and the powers of government and law. None of it existed here, he felt raw and childlike, unprotected. They looked at him now. One by one the thousands stopped chanting when they saw him, the little soldier, the capitalist roader, the man who dared to speak against Mao. They cried, "Why do you fear the masses, Xiaoping? Why do you choose the capitalist road? Why do you want to hold back the power of the people?" The skin of their faces lined with cracks, as if in their young lives they had already endured centuries of pain.

What did they want? What were they trying to do? He tried to shout, but his voice was gone, no sound except sheepish peeps. The crowd jeered, and from what seemed miles away Mao pointed a huge finger and laughed because he knew this was a situation Deng could not win. The Red Guards picked him up and he could not fight and Deng saw himself from outside it all, carried and paraded like a toy, humiliated, disgraced. They spat on him, reached up to punch him as he was passed overhead, surfing the human sea.

Then he was next to Mao on the Gate of Heavenly Peace and the millions were chanting Mao's name, the sound like some great tide crashing repeatedly in his brain.

"These are our people," Mao said, his arm warm and slung over Deng's shoulders. "We give them change, give them what they want."

"Why . . . why are you doing this?"

"I'm not doing anything," Mao said. "I'm following the stars."

Deng was crying. Then he and Mao were riding in an open jeep down Chang'an Avenue through the crowd, Mao's hand held straight and high above him in salute, and Deng sat by his feet, sadly afraid to look up.

*　　*　　*

The next morning he watched Zhao and Gorbachev on television, listened to it on the radio, then read it verbatim in one of the many official reports. Zhao had told Gorbachev that Deng, though retired, was still "the supreme leader of the country." All major decisions, Zhao said, needed Deng's backing before being executed.

He called President Yang, Premier Li Peng, and General Secretary Zhao to his home.

The first to arrive were Li Peng and Yang Shangkun. They were led into the screening room by the housekeeper. They smoked and drank tea and waited. Then came Zhao Ziyang. The housekeeper brought them a platter of sweets. They sat quietly smoking and sipping their drinks. Deng spat in the spittoon he kept by his side. He had it in his mind already—political fissures aside—they were going to decide, once and for all, how to end the situation in the square. He figured the men knew this. They seemed to be waiting for one final signal before they began.

President Yang said, "It's reached the point where we can't conduct national affairs. Not even Gorbachev's welcoming ceremony could proceed as normal. And last night, we were delayed two hours because of the crowds. Finally we had to take him through the back door of the Great Hall!"

"His tour of the Forbidden City," Li Peng said, "had to be canceled because they couldn't get through the crowds on Chang'an Avenue. What a security risk! He went off to see the Great Wall instead. He leaves for Shanghai tonight, then back to Moscow on the eighteenth."

Yang said, "If anybody here takes the position that this isn't chaos, I don't see any way to move ahead."

First the ceremony, now the ruined itinerary. Deng could hear Gorbachev saying to his advisors and even other leaders around the world that Deng Xiaoping and the Chinese had lost their handle, did not have control. The great dragon of the

East, its tail lame, breathing smoke but no flames. He could feel himself slipping in the Russian's eyes, knowing that at some point Gorbachev had witnessed for himself the students, their marching and chanting, with his own ears and eyes.

Deng looked at Zhao, who said nothing. So far he had done a skillful job of paying enough homage to Deng and the Party while exercising his own right to express his opinions and concerns. A great politician, maybe too good. Deng smoked and kept watching Zhao until finally Li Peng said, "I think Comrade Zhao must bear the main responsibility for the escalation of the student movement. Also, I don't understand why you mentioned Comrade Deng with Gorbachev last night. Were you trying to saddle Comrade Deng with all the responsibility for the students, to get them to attack? Didn't you know your meeting would be televised? You have made things much worse." Li Peng was leaning forward in his chair, his neck straining. The loose pale skin around his neck and face seemed to shake.

Zhao sighed. His eyes were dull and he sat uncomfortably, as if he might slip from his chair to the ground. He was a tall man, but his shoulders, neck, and back seemed to sag. "I told Gorbachev what I tell Communist Party leaders from other countries whenever we meet—that we continue to make reports to Comrade Deng and seek his advice. I do this in order to make sure the world is clear that Comrade Deng's continuing power in our Party is legal in spite of his retirement."

"The world already knows that," said Li Peng. "They don't need to be reminded."

"Enough," Deng said. "We'll settle that later. Right now we have to decide on how to take care of the situation in the square. If we don't, the whole nation could take a giant step backward. I think we should bring in the PLA and declare martial law. Suppress the chaos once and for all, return things quickly to normal."

"I am in agreement with Comrade Deng," said President Yang.

"I am in agreement as well," said Premier Li Peng.

"I am against imposing martial law," said Zhao.

They all looked at Zhao, who would not return any of their stares.

"Even among the demonstrators," Zhao said, "there are still supporters of the Party. Martial law will give us total control of the situation, but what will it do to the minds of the people? It will terrorize them. Where will that lead?"

"Comrade Zhao," Deng said, "the minority must yield to the majority."

Zhao looked up. He put out his cigarette in the ashtray, leaned forward, and looked at all the men one by one. He stopped with Deng. "Then my duties end here, today. I cannot continue to serve."

*   *   *

The days now went fast. Gorbachev was gone. Deng did not know when or how he would follow up with the Russian, but he knew he would have to. An official letter of thanks, signed by him, endorsed by the Politburo and the Party. Maybe next was a visit to Moscow by President Yang or Premier Li Peng. Or whoever the next general secretary would be.

Deng received tapes of all the foreign feeds that the Public Security Bureau had intercepted, as well as copies of all CCTV broadcasts. He scanned through it all personally in the privacy of his meeting room: the students mashed together in the square, the marches and ongoing demonstration. The common folk with no affiliation and yet giving their support with smiles and clapping, unabashed cheers. People stuffing money into boxes, donations so the students could eat. He watched the handfuls of student leaders exhorting the masses, calling them to action, as history had taught them, as Mao had exemplified. He paused the tape to read a banner draped over part of the tent city in the square: DENG XIAOPING AND YANG SHANGKUN, RETIRE! WE DON'T WANT AN OLD MAN'S PARTY OF ELDERS!

He watched the meeting between Premier Li Peng and the student leaders. Many of the students were dressed in pajamas, coming straight from hospital beds where they were resting after being rescued from their self-inflicted plight in the square. What drama, Deng thought. Such an arrogant bunch, disrespectful, undisciplined. When in history had a bunch of vagrants and thugs ever had the chance to have a conversation with one of the leaders of their country? Did they believe they were just as experienced, just as knowledgeable about running a nation of one billion people, as the Communist Party? They cut the premier off in midsentence several times, what would have been considered a crime and severely punishable years ago. They said to Li Peng, "This meeting is not only a little late, it's too late." They said, "The topics of discussion should be decided by us." They demanded the promise of an ongoing dialogue between Party leaders and themselves. Deng kept thinking, What could we possibly learn from you?

They said, "The government should take absolute, full responsibility."

He watched the footage of Zhao. After leaving the last meeting, he had tried to officially quit, but Deng and Yang would not accept his letter of resignation. Deng knew what Zhao wanted—to walk away from the Party with an air of moral and humanitarian supremacy about him. He would have an army of liberal supporters waiting to worship him like a saint, a god; it would give him the opportunity to build strength and rise up in the future. The agitators were looking for political legitimacy to challenge the Party, and Zhao would bring that to them. He could read Zhao's every move. He wanted Zhao out, but it would happen on his own terms. He would make no concessions.

Then Zhao went to the square in the middle of the night. Deng watched the video as Zhao marched through the crowd. Li Peng followed shortly after. Dumbstruck by the presence of government leaders, the students gathered with adulation around Zhao. Smart, Deng thought. Strategically, Zhao had entered the hunger strikers' area. Deng listened to Zhao's pathetic pleas, watched the man cry. Is that the way a Party general secretary should behave, should present himself to his people, to the world? Why didn't Li Peng stop him? But what could he have done, knocked Zhao to the floor? If Zhao had veiled his earlier attempts at exonerating himself for all that had happened in the square, he made no attempt to hide it now. He had taken that full step that Deng had been waiting for, the wrong one. Zhao wept like a child, portraying himself as the downtrodden, the sympathetic everyman who lived and died only for the people, with no personal motives. But Deng believed most would know otherwise, see through his act. Zhao was a politician, after all.

It made Deng sick. He fast-forwarded the tape. They put Zhao under house arrest. He would no longer be a factor. He and his family lived in Zhongnanhai, the walled government compound next to the Forbidden City. There was no way he could leave. There were armed guards everywhere. After Zhao's final contribution to the debacle, they would make sure of that.

They declared martial law the same day the students ended the hunger strike. Li Peng gave a speech that was broadcast on national television and radio. The military entered the city. The foreign press was forced to shut down their satellite transmissions. The Chinese Foreign Ministry said, "You are here to report on Gorbachev. Gorbachev is gone. Your task is over." Press feeds continued secretly, and information was being leaked out to the world by a fax network the students had set up across the city, in dorm rooms, in offices, in the homes of people who supported the cause. "Shut them down," Deng said, but there were too many.

Deng watched the tapes. The turmoil and chaos did not subside. The students did not leave the square, because all around the city the martial law troops were being blocked by human waves before they could reach the heart of Beijing. People were running in the streets by the hundreds, waiting for the trucks full of soldiers. Entire convoys were halted like animals caught in a trap. The people would not move and the trucks could not move. The footage showed people climbing up on the trucks and screaming at the soldiers, telling them that they were the people's army, that they could not turn on their own. Deng saw the faces of many of the soldiers—they were lost, scared. Another clip showed a massive crowd offering fruit and vegetables to the soldiers. They tried to refuse the offerings, but the crowd kept shoving and throwing the food at them until they accepted. Another clip of a child giving a flower to a soldier, and the soldier crying. They were shaking hands with the people.

They were not prepared correctly for this mission, Deng thought. In their lack of action, they had defied orders. One segment showed what looked like an entire garrison of soldiers sitting in the street, rifles across their knees. Sitting right next to them, separated only by inches, like an invisible line, were the people, the students, the everyday workers, even mothers and fathers with their children who had joined the fray. They were all singing the "Internationale": "Arise up ye prisoners of starvation/Arise ye wretched of the earth/For justice thunders condemnation/A better world's in birth."

They were trying to *outsing* one another.

Three days after declaring martial law, Deng gave the order to pull the troops out of Beijing.

He watched the footage of students bringing their Goddess of Democracy to the square. It was tall, white, made of plaster. It had long, flowing hair. He thought he could see the shape of a crown. The thing held a torch with two hands high above its head. It was placed at the north end of the square, facing across Chang'an Avenue, aimed at the portrait of Mao hanging on Tiananmen Gate, the entrance to the Forbidden City. Deng knew what they were doing, the symbolism. Their new goddess versus the old gods. People exclaimed and surrounded it like a tourist attraction.

He watched, finally, a tape of a young man in his early twenties. He was taller than average, had longish hair, a lanky frame. He wore jeans and a white T-shirt with small words in English printed across the front. Deng could see the hunger strikers lying on the ground behind him. The boy's face was round but his cheekbones were sharp, sunken, his skin bluish in the light, as if he had lost too much weight too fast. But that was the way all the strikers looked after starving themselves. Unlike many of the other hunger strikers, he did not wear a white rag tied around his head. Deng found this odd. The young man spoke English, but not very well. He thought it brave of him to address the foreign press in their own, universal language. The boy had a pained look on his face, and his soliloquy was angrier and more tense than the others Deng had heard. His voice was moderate, not too low or high. He was fighting off a gaggle of reporters, trying to compose himself.

Deng listened to the Chinese broadcast translation of what the boy said.

"I went to a college in America, but I've come back to be unemployed. The employment bureau officials are all corrupt, trying to extort money from me. But I won't pay. They are all uneducated peasants, and I'm more qualified than them to do their jobs. It doesn't matter under the Deng Xiaoping regime. Only those who are willing to play their dirty games go places. Politicians, bureaucrats, criminals, they are all the same. Communism is a farce, socialism is a joke. The government wants the people to believe in it, but the government is crooked. The people will always be poor under Deng. Deng Xiaoping, listen. You are an emperor without a kingdom. It is time for you to step down."

The broadcaster went on to say they believed that the young man was related to a ring of suspect international groups.

He stared at the screen, then turned everything off. He could tolerate no more of this. It had gone on too long. He and the Party had made as many concessions as they possibly could. Now the people dared to address him directly in front of the world? Who was this boy? He was not one of the student leaders who so blatantly yearned for the camera, always prancing about with a megaphone. The tapes had not shown him before. His voice and face, so bitter, disturbed. The embodiment of the turmoil, the poison. Why? And how dare he . . . He would call the PSB, have the boy identified, see if he had a record, a file, if they had not done so already. It had all gone too far. He could not afford to have one million people like this, rampant and ruling the streets, humiliating him and the Party before the eyes of the world.

This is freedom, democracy. This lunacy. The world had finally gone mad.

* * *

The meeting was between Party elders and the Standing Committee of the Politburo, which included Yang Shangkun and Li Peng. Li Peng did most of the talking in the beginning, reiterating much of what everyone already knew. He blamed the United States and Taiwan and other foreign countries for encouraging the demonstrators. He suggested some of the students were actually working for intelligence agencies in Hong Kong, Taipei, and America. The Party elders cursed and swore that the demonstrators had no respect, no discipline, and deserved no mercy.

When they had gone around the room and everyone had had a chance to speak, they turned to Deng. They had been in the meeting for some time. He had smoked half a pack of cigarettes.

Deng said, "This turmoil has taught us a lesson the hard way, but at least we now understand that the sovereignty and security of the state must always be the top priority. We don't care what others say about us. The only thing we care about is a good environment for developing ourselves, our nation. History will eventually prove the superiority of the Chinese socialist system, and that is enough. Imagine what could happen if we allow China to fall into chaos. If it happens now, it will be far worse than the Cultural Revolution."

Everyone in the room was clamoring, talking to himself and the person next to him. Deng wanted to bring this to an end. President Yang Shangkun and Premier Li Peng suggested bringing in the military once again, properly this time. They looked to Deng for a final opinion.

"I agree," Deng said. "We must explain this clearly to the citizens and the students, asking them to leave the square. Do our very best to persuade them. But if they refuse to leave, they will be responsible for the consequences."

5

Dissident

Grandmother fed me cups of green tea, and soft white rice with chicken soup. She scratched my head and back and mumbled to me, always talking. I felt her hand over mine or on my shoulder, some part of her always in contact with me. Her anger and disgust with me had vanished.

I slept, feeling a quiet contentment, the kind of peace I imagined a dead person would feel lying in his casket having others stare down weeping. For a few days I did not get up to listen to the radio or read the papers. I did not hear from Wong, though he appeared in my hazy dreams. I imagined his voice leading the chanting students, evoking cheers from the Tiananmen crowd.

Grandmother led Grandfather in. They sat down next to me on the bed. Grandfather roughly stroked the top of my head. Grandmother brought us tea. The air about them was different now. I could sense that they did not see me as just their little boy anymore. If it was not pride, then a quiet reverence, because if I had not accomplished anything, at least I had tried.

"I'm sorry," I said. "For putting you through this . . . for everything."

"It's over," Grandmother said. "Everything that's happened in our lives . . . this is just another small step."

As soon as I felt my strength returning, the clearing in my head, I wanted to know what was going on. I knew martial law had been declared, but had anything changed? Were people still camped out in the square?

"Rest," Grandmother said. "This is all going to pass."

"Have you heard from Wong?"

"He's fine. He's gone home."

Grandmother told me not to excite myself. She went to the refrigerator for a plate of leftover spring dumplings.

"You're gaining back the weight." She fed me a dumpling and smiled. "You came home too big, now you're too skinny. Another week and you'll be back to your original self."

I sat at the table, eating, churning inside. Grandmother said, "You have to forget all that now. It's going to be over soon. Then everything will be back to normal."

*   *   *

The paper reported that the crowds in Tiananmen had dwindled, that the movement was on the verge of collapse. Fewer than ten thousand people per day were going to the square, and only a small band of a few thousand remained camped out each night. Maybe things had run their course, already taken too much of a toll. Maybe everyone was just so tired and the government's waiting game had won. I wanted to go to the square and see for myself, but I did not because of my grandparents. They looked skinnier and more tired than usual, as if they had starved with me, our bodies and blood intertwined.

I wondered if Elsie would have been proud of me for what I'd done, or if she would have thought I had behaved foolishly, too irresponsible. Was she the kind of girl who would have stayed with me in the square? Would she have deprived herself of food and risked her life for the cause? I thought I should already know the answers to these questions, but I didn't. And what difference did any of it make? Five months had passed and not one letter or call. It did not seem so important anymore.

*   *   *

The phone rang. Grandmother answered it, as she always did, then handed it to me. It was Wong. I asked where he was.

"In my dorm. Picking up some things."

"My grandmother said you were back home. You have to stop," I whispered. "You're already sick."

"No, I just needed a break."

"What about the soldiers?"

"What soldiers? They never even made it to the square. They were turned back by the people. The soldiers wouldn't have done anything to us anyway."

His voice made me anxious, because I was afraid for him, and because a part of me still wanted to be out there. But at least the hunger strike was over, he would be eating.

Since coming home from the square I had not seen Grandfather take a sip of anything except water or tea. Grandmother was happy knitting and cooking, the things she liked best. When she spoke it was only to me or Grandfather, as if outside voices had never existed to her at all. She did not mention Xiao-An or her father, me finding a job, anything. Things were peaceful, pleasant. Like we were holding all our problems in a pen until life resumed its natural course.

I started feeling nervous. In the afternoon I told them I was going for a walk. Before I left Grandmother stopped me by the door, staring at me. "Be careful. It's not . . . normal yet out there."

"I'll be right back," I said, and gave her a kiss.

On Chang'an Avenue the banners that had hung in the storefront windows and across doorways were taken down like flags at half-mast. Others had fallen and were lying on the pavement or in the streets. No one made an attempt to clear the debris, no public street-cleaning crews or even the owners of the shops and stores. As if the stalemate in the square had brought back the apathy in the people, the dream state of anarchy over; I could feel the scab growing back again. Not until I was close to the square did I feel that tremble, the air loaded with voices, the sun high and hot and unrelenting, all of it seeping back into me.

I navigated the square. Garbage was piled in walls, higher than it had been during the hunger strike. Stray sheets of newspapers, wrappers, and scraps of food littered the pavement. Bathroom stations now overflowed, rank sewage seeping out the closed doors and into the streets. The smell floated everywhere. The listless looks on so many faces, most of them were students from other cities. I could tell by the way they dressed and the signs they carried, their faces smudged with days-old grime, hair and skin waxy with grease and sweat. They stayed in the square not because they were so deeply staked in the cause, but because they had nowhere else to go, did not know what else to do. They had taken trains and buses hundreds, if not thousands of miles, to be part of what they knew was history.

I found Wong by the Monument to the People's Heroes. He was lying on a makeshift bed of newspapers and jackets, in a T-shirt, sweating in the direct light of the sun. When I was close enough I kicked him in the leg. He scrambled to his feet and gave me a hard, long hug.

"I knew you'd be back," he said.

He looked stronger and healthier, of course, than when he'd been dragged off on a stretcher. He told me they'd kept him for a day, pumped him up with an IV, and fed him the terrible hospital food. Then his mother came and took him away.

"She keeps telling me what we're doing is wrong," he said. "I tried to explain to her the meeting with Li Peng, the press reporting on what's going on. None of this has ever happened before. That we made it come about. But she only sees what she wants to see."

Around us there were still students giving speeches to small crowds, but the force of past days had disappeared. I could not tell if people were growing bored, or starting to get scared. But Wong was neither. He still had the look in his eyes. I wanted to tell him to forget about it, let this last phase ride out so we could all go back to living life the way we were used to. But I didn't really want to go back.

"You're okay?" I said.

"Sure, things are great. This is the life. We're having tea with Zhao Ziyang and Li Peng in an hour. Dinner with Deng Xiaoping. Come on, you have to see this thing."

He dragged me through the square, then pointed at the white statue that stood above the crowd.

"Built by the Central Academy of Fine Arts. Amazing, isn't it? They have Mao, we have the Goddess."

It must have been thirty or forty feet high. It wore a long flowing robe and a crown, holding up a torch. I had never seen the real Statue of Liberty. This was as close as most of us would get. People milled about, taking pictures with the statue like it was a celebrity.

"Be careful," I said.

"If my mother calls your house . . . tell her I'm fine."

I went home. My grandparents were so relieved. I could hear it in their voices as we sat at the dinner table talking. They did not mention Wong and I did not bring him up. We all knew I'd gone to see him.

"Any letters from Lu lately?" Grandfather asked. I could feel Grandmother tighten up for some reason. She stood to clear off her plate. She sat back down and shook her head.

"Where is he stationed now?" I said.

Grandmother said, "You don't know? When was the last time you wrote him? Asked how he was?"

"I don't know. He hasn't written me either."

"He's in the army," she said. "He doesn't have as much leisure time."

"I know that. Why are you getting mad at me?"

Grandmother gave me a hard stare, then she went to her room.

"I don't know what I said."

Grandfather said, "Leave it alone. The declaring of martial law . . . Lu is stationed north of Beijing. She . . . she was worried. I shouldn't have brought it up."

Lu and I had not written to each other while I was away. I thought that for us, this was normal. I knew Grandmother would relay anything I said to her, back to him. I wished Lu was here now so I could talk to him about what was happening in the square, with our grandparents, how it related to each of us, all of our lives. Not because he was a soldier, but because this was a point where we needed to be close.

He would not have been proud of me, though he might have shown me more respect, man to man. He would have chastised me, maybe tried to punish me. When we were boys he would tie me to a pole or box in the *hutong*, though not without a struggle. Then I would watch him and the rest of his friends play and get candy. They would not let me have any. He would pinch me or kick me. He would tell my grandparents I'd been bad, that I was too small and stupid and spoiled to understand.

I couldn't remember the last time we had spoken. Had it been before I left for America? Had we called, or had I seen him while he was on leave? How could I not remember? I felt guilty, missed him now, blamed myself for being younger and more spoiled, for having chances that Lu did not have and never would. But it was his decision to join the army, even before I'd decided to go away.

* * *

In the streets I still saw an occasional roving band with conspicuous microphones and cameras. I could see the fear in their eyes, as if they knew they were treading on uncertain ground, committing some sort of crime.

Though I wanted to be back in the square with Wong, I wasn't sure of the purpose at this point—we had staged the hunger strike, had the meetings with the government's leaders, attained a certain freedom of the press. I thought these things were huge, but the student leaders wanted to keep going. But for what? I felt an inner peace, as if I'd resolved some great mystery of my own conscience. I did not bother thinking too much about it, the how or what or why. I did not think about Elsie and it did not bother me. The situation with Xiao-An and her father seemed very distant to me, as if we had lived through many years in the past few weeks. After the student demonstrations came to an end and the air cleared, I would go out and find a job. I told myself that life would straighten out and we would make the best of things, piece by piece, gradually. But things had to calm down first. It would take some time.

On the radio that evening the broadcaster said, "Beginning immediately, Beijing citizens must be on high alert. Please stay off the streets and away from Tiananmen Square. All workers should remain at their posts and all citizens should stay at home to safeguard their lives."

A few hours later the phone rang and Grandmother picked it up. It was Wong's mother. I could hear her crying from across the room. Before she hung up I'd put on my shoes and was walking toward the door. Grandfather said, "Wait. Come here." I went to his chair and kneeled. He held my arms. His face was pinched.

"I'll be fine," I said. He pulled me close and hugged me. He had my chin in one hand and gave me a light slap on the cheek.

The back roads leading to Tiananmen were empty. All the buildings, with black windows, blended into the shadows. As I walked I saw the soft glow of the square, night purple and gold over the trees and houses in the distance. Bicycles and rickshaws lay abandoned, stray toys, vendors' wares left as if a monsoon was approaching and people were scrambling to get out of its way. There were rattles and loud pops coming from the avenue. Were those guns? I recognized the sound, though I'd never heard it live before. It did not seem real. I told myself not to be scared.

I heard shouts and screams, the sound of tiny pecks and thuds, objects being hurled. I wanted to see what was happening on Chang'an Avenue, but I had to make it to the square and look for Wong. If I did not find him I'd turn around and head home. I'd just stay there until what was to happen had happened, then sort out the rest.

I could see the square now. As I scrambled across the street, my body bent low, I heard a distorted monotone voice rumbling from the loudspeakers surrounding Tiananmen.

"The situation has become very serious. There should be absolutely no mercy in dealing with thugs."

It was getting late. The square had not yet been set upon by the soldiers I'd heard coming down the avenue. The remaining students sat at the base of the Monument to the People's Heroes like a giant class gathered to hear a lecture. The night and hazy light seemed to turn the air red. Even from a short distance I could feel the fear emanating, as if only now we all knew this was real.

The loudspeakers said, "You will fail. You are not behaving in the correct Chinese manner."

I approached the students and heard Wong's small voice. There was a rustle as he came down from the crowd. We stood off to the side. No one else seemed to notice or care.

"They're leaving," Wong said. "They're all leaving."

"We have to get out of here."

"No."

"Don't you hear the guns?" I pointed toward the avenue. Wong looked north toward the street. "Wong, we made our point. This is all we can do."

A young man on a bicycle came flying up to the crowd. He dropped his bicycle and ran the last few steps, panting, wiping sweat from his face and neck with a handkerchief. Between breaths he said, "They're blocked from the east, but they're shooting at Muxidi . . . at Fuxingmen Bridge . . . they're shooting everybody."

Wong looked at the crowd. A vote was taking place, who wanted to stay and who wanted to leave. They shouted yes or no and it was split down the middle. No one moved.

The loudspeakers said, "This is not the West, this is China. You should behave like good Chinese. Go home and save your life."

We sprinted across the street and through the dark *hutongs* surrounding Tiananmen. We ran recklessly, the way we used to when we were boys, as if Lu was behind us, chasing us with stones. After a few blocks we stopped. Panting, I felt hot and alive, happy that Wong had come with me. He had not said good-bye to any of his friends still in the square, and I was not even sure there was anyone left from his crew. Wong was stubborn enough to do something like this, even if it meant he was alone.

As we walked Wong said, "They're shooting on the avenue."

"I don't know. Keep walking."

But we walked up toward the lights, out of the protection and darkness of the *hutong*. We climbed a short stone wall and cut through a yard covered in familial debris—a laundry line, wicker baskets, chunks of cement from a broken part of the wall. I told myself repeatedly, I don't want to get shot. Then we were in an alley between two stores. We could see onto the wide dark spread of Chang'an Avenue. A procession of armor, marching soldiers. Stones and bottles flew out of the night and blew up in flames. The soldiers lifted their rifles and fired. I felt something in my head, a numbness or lightness, cold fusion in my brain. What was going on? The soldiers were really firing at the people. The people had no guns, but the soldiers were shooting anyway. We watched as the crowds continued to come at them, dozens of young men jabbing wave by wave, as if the stones and sticks and firebombs they threw could match the bullets and cripple the tanks. On the side of the street I saw a pile of bodies and mangled bicycles, arms and legs, glittery red painted frames and spoke metal twisted in a heap.

We ducked back into the cover of the *hutong*. I heard Wong's heavy breathing beside me. "They're shooting," Wong said. "They're really shooting." Then we heard the footsteps in front of us. I looked to the sides. There were low stone walls. I knew we had already been spotted.

The voice said, "Stop! Don't move!"

We broke off in opposite directions, but the fire was only aimed at Wong. I heard the bullets thump into him. He did not cry out and I turned, watched him stumble and fall. I darted back. By his side I could see his face, the clear sheen in his eyes. My hands were wet, the warmth leaking out of him.

I said, "Okay, okay, okay." I felt a hole in his side and tried to plug it with my finger. He was heavy and hot, his blood on my chest and arms, his breath wheezing.

I said, "Look at me. Come on, look at me."

"Damn it," he said. Then again, "Damn it," though lower now, almost a whisper.

"Look at me," I said, but he wasn't anymore. His eyes were still open and his chest had stopped heaving. He made no more noise. I was still holding him. Flecks of blood stained the glasses hanging off his face. The soldiers' footsteps coming closer. I tried to pick Wong up but couldn't. The red scream of a single bullet by my ear. I stood and ran.

I thought they would follow me but they did not fire after me or try to chase. I ran with my clothes wet with Wong's blood. In my back and legs I imagined the weight of his body draped over my shoulders. I believed I could bring him back safely to my home, his mother. Things would be okay. He was a good boy and he did not deserve to die. I believed I would save him because that was my job.

I reached the *hutong* and walked slowly to the front door. Grandmother was at the table crying. Grandfather was in his chair, a full glass in his hand. When I walked in they looked at me like I was a ghost. I said, "I'm okay," and Grandmother put her hands on my chest. Grandfather stood when he heard the thud of Grandmother's body hitting the floor. I could not think, did not have the energy to try to grab her. I watched her crumble and collapse in slow motion like a broken mannequin.

Grandfather was trying to move across the room. I wrapped my arms around Grandmother, scooped her up and sat her down, blood smearing the front of her dress. Then I took Grandfather by the hand. He said, "Are you hurt? Your hand, what's on your hand?" I sat him next to Grandmother and put her hand in his.

I went to the sink, the water running pink, bits of earth and grass, blades of hair. Wong's blood hardening on my skin. Nothing would come clean.

Grandfather said, "What's happening? Why is this happening?" He was crying and reaching around the table for his glass.

I said, "I'm not hurt, I'm okay."

I said, "Wong's dead. I left him in the street."

*   *   *

I washed myself with near-boiling water, Grandmother scrubbing my back, my skin burning hard and raw. I wanted to cry but I could not. I focused on the scrubbing. When that was done, Grandmother dropped my clothes in a metal can and set the pile on fire. After the flames died we threw the ashes into the street.

We didn't know what to do, so we waited. The phone rang. We knew it was Wong's mother. Grandmother did not pick up the phone. It stopped ringing.

"Did they see you?" Grandfather asked.

"No. Too dark."

"You're sure?"

"We were just walking home," I said.

I kneeled at Grandfather's side and let myself cry, felt the hard wall I'd built up crumble. I howled into him, felt his old body, the light smell of his sweat and rice wine. Grandmother held me, too, as if this pain were too great for one person to bear.

The phone rang again. Grandmother went to it this time. All over I felt cold. When Grandmother hung up she sat and wept. Like a bad dream escalating, none of us were equipped to deal with this, not even my grandparents, who had spent their entire lives conditioning themselves to endure.

Later that night we went outside with a small flashlight and kicked dirt over the drips of blood I'd trailed back, rubbed it into the street so that the stains grimed over and disappeared. We checked the rest of the house for incriminating evidence but found nothing. We listened to the commotion outside, the random shots and caterwauling from the streets, soldiers and their machines, the discordant cries of our city gone to hell.

*   *   *

The next morning Grandmother said, "I'm going to Mrs. Wong's."

Grandfather said, "Have you lost your mind?"

"I'll go with you," I said.

"No, don't . . . but I can't let her suffer like this. Not by herself."

I watched Grandmother wind her way out the *hutong* toward the main streets. Grandfather said, "So damned stubborn."

He reached out for my hand and I gave it to him. I wondered what it was like for Grandfather to have lived all these years without his eyes: for him to have had sight through the first half of his life, to know what we looked like as children, and now to guess our shapes and the details of our physical lives. To have had this part of his world taken away.

"Get me a beer, would you," he said. I didn't hesitate.

We thought they would come looking. The streets were flooded with soldiers. We decided on an alibi: the three of us had stayed in and locked the doors, the way the radio announcements had demanded. No one here was looking for trouble.

We waited for Grandmother to come home. When she finally did in the afternoon she was choking back tears. She said, "I don't know what to do." She turned to me and hugged me hard around my neck. I wanted to cry, too, but could not anymore. Wong was dead. I'd let him die.

"Did she . . . see him?" I asked.

Grandmother wiped her eyes and nose with her hand. "No. She went to two hospitals. No one could help her. They said there were . . . too many."

A few hours passed. I got up because I needed to move. Grandfather was asleep in his chair. Grandmother had gone to her room and dozed off. The phone was off the hook. Outside in the *hutong* there were no gunshots, no running or people yelling. It was almost like a normal day.

I grabbed my satchel and a light jacket, slipped out the door. I couldn't stay put anymore, or I'd explode. The surrounding houses were silent, as if they had been evacuated. I walked toward the street where Wong had been shot. I saw no soldiers, heard no signs of danger. I felt my pace quickening, as if someone else were controlling my body. The heat was heavy and thick in the late afternoon. Why did I bring a jacket? I walked faster still. When I came to what I thought was the spot, there were no stains, no rubble. It was as if the army had never been there at all. I stood on the spot where Wong had died. The pavement was cracked and dug up, tiny pieces of gray and black stone. I headed toward Chang'an Avenue.

I saw random huddled packs of civilians in twos and threes. On the main corners were APCs and trucks, soldiers standing guard. They were towing away the burned buses and metal rails that had been dragged into the main streets. When I saw other civilians I wanted to ask them what they had seen, what they knew. If their friends had been shot, killed—why the army had turned on us. I wanted to share with them my disbelief. Beijing so desolate and quiet, the fragile hum of life suppressed, except the smashing of metal and breaking glass, roadblocks and cars being towed.

As I continued I heard the sound of metal treads on the concrete, shots ringing in the background. I saw tanks in a line down the avenue, the long guns pointing forward. They were moving fast. I was close to the square and felt something inside me burst. The tanks came closer. I could see at least three, maybe four. I stopped walking, caught in the sound of the treads, the roar and rumble of the engines, their procession a spectacle in itself.

I walked into the avenue and they did not slow down. When I was in the middle of the street I wondered if they could see me. I heard voices around me: "What are you doing? Get out of the way . . . they're going to run you over!" I felt the vibration of the earth. I started waving my arms. People were shouting.

I thought of Wong, my grandparents, and all they had gone through and done for me; I thought of Elsie, Xiao-An, the promises I'd made to everyone and broken, the promises her father had made to me and broken as well; the life I'd adopted and left behind, and I hated myself because it had all been my fault. I felt this electric, boiling anger, this frantic rage. I stood there and did nothing, waiting. I wanted them to kill me the way they had killed Wong and how many others, without reason, in cold blood. The tanks had slowed and were creeping forward. I felt cool, though I was sweating. The lead tank stopped no more than fifteen feet away. It was trying to maneuver around me. I slid along with it, could hear the treads and coils screeching and grinding. It tried to turn to the other side and I hopped in its way. I thought I might be shot in the back or from the side. I stayed aligned with the nose of the tank's cannon, told myself this was not a humiliating way to die. My arms were pressed to my sides. I shuffled my feet to stay dead center to their guns.

Everything stopped. I stared into the green metal and waited. The people were still shouting for me to get out of the way. I was frozen, could feel Wong watching. I wanted to show him that I had not left him because I was selfish, only because I was scared.

"GO BACK! TURN AROUND! STOP KILLING MY PEOPLE!" I stepped forward, climbed the side of the tank, reached the top door. I pounded on it and screamed until a soldier's face popped through. He had on a white helmet and plastic goggles, red pimples on his chin. I could see his eyes through the clear goggles. He stared at me as if we knew each other.

"Get out of here!" I could hear angry voices beneath him inside the tank. "Just go!" He had climbed halfway out. I did not think he was going to attack me. He looked tentative, scared. I heard running footsteps from behind as I climbed down. The soldier closed his hatch. A man had ridden his bicycle up to me, a few feet to my left. From behind three men dragged me away. We ran off toward the side of the avenue.

*   *   *

That night when I returned to the *hutong* I realized at some point I'd dropped my satchel and jacket, along with my wallet, while being dragged away by the crowd.

Grandmother was sitting at the table, Grandfather in his chair. When Grandmother saw me she jumped up and tried to hit me, screaming something unintelligible. I grabbed her wrists, felt her body go limp. I helped her back to her chair.

"Where the hell have you been?" said Grandfather. Grandmother was getting hold of her sobs now, breathing hard. I sat down between them. I was not sure how to begin, what to say.

I told them what had happened on Chang'an Avenue, with the tanks, the soldier who had come out to warn me away. As I told the story I wondered why the tank driver had not just run me down. What would have been the difference? They had killed Wong for nothing, and how many others? The confused look on the soldier's face, trying not to be scared. Grandfather shook his head. Grandmother screamed, "What have we done to you? Why do you want us all dead?"

I stared at Grandmother, did not have an answer. She railed and wept and went to her room, where I could hear things flying about, whatever scant decor she did have on her walls broken and smashed. I didn't try to calm her down. Then she was singing, chanting the way she did when Grandfather was too drunk to listen. We were starting over again.

We sat listening to Grandmother's humming and chanting. Then I said, "I have to go. They might come looking. I . . . I can't stay."

Later that night I grabbed a small bag and stuffed it with two shirts and a pair of pants. It was nearly midnight. I hugged Grandmother, felt her body shaking. We wept quietly, lest someone outside hear and grow suspicious.

"Stupid boy," Grandfather said, his arm locked around my neck.

"When they come just say you don't know. But if they press you too hard . . ."

"Tell me you're going to be okay," Grandmother said. "Just say it once."

I paused and looked at her. I tried to look confident and brave.

"I'll be fine," I said. "We'll all be." I held their hands and squeezed, could not feel them squeezing back.

"You need something to eat," she said. She went to the refrigerator and pulled out two eggs and a head of cabbage.

"Grandma, there's no time."

"I'll be fast . . . just wait . . ."

I went over to her. She burst into tears against my chest. I let her go and she reached into the refrigerator again. She wedged two wrapped packs of leftovers into my bag and pushed me toward the door.

PART II

The world is yours, as well as ours, but in the last analysis, it is yours. You young people, full of vigour and vitality, are in the bloom of life, like the sun . . . . Our hope is placed on you . . . . The world belongs to you. China's future belongs to you.

—MAO ZEDONG, AT A MEETING WITH CHINESE STUDENTS AND
TRAINEES IN MOSCOW, NOVEMBER 17, 1957

6

Soldier

June 4, 1989

They had locked down the main intersections of the city and moved into the square. They surrounded the Monument to the People's Heroes where the rebels sat waiting. Two rebel leaders were talking to Platoon Leader Ji, trying to negotiate a safe exit. Others were taking yes and no hand votes as to who wanted to stay or go. Many were crying. They sat on the concrete with their arms wrapped around their knees pulled tight to their chests, heads ducked down, hidden away.

Dawn was nearing. The more the rebel leaders talked to Platoon Leader Ji and the other captains, the more scared they seemed. The rebels yelled at the soldiers, said they were killers and animals, fascists. Lu told himself, This is the enemy. They have broken laws and created turmoil, brought this punishment on themselves.

Platoon Leader Ji said, "Don't talk back and do not fire. No shooting in the square."

But the soldiers did shout back. They called the rebels pigs, kicked and speared the louder ones with their rifle butts. In the rebel crowd some were bleeding, though no one in the square had been fired on. Lu could still hear the bursts of machine guns, random spurts echoing from the roads surrounding Tiananmen. The trucks and sweeper crews were moving through from the north side. The tall white statue—the Goddess, the rebels had called it—was tipped over and crushed into white dust by an APC. All the men cheered. A wall of APCs and tanks rolled through methodically. He looked for Xiao-Di's face in the crowd. He had not seen him since before his little brother had gone away to America to be a college student, to better himself in the West. He didn't know if his hair would be long like some of the rebel vagrants or short and cropped tight like his.

If he was fat or thin, bigger or just the same. He wasn't sure if Xiao-Di was a part of this at all, but he had a feeling. He would know his face, but Lu did not see it. He imagined what he would do if he spotted Xiao-Di. Lu could not say for sure.

*   *   *

By daybreak an agreement had been reached and the remaining rebels filed out through two columns of troops. They jeered back and forth with the rebels. They were weeping and falling on one another, being carried out like the sick or dead. Acting, Lu thought, for who? They were lucky. He poked a few of them in their backs and sides with the butt of his rifle. No more Molotov cocktails and rocks, no more chanting or haranguing in the dark. They did not look so dangerous anymore.

"Where are we taking them, sir?" asked Lu.

"We're not taking them anywhere," said the platoon leader.

"Sir?"

"The order is to clear the square," said the platoon leader. "Just get them out."

The tanks and APCs rolled freely over the massive plain of concrete. The men and trucks and tanks surrounding created a tight wall. Platoon Leader Ji addressed the platoon. "You have all served the people well. Be proud of your actions and bravery." Lu listened to the tanks crushing metal and wood, tents and boxes left in the rebels' wake.

He watched the rebels file away as the sun broke gold and red over the buildings ringing Tiananmen. They were going away, home. He did not understand why the rebels were not being taken into custody. They had created such turmoil, chaos. All the fighting on the avenue to get to the square, and now they were being set free? It didn't make sense.

He was tired and hungry, wondered if they would get a chance to sleep. A part of him wanted to go back home as well. Grandmother and Grandfather would take me in, he thought. They would not talk about what he did as a soldier. They respected him, understood. But he couldn't go back—not now—even if he was allowed. What if Xiao-Di was there? They would be pampering, babying, him, as they had his whole life. It made him sick, how weak they were with him.

Platoon Leader Ji was shouting directions. The tanks and APCs in the square were drawing closer. They were ordered to collect as much rubble and debris as possible after the tanks had rolled through. Put it all in a giant pile. He found the crushed jade of a Buddha the size of a coin still wrapped around thin red string. He found books and torn clothes and shoes. It was all tossed in a pile that was growing big very fast. The mangled frame of a bicycle, the bloody rag remnants of a shirt twisted in the spokes. Without the rebels the square was quiet and eerie. The tanks had flattened anything that was left. They worked fast and soon the sun was high. All of them were sweating. A large portion of the square was cleared. Gasoline was poured on the heaping pile and set ablaze. Lu could sense a quiet exhaustion among them all, a certain kind of freedom watching the rubble burn. All around him was fire—in the square, on the streets, the avenue—columns of black smoke twisting into the sky.

* * *

They were given an hour to eat and rest, then they were rounded up again. Platoon Leader Ji said the city needed to be stabilized. The entire division would stay in Beijing until that part of the mission was complete. No one was bothered by this, no one seemed to care. The men took their orders, then separated.

He saw that by day, the city was a different world from the one they had entered just hours before. As a boy he remembered Beijing and the center of town: constant commotion, cars and buses, rickshaw drivers and bicycles, always some kind of life and noise. Now it was silent, motionless. All he could hear were the voices of the men and the sounds of the army vehicles moving through the streets.

Tanks were aligned in formation over the main bridges to the east and west of Chang'an Avenue. They were given sections of the city to patrol. "The situation is still very dangerous," said Platoon Leader Ji. "The rebel thugs have been decentralized but they remain in hiding and should be taken very seriously. Do not be fooled by appearance. Use force as necessary."

Up and down the avenue Lu saw only soldiers. The sight was bizarre. The army was only present in the city on National Day, October 1, when a parade marched down Chang'an Avenue each year to celebrate the founding of the People's Republic of China. A great ceremony was held over the Gate of Heavenly Peace and in the square. He and Xiao-Di and his grandparents never got to see the parades officially. They had to sneak out and line the back of the crowd, farthest away from the road, catch glimpses over the shoulders and heads up front. Crowds for such occasions were preselected, and the majority of citizens were ordered indoors by the government. His grandmother always hated these celebrations. Even before what they did to his grandfather, and a thousand times more after. As a boy, Lu had wished he could join the parade, be part of the national spectacle. For a little while he thought wearing his Red Guard uniform would qualify him. No one ever told him otherwise. But even as a soldier he had yet to march in the National Day parade. Many of his fellow infantrymen—younger and less experienced—already had. Always some kind of penance to be paid: for fighting with another soldier, drinking after hours, or that time with the loose girl from Changsha. All adding up to such a dishonorable punishment. He believed he deserved to be among the best.

They split into groups of four and walked with rifles ready at their shoulders. They encountered a small band of teenagers who glared at them. They warned the teenagers to go away, and they did, though they moved slowly. This bothered Lu very much. When they were nearly out of sight, Lu heard them shouting,

"Murderers! Killers!" Lu shot down the street but hit nothing. The boys had disappeared. No one tried to stop him from firing. Off the avenue his unit circled into the smaller streets near the shopping district, Wangfujing. The other men were from different provinces and cities. They had no link to Beijing. Lu did not tell them this was his home. He was trying to block it out, treat the area like a different city, a foreign world. Down the street they heard gunfire and ran toward it. Another unit was shooting into an alley. Then they stopped, did not go down the alley. When Lu looked the alley was empty.

He could feel the city watching, from windows, cracks in the walls, rooftops. Random fire rang out every few minutes. As the day extended he began to feel the heat and the weight of the equipment strapped to his back. Other soldiers were taking potshots into buildings and shooting into bushes and cars. The burned-out husks of empty buses and a few overturned army trucks. What had happened to the men inside the vehicles?

Lu heard screaming. A crowd sprang from nowhere. In their hands were pipes and rocks, bottles and knives. They had surrounded a patrol close by, swallowed them up, arms and legs pumping, kicking, thrashing.

He ran toward them and fired off three rounds, saw a woman hit, the side of her body burst open. Another shot and a man fell. The crowd turned and ran. Another patrol had come to help. They grabbed the ones they could catch, but most of them scattered. The woman Lu shot lay at his feet, her eyes still open. He stared down at her crooked yellow teeth and flat nose. She was still very young. Lu stepped over her and saw what they had done to the soldiers. Their uniforms were torn. He could see blood and smell the thick odor of their bodies. One soldier's eyes had been gouged out. There was blood streaming from the holes in his face. The other soldier's forehead was cracked the way a plank of wood might break. He had seen dead bodies up close before, dragged from lakes and rivers, the poor farmer or peasant unlucky enough to fall in or be swept away. Or fires in the bigger villages where they helped sort through the rubble and fields, victims blackened and unrecognizable. But this was different. These were soldiers, and they had died because the people had wanted them to. He helped move the soldiers to the sidewalk, called in medics. They left the bodies of the rebels in the street.

As they waited for the medics more patrol units came over. They saw and shook their heads, traded consoling words, then moved on. Two of Lu's partners sat on the curb crying. Their friends had been killed. Lu thought that if Platoon Leader Ji was here he would have told them that their friends had given their lives for the revolutionary cause, had died for the people, and there was no greater honor than that. But Lu had no tongue for this. It was not his job to talk; he was just a soldier. He sat down on the curb next to his partners. His leg hurt, his throat dry. He scratched at the scar on his face. He wiped his forehead with the back of his hand. The medics came and asked if anyone else had been hurt. "No," he said. They wrapped the bodies of the men in black plastic and took them away.

*   *   *

From the truck Platoon Leader Ji said to Lu, "You have two minutes. Clean yourself up."

They had been in the city for nearly forty-eight hours. There were several reports of mob attacks on the PLA. More than two dozen men had been hurt so far, and at least six Lu knew were dead. No assessment of rebel casualties. Right now the city was soundless. They spent hours clearing the roads, tearing down roadblocks, and finding bodies, removing them from street gutters and alleys. Each body he came upon, man or woman, he looked to see if it was Xiao-Di or his grandparents. Maybe that ugly girl Xiao-Di used to date, or an old forgotten friend. He was steeled for the shock, though he found no one he knew. They worked wearing masks and gloves, threw the bodies on the backs of trucks.

He took a canteen of water and splashed a handful on his face, rubbed his hands together to wipe away the dirt. Why was he being called for, singled out? You were only called out when you had made grave errors or had performed incredible acts of bravery. He had done neither. His leg had not stopped hurting since they had entered the city. Not pain, but nagging, throbbing through the bone. He doused his boots with water and rubbed away some of the grime. He raked his hand through his hair and put his helmet back on.

Platoon Leader Ji came back. He led Lu to a car. Lu sat in back with Platoon Leader Ji, wanted to ask what this was all about. The car started and they drove. The glass all around was black.

"You've done well," said Platoon Leader Ji. "The entire unit."

"Thank you, sir."

"It has not . . . been easy."

"No, sir. It has not."

Out the black windows he saw that some civilian cars and trucks were back on the street. People on motorcycles dodging the debris still left in the road. Most of the roadblocks the rebels had set up had been cleared. He thought of their men attacked by the rebels and killed in daylight with pipes and glass, wood and stones. The rebels didn't care if they were shot or arrested, beaten down. Like animals. The stories were circulating from all parts of the city: soldiers dragged from APCs, beaten, set on fire. Bodies hung from a bridge, still smoking. Thugs running about wearing PLA helmets, reveling in victory. Didn't the people know they were here to help? What had happened to respect for the PLA?

The car made its way onto the highway. Platoon Leader Ji lit a cigarette. He offered, but Lu declined. After a few minutes they got off the highway, onto a series of suburban side streets. Lu was not sure where they were. The car drove through a gate and stopped. He felt odd balancing his way out of the backseat with his pack and rifle. He shook himself, looked across the small parking lot at a row of gray buildings two stories high, more buildings farther off to the left, all inside a high wall with razor wire sprawled across the top. There was a cluster of big black cars parked close to the buildings, some military jeeps and trucks. The gate closed behind them with a loud clank. He could see sentries with rifles at various posts lining the perimeter.

He and Platoon Leader Ji walked up to the center building, the largest one. Two uniformed men with rifles and white helmets stood at the front door. Platoon Leader Ji showed them a piece of paper. The men saluted and stepped aside. Platoon Leader Ji gave Lu the paper and said, "Go."

"You're not coming, sir?"

"They asked for you. The room number is on the paper."

He walked down a long hallway, no paintings or plaques on the green drab walls, only offices with closed doors. Lu could hear one man talking loudly on the phone. He entered what he thought would be an office but was really a small auditorium with a large projector screen. It was dark.

He waited. Lu saw two heads toward the front, smoke rising around them, chatting. He covered his mouth and coughed. The men in front stood, came forward.

"You're here," the older one said. "We can begin."

Lu looked at the two men. One was taller, younger, with deep acne scars on his face. His skin was dark, southern Chinese, his eyes narrow and yellow. Lu noticed that he slouched when he walked. The older one was stocky, thicker, his hair thinning, but Lu could tell he was still in good physical condition, strong like an ox. He had a round white face, flat cool expression. They both looked older than Lu.

"Soldier Lu," said the older one, "thank you for joining us. I am Agent Liang. This is Agent Fen. We are with the Ministry of Public Security." They each showed Lu their identification cards. "We need to discuss some matters with you. Please sit."

They all sat. "How is the situation in the city?" asked Agent Liang. He leaned forward and lit a new cigarette. Lu could see the yellow of his teeth, small moles and flecks on his skin.

Lu said, "Under control, sir. The situation is being handled properly."

"We admire the work the PLA has done so far. What's happening out there . . . it's terrible. It needed to be stopped."

"Absolutely, sir."

"Have you seen action?" asked Agent Fen.

"Action, sir?"

"What have you done out there?"

Lu thought it was an odd thing to ask. He said, "Upon entering the city we encountered groups of thugs and rebels who attacked us. We turned them back. Then we cleared the square of rebels. Since then we have been patrolling the city for disturbances, tearing down roadblocks. Restoring order primarily, sir."

"And you have not had any conflict with this?" Fen said.

"Conflict, sir?"

"You are from Beijing, aren't you? You haven't felt . . . guilty. Or bad about what you are doing." Fen stared at him and took a long drag on his cigarette. Lu did not like the look on his face.

"No, sir. These are rebel thugs out to create turmoil, not the good citizens of Beijing. There is nothing to feel guilty about, sir."

"Very good," Liang said. "We're going to show you some footage of the recent turmoil in Beijing. Watch very carefully."

The lights went down. The projector screen came alive with a shot of Xiao-Di standing in Tiananmen Square. Lu could see masses of rebels behind him, some standing, many sleeping on the ground. Those were his high thin eyebrows, his round nose and face. His frame was bigger, his shoulders and chest, his legs, as though his body had expanded into manhood. Not the stick-boy he remembered in middle school. But it looked like Xiao-Di was sick, his cheeks sucked in, lips pursed. The same Little Brother, but older, more weathered, almost like a man. Xiao-Di was speaking English. Lu listened to the Chinese broadcaster translating his little brother's words: " . . . officials are all corrupt . . . Politicians, bureaucrats, criminals, they are all the same . . . Communism is a farce, socialism is a joke . . . the government is crooked."

He listened to his brother say, "Deng Xiaoping . . . You are an emperor without a kingdom. It is time for you to step down."

He did not want to look at the agents who were sitting to his left and right. He could believe it was Xiao-Di running his big mouth, but the things he said, that was what Lu did not want to believe. Where had he learned such thinking, grown such opinions? In America, at that liberal, capitalist college. To speak against his country, the people. Did he no longer believe he was Chinese? He would be stupid enough and have the audacity. Privileged, better than the rest of us. Lu wondered where all this footage had come from, if his grandparents knew about this. If so, why hadn't they tried to stop him?

The scene changed to Chang'an Avenue. Lu recognized it from the high white streetlamps and the backdrop of buildings and cars. The quality of the film was grainy, shot from a distance, as if from a camera perched atop a short building. A line of tanks rolled down the street. He watched his little brother stride before the tanks, and Lu felt like some chemical was seizing all of his muscles. For a moment he forced himself to breathe. Xiao-Di's hair was floppy, he could tell even from this distance. He looked much thinner now. He was holding a small bag in one hand, a jacket in the other. He was waving his arms at the tanks even as they neared. All he could see was his brother's back as the tanks tried to maneuver around him—left, right, left again. His little brother kept jumping in the way. Didn't he know what those things could do? Of course he did. The only sound was of the tank treads, their engines, and the exclamations of bystanders watching.

Lu and the two agents watched in silence as the lead tank stopped moving. Xiao-Di climbed the tank and knocked on the hatch until a soldier came out.

They traded words and then he got down and was swept away by a small crowd. Lu tried to make out his brother's expression from one shot just before the end, before he disappeared, but could not.

The tape ended and the lights came back up. They stared at the blank screen until Liang stood and walked into the aisle.

"Is that your brother?" he said.

A pause, then Lu said, "Yes, sir."

Fen stood as well. "Both incidents, correct?" His voice was raspy and high, grinding.

Lu looked up at Fen. "Yes."

Liang paced the aisle, a few steps up, then back. He said, "Your brother is suspected of being one of the main conspirators and leaders of the recent turmoil. For helping to start the riots, for perpetuating the hunger strike, and for obstructing martial law. This evidence is very hard to disprove. Do you agree?"

"Yes, sir."

"Soldier Lu," Liang said, "there is no need to call either one of us 'sir.'"

Liang blew out a cloud of smoke, kept looking at the blank screen, as if expecting the footage to reappear. Lu wanted to see it again, though he knew it was Xiao-Di.

"He had not been considered a threat early on," said Liang. "We didn't even know about him. But his actions in recent weeks . . . it is important he is found, brought back. He is a danger to the people. We have very little information on him. His file only dates back to fall of last year, when he was still in the United States. It was opened after an inquiry made by a member of the Ministry of Labor and Social Security. His mail was monitored. We saw the letters your brother was writing to a girl in Beijing when he was still overseas. And another friend, a male we have identified at one of the hospitals, also a conspirator. A young man named Wong, now deceased. Your brother was having problems with the girl, and her father. Some personal conflict over his return. The father is the one who he claims tried to extort money from him. Since your brother has been back there have only been letters to some American girl. Love letters. Besides that, all we have are his school records."

Fen said, "Your parents died when you were children?"

"Yes."

"Had your brother ever shown any counterrevolutionary behavior in the past?"

"No . . . I mean . . . I don't believe so, sir."

Liang said, "Soldier Lu, we need your help. Because we have no real record of past criminal behavior, or any pertinent information in his file, we believed it would be best to use your experience and knowledge of him. This order comes from Party Central. Your brother has committed capital crimes against the state, slandering Comrade Deng Xiaoping and the Party, inciting public riots and chaos, and endangering the lives of thousands of innocent citizens. We believe he has information or contacts that will help us solve the causes behind all the recent turmoil. He is not to be . . . he will be treated properly. We need to find him, so we can prevent this from happening again. Will you help us?"

The agents looked at him, waiting. Lu knew this was not a question. His throat felt dry, as if he had swallowed a blast of sand.

"Find him," Lu said. "Yes, sir."

They briefed him on the next steps: They would begin tomorrow, to gather initial clues as to his brother's whereabouts, possible escape routes. Stills of the video footage were being circulated to roadblock teams around the city, along with photos and information of the other leaders on the blacklist. Assistance would be called in as needed. But they had to move quickly. They asked Lu if he understood that their activities were confidential, classified. Lu told them that he did.

Liang said, "You have been in the PLA for six years?"

"Over nine years, sir."

"Your rank?"

Lu paused. "Infantryman, sir."

"After nine years?"

He paused again. "Complications, sir."

Liang nodded slowly. Fen was smiling. Liang said, "I'm sure Comrade Deng Xiaoping and Party Central will be very pleased when our objectives have been completed and are successful. We will see what can be done at that time."

"Comrade Deng?" He looked at Liang, who was staring back at him, nodding. Lu said, "Yes, sir."

*   *   *

They had no money, no toys, so most of the time they played hide-and-seek or tag. They did not need toys or balls, fancy things. He, Xiao-Di, and Wong would often play, just the three of them. Things were simple and they were simple. Even during the winter when hiding meant being silent and still for long minutes lying on the hard dirt, breathing the cold. Or in the summer when the stink of the communal bathroom rose into their noses and the heat and dampness lay on them. But they loved it. When they were really bored they had rock fights. Until the day Xiao-Di kicked Lu out of the tree.

It was hard for him to remember everything now. He had been chasing Xiao-Di, but he was smaller, faster than Lu, able to go over the low walls and through the bushes with greater ease. Lu kept chasing, was getting angry. Finally Little Brother climbed up a tree—a bad move, now he had him—and Lu went up after him. He grabbed Xiao-Di's foot and started to pull. He remembered the sound of Wong's small voice in the background. He could feel Xiao-Di kicking at him. Xiao-Di's foot nearly caught Lu in the eye, and Lu lost his balance. He remembered the odd feeling, for a split second, of being suspended in midair before landing:

the tree branch slamming him in the face like a punch, then the crack of his leg breaking on the ground. He had never, to this day, felt such pain. He screamed until he could not breathe. When his leg ached now it was only a trace of what he could slightly recall.

For weeks his whole body hurt, like fire set to the web of his nerves. They did not have painkillers, except for the strange potions his grandmother mixed up. She rubbed a soft, grainy salve over his face and would not let him look in a mirror until the stitches had been removed. But Lu took peeks and saw himself in reflections. First he was shocked at the size of the bandage covering half his head, the area over which his grandmother had spread the dark paste. Eventually the thick black scar looked like a ribbon stitched over his skin.

Sometimes he thought he would have preferred breaking both of his legs just as bad, being laid up for a year, several years, rather than have that scar on his face. The looks and double takes, the questioning eyes. Little boys and girls he was friendly with afraid to talk to him after, scared to look. Even now, a man who children and women might look at like a monster. He wondered why people looked at him as if he had done something wrong.

Then they grew up. Xiao-Di was sent away to America. By then Lu was already a soldier. His grandmother wrote him and told him that Little Brother had won a scholarship. She included a picture of the girl Xiao-Di had been dating; she said they would get engaged, then married when he returned. The girl was ugly. Lu felt neither happy nor sad about any of this. But it made sense. He could hear his brother babbling, going out of his way to talk fast and say vague things that sounded smart, to confuse them. He had been doing it since he had turned twelve or thirteen and his vocabulary had expanded. That, plus the fact that he never thought he was wrong about anything. If you challenged him he would not back down from an argument, a fight. The little brother would bully his way into getting what he wanted, tricky because it didn't seem like bullying. They all thought he was so smart. He was like this, even with Lu, five years his senior. Taller, bigger, stronger. But he had given Lu the scar on his face, so what was Xiao-Di scared of? They fought often. Xiao-Di would come at him like a small monster, swinging and kicking wildly, screaming, lunging. Lu could have crushed him easily, hurt him. But his grandparents would have never forgiven him if he had hurt their baby grandson.

Back then he tried to imagine the reasons why Xiao-Di would want to go to the West, move across the world. What would happen to him there? What would he learn? How would it make him better? What about now: what good had come of it? Look at what was happening. Lu had heard stories from some of the men in his division who had traveled overseas, how the West was loose and frivolous. Yes, there were many exciting, glamorous things—brightly colored and fancy clothes, women with daring makeup, long legs, luxurious hair. Fancy electronics, gadgets they said could change your life. Money, food and drink, cars. But there was no discipline, the people did not understand the need for it. It showed in their societies, the crime, drugs, and violence in the crash-mix of races. It showed now in Xiao-Di and the other rebels who had gone out of their way to destroy so much. Wong was dead, they said. He wondered how it had happened. It did not surprise him. The calamitous mix of their misdirected ideas. Lu thought, Look at all the evidence.

But it also made sense. Little Brother was the chosen one in the family, as if he had to go away, had to be different. They'd found him Xiao-An, that girl, and her family had given him the chance to go abroad. In letters sent to him, his grandparents did not hide their joy. Lu wasn't good in school, and his face was ugly. Xiao-Di was always the light: smart, handsome, the intellectual. Lu knew he was a soldier, the natural order of things. He told himself even back then it would be easiest to accept this.

My brother who stops tanks. He was sure Little Brother had lost his mind. Or else he wouldn't have done the things he had done, said what he had said. As if he had gone to America and contracted some untreatable disease. All these years in the army and still an infantryman. But now he was working with the Ministry of Public Security, state affairs. Even Platoon Leader Ji was unaware of exactly what was going on. He was told only that Lu was needed by the Ministry, that was all. Platoon Leader Ji understood not to question authority. His little brother had a file. He would never have known. He was not the same and yet Lu knew him when he saw him. If he was alive, he would find him. He thought of Xiao-Di challenging the nation's army, metal to skin.

*　　*　　*

At six in the evening he reported to Platoon Leader Ji. He had changed uniforms and cleaned up as best he could.

"I'm leaving, sir."

Platoon Leader Ji looked him up and down, said, "The car will be here shortly."

A pause. The two men did not look at each other. Then Lu said, "I'm not sure how long I will be gone for, sir, but I'll be sure to report back as soon as possible."

"We will try to make do without you," the platoon leader said.

The car came and took him back to the building he had been to yesterday. He was led to an empty room, where he waited alone for nearly thirty minutes. Then Liang and Fen came and told him it was time to go. The three of them sat in one car. They pulled out of the parking lot, through the open gate, with a car in front of them and a car behind.

Liang said, "To your house."

"Sir?"

"Your grandparents. There first."

"I doubt he'll be there, sir."

"We just want to talk to them," Liang said. "See what they might know."

Once they were off the highway Lu directed the driver. As they drove he inspected the city again through the black windows. They would never fit these cars down the *hutong* but he did not worry about this. He had been in the city for three days now, felt like his grandparents already knew he was here. They would be angry, like he had taken leave from the army and had purposely not come to see them. But he did not owe this to them, or anyone. Xiao-Di had always been the good boy, their saving grace, but what was he doing to them now?

They would find him because that was the objective, the order from Party Central. Liang had said Lu's rank would be considered when it was over. He could not believe this stroke of luck. No, he deserved it, had worked for it since the beginning. Now he was being recognized. He thought of a military career like Comrade Deng Xiaoping's, which they all had studied vigorously in school and in training. Comrade Deng had fought the Japanese, the Nationalists. Lu thought of the nine years he had served, how that was barely a speck in the great leader's life. Had Comrade Deng and the Party personally given the order for this mission? Would he meet Comrade Deng when it was all done? He could not imagine the honor.

"Your grandfather is blind," Liang said. He was driving.

"Yes, sir."

"An incident . . . from the Cultural Revolution."

"Yes, sir."

"And your face?" said Fen. "What happened?"

"Childhood accident. Looks worse than it really is."

They had a file on him as well, obviously. Lu wondered how detailed it was, if it would contain each demerit he had received over the years. He did not want the agents to see this.

He could feel the agents' thoughts close like a protective cloud. Lu crossed his arms and leaned closer to his door. The cars went deep into the back streets until they could not move in the darkness and the winding *hutong*. Lu said, "I'll go check, make sure they're there."

Fen said, "Where else could they be?"

The men in the other two cars stepped out. Lu told them what he was doing. They nodded and made a small circle. Walking through the dark *hutong* he listened to the crunch of pebbles under his boots, a dull wind sweeping back the weeds. As he approached the house he felt his leg burning, held his breath. He had not been home in so long, didn't know what to expect. Maybe Xiao-Di would be sitting right there, waiting. After all that had happened, all Lu had seen on tape, Xiao-Di would know this was coming. Lu thought, End this quickly.

Lu opened the door without knocking. Music played loudly though he didn't hear it until he had stepped inside. It stank of days-old garbage. Something was burning on the stove, greasy smoke building and drifting out the window. His grandfather was in his chair in the corner, head lolling to one side, a clear empty bottle on the table next to him. He could hear his grandmother singing from one of the back rooms. He called to her. His grandfather stirred in his drunken sleep. His grandmother came pattering out into the room, wide-eyed. Her hair was tangled, as if she'd been running through rough bushes or rolling about in the woods.

She said, "You're late! Where is your brother? I can't trust you two to come home on time, then you'll both just stay in!"

"Grandma . . . where is Xiao-Di?"

"He's with you, isn't he? Don't tell me you've lost your brother! What am I going to tell your mother?" She turned and started humming. Lu couldn't pin down where the music was coming from. He remembered it all now, why he had to join the army, escape. He sat next to his grandfather, careful not to knock things over with his pack. Everything seemed so small now. He patted his grandfather's face, could smell the heavy stink of wine, as if he had doused himself with it.

"Grandpa, it's Lu, wake up. Where is Xiao-Di?"

His grandfather put his hands up, as if warding off an attack. Lu grabbed his grandfather's hands and put them on his face. His grandfather massaged Lu's cheeks and forehead, his chin, one hand resting on the bad side of Lu's face. He said, "It's me, it's Lu." It calmed the old man down. His grandmother was moaning and howling in the back. She said, "Lu, go find your brother! I can't have him running around. It's dinnertime!"

Lu went to the stove and turned it off, placed the burning pan in the sink and let the water run. Then he went back to his grandfather and held his hands. "Grandpa, tell me where Xiao-Di is." His grandfather opened his mouth but no words came out. His breath sour. He said in a quiet voice, "He's gone, Lu. Xiao-Di is gone." Then he said, "What happened to my little boys?"

His grandfather's head fell back. His grandmother was still singing. Lu walked outside and tried to think of what to tell the agents. He went back to the car. Fen was standing in the midst of all the men, smoking and telling a story. They all watched him and listened. When Lu walked up Fen stopped talking.

Liang said, "Okay, let's go."

"Sir . . . they're not feeling well."

"Are they sick?" said Fen. "Do they need to go to the hospital?"

He could feel the eyes of all the men pressing.

"No, sir. But they're not in good shape. And my brother, he's not in there."

"I know he's not," Liang said. "Let's just make sure."

They began walking, the two of them with Fen trailing behind. Liang told the rest of the men to follow only if they heard a disturbance.

As they approached Lu did not hear the music anymore. He opened the door and peeked in, as if things might have changed in an instant. He wanted to see his grandmother cooking in a clean housedress by the stove, his grandfather resting in his chair listening quietly to his music. But he saw neither of these things. They moved in quickly. His grandfather's chair was empty. The water was still running into the pot he had taken off the stove. The smell of garbage and whatever had burned itself into the pot was everywhere. "Grandma? Where are you? Grandpa?" Fen walked over to the table and picked up the empty bottle, sniffed it, then set it back down. Liang looked around the filthy house, shaking his head.

In his grandparents' bedroom Lu found them on the bed. His grandmother was sitting up, his grandfather lying with his head in her lap. She was stroking his grandfather's hair the way she used to stroke Lu's and Xiao-Di's when they were children and sick. His grandfather was crying and garbling some strange noise. His grandmother said, "That's all right, you'll be fine. Everything will be fine." Then she saw Lu and shot him a rude glance, as if he had broken her concentration. She said, "Why haven't you cleaned up? It's almost time for dinner."

Lu stepped aside. Liang walked into the bedroom. At first the old woman did not look up. Then she did and her hands stopped moving. Her eyes grew wide and her mouth came open.

Liang said, "Hello." The old woman said, "I'm not dressed! You dirty pig, I'm not dressed at all!" She tried to cover herself with a blanket.

Lu's grandfather had stopped crying. He teetered and sat up, his hand on his wife's shoulder. "What's going on? Who's here?"

The old woman said, "Not again . . . they've come back. It's happening again."

She was hysterical now. Liang walked toward her slowly. She watched him as he came closer. Liang took her hand. He said, "Nothing is going to happen to you, I promise." She stared up at him, grew quiet, the calm and peace instant around her.

The old man said, "Who's there? What's happening?"

They led them to the table in the kitchen, where Fen was waiting.

*   *   *

He remembered it this way: how his grandmother could snap herself back in a second, as if it was just one short step between her fantasy and reality.

She prepared a pot of tea. First she helped his grandfather sip. Then she served Liang and Fen. Fen did not drink his tea. He did not sit down. He left the cup sitting by the sink. Lu sat next to Liang. He felt like a stranger trapped in a dream.

His grandmother said, "You look so thin."

"I'm fine," he said. He looked at Liang, then back at his grandmother. "We're looking for Xiao-Di."

He could see his grandmother's hand tighten around his grandfather's, could feel his grandparents connecting, the form of silent communication they had developed over a lifetime. His grandfather sighed.

"Your younger grandson," said Liang, "was involved in the recent turmoil. Did you know about this?"

"Yes," the old woman said. "But it wasn't his fault. His friend . . . his best friend was killed. All those kids . . ."

Lu said, "Grandma, we don't have a lot of time. You have to tell us where Xiao-Di is. Did he go to Xiao-An's? Where did he go?"

"Lu, you . . . you were in the square?" She stared at him. She looked very sad, as if she already knew. Lu tried to think of something to say.

"Grandma, we need to find Xiao-Di. It's very important."

His grandfather said, "He was going to try to get to Hong Kong. That's what he said."

Fen had walked over to the table. He and Liang were looking at Lu. His grandfather was still drunk, lying.

"If you find him, will you bring him back?" his grandmother asked. "He's just a boy. He doesn't know what he's doing. He didn't mean to hurt anyone, cause any trouble. He apologized to us. He knows he was . . . confused! He's a young man. He doesn't know how things work. Please . . . don't." She had moved her chair next to Liang and had taken his hand in hers. Fen was now smoking by the door.

Liang said, "If you have any idea where he is, you must tell us. This is a very important matter. If it wasn't, we would not be here."

Lu's grandmother stood and walked over to Lu. She put her arms around his neck, her face against his cheek. She ran her thumb over the scar on his face, started to cry. She said, "My boys, my baby boys." Lu was not sure what to do. He stood so his grandmother could put her arms around his waist. She cried into his chest. Both Liang and Fen had turned away. Lu took in a deep breath and let his arms hang at his sides.

His grandfather said, "Now I wish I had my eyes." He had turned toward Liang. "So I could see all of you, face-to-face."

7

Comrade

The Public Security Bureau confiscated the video footage from foreign reporters and some local news stations. Of course it would not be shown by the government news agency, but the PSB told Deng they suspected that the footage had already been transmitted out of the country, back to Europe and the United States, even though they had shut down most of the satellite feeds.

Deng went to his meeting room, turned off the lights and watched the tape again. He had viewed the footage nearly a dozen times by now, had begun to memorize the exact movements and moments of the tape—how the young man shuffled to stay before the lead tank, and how the tank shifted left and right, slowly, mechanically, trying to go around him. Until finally the tank and the man were so close that the dissident just stopped and stood motionless like a statue with his head held straight and high. How he seemed to fidget for just a few seconds before climbing the tank, like his body was fighting the urge his brain was transmitting. But Deng had to watch it again.

Was it the act, the sacrifice? It enraged him, the stupidity and flagrant nature of it all. The outright challenge, far greater than any plaster goddess could ever pose. Deng went through the thin file they had pulled on the fugitive. He had studied in America—as the fugitive had said himself—for three years. Maybe he was one of the real instigators behind the movement, outside of the headlines, being backed by people he had met overseas. He was not a glory hound like the others. When Deng watched the footage of those leaders he could see in their young eyes the stardom that they yearned for. They loved the cameras. They wanted to talk and be on television. They wanted the country and the world to hear their voices, recognize their names. But not this one. Deng could tell simply by the dissident's voice, how its tone was not powerful and full of its own message. The dissident was tired, in pain. He was angry. As if he did not want to be in front of the cameras, but had been forced by something inside him he could not control or name. The file mentioned the brother in the PLA, the parents killed in Shandong, the grandfather blinded during the Cultural Revolution, how they were peasants and the family had been stripped of Party membership. He read about the ex-girlfriend, who they would have to interrogate. It detailed the fugitive's leave for America—he was a math specialist—how his girlfriend's family had helped him get his scholarship. Deng looked over the contract the fugitive had signed before leaving, the one that promised he would return and do good for the people.

He has no idea, Deng thought. His ridiculous, fantastic luck.

The tape ended and he played it again. In the screening room he sat close to the door and listened for footsteps or voices outside. He heard none. He looked at his watch. It was late. He lit another cigarette.

The search had begun, the soldier-brother and select agents of the Ministry of Public Security. Though all the student leaders were being searched for, this one specifically Deng wanted to find, did not understand. If he started behind the scenes, why did he suddenly step forward so brazenly? The things he said to the foreign press during the hunger strike, then this incident with the tanks. As if tempting fate, the government, everything around him. As if he wanted not to be famous, but to be caught. The tape ended and he played it again. He wished there was a way for him to zoom in the focus so he could see the dissident close up, the fine details of his being as he dared the tanks to run him down. This was not an act. He read the reports on what the dissident's letters to America had said, but Deng was having them translated now, verbatim. He wanted to study him, know him, needed to feel a certain bond with his opponent, if he was going to understand him and be able to stop it all from happening again. He felt that pang he used to feel when he was a younger man, that distant urge and hunger that consumed him before battles he knew were inevitable.

The people were blaming him, Li Peng, Yang Shangkun, the entire Party. But this was not their fault. These protestors, these rebels, they all had parents. He felt sad for them because of all that had happened, the place they were at now. But he believed it was the fault of each individual, and their parents, not the system. The system had come further in the last ten years than Mao's reign had ever taken them. These students should have been taught better. They had lost sight of reality and structure, and this had left Deng with no choice. What else could I do? Step down to these kids who rant and rave? Do they realize what would happen if the stability of the Party, and all they had worked for over the last half century, were to be shaken apart? Absolute calamity, disaster. This was the only way to bring back order and peace, for the future.

The tape ended and he let it wind to a finish. He leafed through the dozens of reports that were coming in from the Central Military Commission, the Public Security Bureau, the People's Armed Police. First the detailed report from the thirty-eighth group army, which had cleared the square. Then the reports from various municipal Party committees from cities around the country. Students were protesting in Shanghai, Changchun, Shanyang, Nanjing, everywhere. They carried signs, posters, banners, that read, REPAY THE BLOOD DEBT, DOWN WITH REPRESSION, PUNISH THE MURDERERS. Mass memorials were being held. Dare-to-die teams were lying on railroad tracks, stopping all trains. In Chengdu demonstrators set fire to a shopping mall and a restaurant, then a movie theater and two police stations. They firebombed an exhibition hall and looted a jewelry store. Beijing had been quieted, but now the rest of the nation seemed ready to implode. The mayors calmed their cities by assuring the people that the military would not be called in, but that the city, and the country, could afford no more turmoil. After two days in all the cities, the protests and rioting stopped.

He read the official statements from foreign governments. The United States was the loudest condemnation—he knew it would be—saying they would temporarily halt weapons sales and commercial exports. They would extend the visits of Chinese students who requested to stay. After that came expressions of shock and regret from England, France, Germany, Italy, Sweden, Canada, Japan, Australia, Taiwan, Hong Kong, South Korea. Even Brazil. Even the Soviet Union, who had helped make China what it was.

But what did they know of what had happened and why? Their reporters told lies to sell papers. Deng knew this. The world did not have all the facts. How could they if they had not lived China's history, and were not Chinese? The West had been scrutinizing China for as long as he could remember, and even further back, raiding the country for riches in the nineteenth century, forcing China to trade and use opium, pillaging the Old Summer Palace and taking historical artifacts for their European museums. If they could have, they would have destroyed China and turned it into a puzzle of satellite nations, puppet states, and mined China of all its riches. But they had not, and China still stood on solid ground. The world had failed, Deng thought. The West didn't understand that the Chinese were different—in history, culture, values, tradition—too stubborn and strong, and always would be.

He was very tired. It was late enough for him to fall asleep now, but he knew he would not sleep because there was too much action in his mind. The house was dark and quiet, and in his bedroom he found his wife asleep.

Deng smoked one last cigarette in bed before turning off the nightstand light and closing his eyes. He dreamed he was hiding in a cave during the Long March. The dank, musty smell of the stones and earth surrounding, the crackle of gunfire, and the glowing hue of night all just beyond the face of the cave. He held his rifle too tight. He knew he should be out there fighting with his men but he hid in the cave alone and wrestled with the terror that gripped him like shackles. He heard them outside, screaming, shouting, the sounds of warfare and dying. Then to his side he saw the dissident sitting next to him, in his white shirt and dark pants carrying the satchel in one hand, a jacket in the other, the features of his face blurred by darkness.

Deng said to him, "What are you doing here?"

"Hiding. The same as you."

"I'm not hiding . . . I'm just waiting."

"Right," the dissident said.

They kneeled in the cave together, side by side. Deng offered him a cigarette. He laid down his rifle to dig through his pockets for matches and the rifle was swept up and in the hands of the dissident. Deng did not look, could hear the weapon being bolt-locked and aimed, feel the pressure of the muzzle against his cheek. He turned his head slowly and stared past the rifle and into the eyes of the boy.

"We are going to find you," Deng said. "All of you."

Then he was in a space by himself. Where there should have been walls and a floor beneath him there was nothing, only darkness, void. He stood in the midst of it and wondered what supported him or held him in place, or if he was now drifting in a vacuum with no time or name. He saw his first wife and first child, both of whom had died when he was very young. He saw himself taking care of them. They lived in a small home, on meager means, and yet everyone was healthy. Together they smiled with a radiant strength. He was not the Deng Xiaoping he had become, but a different man with no Party affiliations and no ambition or revolutionary drive. He was a peasant, a market worker, no education or knowledge of the world. His wife was smiling. The child was laughing. They were all very happy.

Then they were gone. He saw them in their deadness like stone statues arranged in the passing hall of his life. He was Deng Xiaoping again. These people around him he had loved and they were dead. His oldest son was a man in a wheelchair; he wished Pufang were a child and he could hold him and love him and tell him things would be okay. He wept in his dream and he wept in bed as he dreamed next to his wife. He woke reaching into the darkness.

8

Dissident

I left my grandparents, turned out of the old *hutong* and walked west. I was afraid there would be soldiers parading down the avenue and side streets, but it was quiet. I couldn't even hear that awful hum of machines and the distant cackle of voices I'd grown used to since the army had entered the city. As if they had just pulled out, finished their duty and gone back to their camps. But I knew they were still here, somewhere. Had word spread about what had happened with the tanks? Were they looking for me already, just hours later? Maybe there was too much going on all over the city, just another incident, another casualty. Or maybe not. I kept my eyes moving in the darkness for flashlights, my ears pricked for dangerous sounds.

I tried not to think of my grandparents. I remembered when I was very small, no more than six years old, I tried to run away from home. I'd taken a small bag full of clothes, a few cookies, and began my own long march. Grandmother was very angry with me, though today I could not tell you why.

Lu chased me down and said, "Where are you going?" He was dressed in his green Red Guard uniform, the afternoon sun sending sparkles over the Mao pins on his chest and hat.

"I'm running away," I said. He stared at me curiously, then he said, "You can't. We'll get in trouble."

"I don't care." I started walking. Lu grabbed me and I kicked him in his left leg, the one he had just started walking on properly. I didn't realize it was his bad leg until he fell and held his shin. I thought he was going to cry, but he didn't. He was breathing hard. Then he stood and hobbled back toward the *hutong*. I circled the streets surrounding our *hutong* because I knew our allowed perimeter by heart and did not risk crossing it. I walked for over an hour until I grew hungry. I ate the cookies.

When dinnertime neared I went home. Grandfather grabbed me and slung me over his knee, giving me a hard, loud spanking while Grandmother chastised me. There were Red Guards all around these days, and did I know what they did to stray children wandering the streets? Lu was hit because he was the older brother who was supposed to watch after me—stop and correct me when I did stupid things. I watched Lu take a paddling for my mistake. He had not told them that I'd kicked him in his bad leg and knocked him down. For many days after I felt I owed him a great favor.

The kickback fire from a truck exhaust brought my attention to the avenue. I needed to get to the highway. I felt dizzy, hot, and hollow. I moved through an alley and between two small buildings to look out onto the main road. All the roadblocks the demonstrators had set up were gone. There were no trucks, no soldiers. Cars flashed by intermittently. It was almost as if this part of the city had returned to normal, as if it had never been infected at all. All along the avenue buildings glowed with light and the night hung heavy and black, dotted with stars.

A truck had pulled over to the curb. The driver climbed down and pissed at the side of the road by his rear tire. I ran across the avenue, felt strange running across roads that should have been jammed with cars. The driver did not see me. I kept my head swinging back and forth, eyes darting. I came up behind the driver as he was shaking himself off and zipping, wobbling slightly. He turned, I startled him, and he nearly tripped over himself. I could smell the alcohol from ten feet away.

"Who are you?"

"A friend," I said.

"A friend? Leave me alone."

"Listen, let me ride with you." I held out my hand, watched him assessing me with his drunken eyes. I did the same: he was in his forties, skin dark, his face covered with stubble and wrinkles and the smudged grime of hard labor. What was left of his gray-black hair stood in short bristles on top of his head.

"You're one of them."

"I need your help," I said.

I glanced around to see if police or army vehicles might be nearby. There was no one except a few other cars and trucks that moved with seeming freedom. The driver told me to lie down in back.

I lay among small piles of concrete and wood, boxes of tools and other supplies cased safely away. Was he a mason, a construction worker? Or was he just transporting supplies? I tucked myself between the wood and boxes, breathed in the dusty sour smell of the metal. I felt lucky to have found him. I ripped a small hole in the plastic tarp by my face so I could breathe more easily as we drove.

The truck did not sway violently as I thought it might and we moved at a considerable speed. The wind whistled through the various holes in the tarp. I did not know how long we would be driving, so I pulled from my bag my old

Cornell T-shirt, gray and heavy, soft from so much wear, crimson letters spelling CORNELL printed across the chest. It had been one of Elsie's favorites; she wore it constantly, like it was some kind of physical solace. Now I wrapped it around my head so it covered my eyes, a poor-man's pillow.

The brakes started to squeal and the truck came to a stop. I could hear the driver singing through his open window. I held my breath and remained still. Footsteps outside, the heavy clop of boots.

A man's voice said, "Where are you going?"

"Changping. Delivery."

"Delivery? Now? Where are you coming from?"

"The Wuhan Factory. I've been trapped by all that mess going on in the city."

The soldier said, "Mess, eh? What a mess."

I could hear others circling the truck, but no one stuck his head in or tried to lift the plastic tarp. Random pokes, the clink of metal against one of the piles near my leg. I pulled the shirt down past my eyes and tilted my head enough to peer through the hole I'd gouged.

"We're looking for rebel thugs. Have you seen anyone suspicious-looking? Acting oddly?"

"Not more than usual," the driver said. "I'm a country boy. Everyone in the city looks strange to me."

The soldiers laughed. The lead soldier said, "Is your truck filled with things you stole during the riots?"

"Do I look like I could steal a truckload of stuff? If you want, strip the whole damn thing and take it all. But I have a delivery to make. At least give me some papers I can show my boss so he can come back and claim his things."

Did they know he was drunk? They had to, drunk enough to talk to them in such a way. Through my hole I could make out the green garb and red trim of army uniforms. The soldier's voice said, "All right, move on. Be careful, country boy."

The engine fired up, then we were moving and back to a high speed. Minutes later we were on the highway. I could barely see the rails guarding the road, but I could feel the new cool winds outside the city as we made our way beyond Beijing.

*   *   *

Somehow I dozed after the roadblock. Maybe it was the soothing calm of the wind and the rumble of the road. Then there was a loud pop and the truck was bouncing. I tried to brace myself against the piles of wood and metal but they were shifting and sliding, as if everything was being sucked into a pit. Another bang and crunch and I could feel myself in midair, then drop and hit the ground. My arms were wrapped around my head, my knees pulled up to my stomach. Pipes and bricks and beams rained over me, landing on my arms and thighs. Something smashed across my ribs and side; I felt a sharp sting go through my stomach and chest, into the back of my head. I heard noise outside the tarp but was not sure who or what it could be.

Everything stopped. First I lay still, slowly uncoiling my arms and legs, testing to see if anything was broken. Then I slid my way out from underneath the metal and wood, the tarp. I felt pain in my chest and head, an instant soreness all over my arms and legs. The road had no lights. I put my hand up to my forehead and felt it slick and warm, a trickle down my temple. The shirt had come loose but was still draped around my neck and shoulders. I rolled it up and tucked it inside the waist of my pants.

I looked at the back of the truck to see if we'd been struck, but I could not see any damage. I managed to stand and circle toward the driver's side. The front right tire had blown out, the body of the truck dipped to that corner. Smoke hissed out from beneath the hood. The fender was curled from where we had struck the iron rail. Had we been on the elevated part of the highway or an overpass, we would have been dead.

The driver was in the grass, on his hands and knees. I limped over to him and said, "Are you okay? Are you hurt?" He did not look up. From behind, his shape was round and squat like a big pig feeding in the mud. Then he stood. In the darkness I could barely make out his features or see the expression on his face.

"What happened?" I asked, but he did not answer. He looked around, dazed. "Did you hit something? Are you all right?"

I knew he was not drunk anymore. All those years of living with my grandfather, it was not only the look and smell of a person that told you their state, but a sense.

My body inside felt like a torch. I could feel the wound on my head pulsing, blood wetting my hair and face. I felt queasy and dizzy and knew we had to move on.

"What are we going to do?" I asked.

The driver looked newly aroused. I could make out his wide eyes scoping the night.

"You, it's your fault," he said. "I knew it when I saw you. I shouldn't have picked you up. I was just too goddamned drunk." Still he did not look at me. He raised his head slowly and pointed north. "About ten miles and you'll hit a village. Stay off the road, stick near the brush. They're going to be searching for all of you. Don't let them catch you."

"I think I'm hurt." My breaths were coming faster, harder. There was a hot burning pain in my side just above my stomach. The driver, besides being startled, looked fine. I tried to stand up straight and could not.

"What you all did," the driver said. He shook his head as he stared at me. Then he turned and started walking back in the direction we had come from.

"Wait! Where are you going? You can't leave me here!"

He turned and shouted, "There's nothing else I can do! Just go!"

I knew I could not follow. I watched him walk. Moments later I could no longer hear his footsteps or see any shadow of him.

In the dark I looked at the broken shell of the truck, the wood and metal strewn on the side of the road. Broken glass and bricks, the ripped-up tarp. I thought to take a piece of that tarp with me, cut it up in case I would need it for shelter at some point. But I had no energy. Every inch of me hurt from bone to skin, as if my flesh had been pulverized. I walked away from the shoulder so that cars passing now would not be able to see me.

I imagined hearing the driver's footsteps as he ran back toward Beijing but I looked behind me and I could see nothing. I was hungry. I realized my bag—the clothes and the food Grandmother had sent me off with—was lost somewhere back in the wreckage.

I felt my scalp for the wound, through the mush of bloody hair. It was more than three inches long and very close to my forehead. I pulled the shirt from inside my pants and tied it around my head. I tried thinking of the village the driver spoke of and how someone would take care of me. Who? Who would take in a fugitive who had crossed the government? I stopped thinking, kept walking. A few times, along the wooded side, I just stopped and sat but kept my eyes open. If I closed them I knew I might not wake up.

I ducked deeper into the woods when I needed to rest. I did not know where I was. I had not heard any cars pass in either direction since the accident. I took down my pants and pissed on a tree. Since I could not see, I thought I would feel it if I was pissing blood. But I felt nothing wrong except in my torso and head. I imagined cracked bones and damaged internals, a fractured skull. I rested a few minutes more and moved on.

I walked for what seemed a long time, until I knew I could not move another step, had to lie down and rest. I looked for a spot inside the brush by the side of the highway. I knew there was a chance I would lie down and not get back up. I sat against a small tree. The ground felt soft but dry beneath me. I gripped the dirt in my hands and rubbed it between my fingers. The shirt tied around my head sagged with blood. Would I die from losing too much? What a waste, the injured fugitive found dead against a roadside tree.

I found myself cursing Elsie, calling her a bitch and a slut, a whore who had used me. But for what? I had no money, no power. I heard her voice saying, "I don't know . . . How am I supposed to know?" I wondered what had made her say those things, and what had made me do the things I'd done? I had been given a chance to bring pride to the family, help find a way out. Instead I'd come home and treated my grandparents poorly; I'd left my best friend to die; I'd destroyed any chance at all of us escaping our miserable lives. I cried for them, and kept crying. My parents, I knew at that moment, were ashamed of me.

*　　*　　*

I woke to the sound of birds and whistling wind. I tried to jump to my feet, but the pain in the middle of my body stopped me. I did not know how long I'd been asleep. I'd slumped to the ground and was lying with my face against the dirt. My stomach was growling, eating away at itself, as if once again I was starving in the square. I worked up to my feet and looked around, brushed off my face. The shirt was still tied around my head. It was heavy but dry and crusted with blood. I needed to find food but was not sure how or where. Looking around I realized what a city boy I was, how I'd imagined myself harder and tougher from the things I'd seen and endured so far. But here I was, useless, helpless.

The highway was peaceful. I heard an occasional car rushing by, but no one stopped. I wondered when the overturned truck would be found and by whom. I thought I was far away from it by now, or maybe I was just down the road, the distance I'd walked nothing but a spit away for someone to track me down. My head was buzzing, my legs weak. Slowly I pulled up my shirt and pulled down my pants. My chest, legs, and arms were covered with big red-and-blue bruises from where the metal and wood had struck. The pain inside my chest and near my stomach was worse, from hunger or injury I was not sure. I walked deeper into the brush. No one would see me in here unless they came specifically on my trail.

It was early morning, I suspected from the light of the sun, the feel of the air—not so hot and intolerable just yet. I beat a path through the bush and walked as best I could. A few times I stopped because of the pain shooting through me. I saw berries on bushes and remembered the stories Grandfather used to tell us of travelers in the wild, how they ate whatever they could for sustenance, how they knew to boil the bark of certain trees and leaves and roots for tea, the kinds of bugs you could devour and the kinds of berries that might make you go blind. My grandparents knew these things. I thought Lu might also. I'd believed it all to be a myth and now I felt like an imbecile walking about in this strange part of the land. It made me angry to think that this was what I'd been reduced to.

I heard the sound and knew what it was. I hustled toward the break in the brush where I could go back to the highway. I didn't want to run out because I was not sure, so I kept my head ducked. As I watched the old man pedaling I could hear him whistling, the cackling noise of the livestock he carried behind him, the bell on his handlebars ringing like an instrument. As he was about to pass I jerked myself out of the bush and shouted to him, not words, just loud sounds. I realized how thirsty and dry I was. The driver whipped his head around. He did not stop pedaling, the path of his carriage veering.

"Come back!" He'd gone past me twenty or thirty yards by the time I'd made it to the side of the highway. He stopped. I was catching up to him as fast as I could, bumping and dragging along, my sides and skull splitting. The old man had stepped down and was walking toward me. When we were close enough to see each other's faces he motioned me toward the brush.

"I need your help," I said.

"You . . . you're from the city."

"Yes."

"Your head . . . my God."

He had a pleasant face, tanned and wrinkled from work in the sun, gray hair receding. He was short, thin, and old, but not as old as Grandfather. He looked strong, the angular structure of his body like some man-made tool. He dug into his pocket and pulled out a chunk of hard candy.

"Suck on this," he said. We hurried to his carriage with the massive load on the back, something constructed out of old bicycle parts, the flatbed and axle of a small truck. In the rear were high-piled cages of wild squawking birds.

"Get down there." He pointed to the underbelly of the carriage, coated with bird shit. He helped me angle in between the high main board of the carriage and the slats of wood beneath. I was barely thin enough to fit, could feel small bursts popping everywhere inside me. I thought the person who had come back from America, thicker, with new muscle, would not have been able to fit. One small saving grace. The birds sensed me and squawked high and loud. The man said, "We're close to the village, don't worry. No one's looking up here. At least not yet."

The man started pedaling. The birds were going crazy, shitting on me furiously. I closed my eyes and tried not to breathe. The bumps in the road made my nerves go white-hot. But there was a certain safety riding in the gut of this carriage, like I'd become invisible to the world in this cloak of shit and feathers. The man up front was singing and whistling, ringing his carriage bell.

"Don't worry. When I was a boy we hid soldiers from the Japanese," the old man said, "and they never found them. Just like they'll never find you."

9

Soldier

Chang'an Avenue had been cleared since they had entered the city. In the streets were people and bicycles and cars. They swerved and stopped in their paths to avoid the three black cars, curious faces looking in.

Xiao-Di's ex-girlfriend lived near the university district, to the northwest. Lu gave directions, but otherwise did not talk. He did not want to risk the chance of saying something stupid and ruining his moment. After all the years spent trying to move up through the ranks, the mishaps that had held him down, he looked back on all of it like obstacles in a training course. The shame of his brother's crimes, his own leg and face, the condition in which his grandparents lived—all that had seemed in vain but was finally paying off.

As they twisted through traffic, Lu remembered his grandmother telling him how Xiao-Di used to complain about Xiao-An. So ugly, those pimples and acne scars, her fat face and fat body, like a tree stump, a big rock. She lived too far away, Xiao-Di would say. "It's where rich people live," his grandmother would say. She talked too much and didn't understand the world. A rich girl with a small brain and an overblown sense of her own importance. Because her mother took her to the hairdresser and bought her pretty clothes. But he had someone, and Lu did not. Ungrateful dog, Lu thought, how could he not know that he had been chosen for this? The guts to complain . . .

They reached the house in the afternoon, sun hanging midsky, air damp and warm. Children were outside playing a few houses down. They saw the cars and men and ran back to their homes. The agents left the cars parked on the street in a row. The others stayed behind as Lu, Liang, and Fen made their way inside the gate.

Lu banged on Xiao-An's door. A young woman opened it slowly. Lu remembered her face from the picture his grandmother had sent him. Her face was big and round like a white melon. She still had the craters in her cheeks, but no more the big dark pimples on her chin. Her hair was much shorter, cut in a bob that hung just below her ears. She did not know who he was. Her eyes widened.

Liang said, "Miss, we are with the Ministry of Public Security. May we come in?"

There were framed paintings on the walls, a calendar, carved jade and red-tassel banners, a thick gray carpet. The wood of the tables and chairs and even the upholstery of the sofa seemed to glow with new polish. Lu thought he knew the house from Xiao-Di's stories, retold to him in his grandmother's letters. He felt familiar with every piece of it, though he had never actually been there before.

He could hear people shuffling in a back room. Xiao-An asked them to sit.

Lu said, "Where is your family?" and then, as if on cue, the parents came out, first the father, then the mother. Her father, short and fat, like an overstuffed goose, the mother tiny and so pale you could almost see through her skin. They stood together, paralyzed.

Liang introduced themselves again. The father said, "We haven't . . . we've done nothing."

Lu said they were looking for a fugitive from the rebel turmoil. Liang showed them pictures of Xiao-Di, color stills from the video interview in the square. Lu described his little brother's height, looks, and build. They did not show pictures of Xiao-Di in front of the tanks.

Lu said to Xiao-An, "You were his girlfriend, weren't you?"

Xiao-An's face flushed. She looked at her parents as if they had the proper answer. Her mother nodded and the father still had that stunned angry look on his face. Lu was glad they did not recognize him.

The father said, "They have been separated for some time now. Our daughter is now engaged to a public security officer. We've been Party members since before . . . You have no right to do this! We're good citizens. We're not hiding any fugitive."

"Has he been here to see you?" Liang asked. "Have you had any contact with him recently?"

"I told you they have been separated—"

"He was talking to the girl," Fen said.

"You helped him go away to America," Liang said. "You used your connections to get him a scholarship. We know this." Liang turned to Lu and Fen. "Get some of the others. Search the place thoroughly."

"We were trying to help him!" the father said. "And look at what he did to our family, our daughter! That ingrate!"

"He accuses you of trying to extort money from him. You work for the district employment bureau, don't you? You had a file opened on him, one of your superiors in the Ministry of Labor helped you do it."

Xiao-An's father said nothing. His face had lost its color. He looked at his wife and daughter, then away into the wall. The mother had grabbed his arm. Both of them ducked their eyes. Xiao-An was looking back and forth at her father and Lu.

The mother said, "He came to our house to apologize . . . for what had happened between our families. But my husband told him Xiao-An was engaged. We haven't seen him since. Right?" She looked at her daughter. "Xiao-An, we kept her inside the whole time . . . . She was never out there."

"That is not why we are here," said Fen.

Xiao-An was staring at Lu. She said, "You're . . . Are you his brother? I remember him telling me about . . . your face." She looked away, paused. Liang was looking back and forth from Lu to Xiao-An to her parents. Fen was tapping his foot, reaching into his pocket for a cigarette. All of them were silent.

"He's in real trouble," Xiao-An said.

"Yes," Lu said. "We have to find him."

* * *

A guard stayed in the kitchen with the family. They rummaged through the closets and back rooms, under the beds and in the backyard. In each room Lu wondered if Xiao-Di had spent time there, maybe lain on the couch with Xiao-An, kissing, living and loving his life. Or if he'd sat reading and brooding in their study the way he did in their own home. What kind of boy was he in someone else's life, outside of theirs?

They found nothing. Lu looked back at the family one last time to see if they would stop him, ask a question. They were angry, scared, and tired, the three of them together like one body. He heard Xiao-An crying the whole time they were searching the house. As they left their eyes met for a moment, but Xiao-An looked away.

Liang told a few of the men to take Xiao-An and her parents outside. "We need to ask you a few more questions. But not here. Please follow these men."

"I don't understand," the mother said. "We've told you already . . . and you've torn the house apart! We're not hiding anything from you."

The father said, "Just do what they say." He took his wife and daughter by the hand and went outside. They got in one of the cars with two men and were driven away.

In the car Lu tried to picture Xiao-Di hiding in an alley or the lot of some empty warehouse. Maybe he had gone back to their grandparents' home, but Lu thought that would be too brave of him. In such a situation he could not predict what Xiao-Di might do next. If he was more like myself, Lu thought, then maybe. But since they were children he could not tell what Little Brother was thinking or feeling.

They circled back to Lu's neighborhood because that was where Wong's mother lived. His father had died years ago. Even being away in the army Lu knew this. His grandmother wrote so often and loaded her letters with every detail she could muster. Wong's father had been a factory worker and after too many years of smoking and the chemicals he'd unknowingly inhaled, a disease grew in his body and he died. Wong, Xiao-Di's little friend, dead now. Also a rebel instigator. What had happened? They were all decent boys. He tried to think of memories, and could only recall being carried to the doctor by Xiao-Di and Wong after the fall. It was factual, nothing emotionally engaged. Then he thought his grandmother might be there consoling Mrs. Wong. They were best friends.

He thought it would be so easy to let Xiao-Di run away. Disappear, live a hidden life in a smaller city like Chengdu or Changchun. But this was not something Little Brother would do. He knew it. If he was smart he would make it to one of the port cities, Hong Kong or Shanghai, pay off a snakehead, and take off for his beloved America. Climb into the bowels of a tanker ship and somehow return to his old college town, wherever he might feel safe. Begin a search for his sweetheart, this white girl with the gold hair that his grandmother had written him about but he had never seen a picture of. Lu could only imagine. Then Xiao-Di could live the life he truly wanted. He was surprised when his grandmother told him Xiao-Di was coming back to live and work in Beijing. When he left for school, Lu believed he would never see his little brother again.

He did not have to give the driver directions, they knew where Wong's mother lived. In the back-street slums along broken narrow roads, like his own home, in poverty. It was one of the good things about the army: the order and cleanliness; knowing there was food, knowing you had that certain slot of time, even if it was only three or four hours, to sleep. Your duties laid out for you, you knew where your life was headed if you did your part and played the role. These were things Little Brother never appreciated, never understood. Which was why they were where they were now.

Liang looked tired, his face sagging and his eyes half closed, sad and pale. Fen looked impatient, his teeth grinding. He was smoking his last cigarette. Lu thought to say something but did not. Help execute the mission. That is all I'm here for.

"Did you know he wouldn't be there?" asked Liang.

"Excuse me?"

"The girl's house. Did you know?"

"I wasn't . . . sure, sir. It was a possibility."

"If you know, say something."

He paused. "Yes, I will, sir."

"Feel anything now?" Fen looked back at Lu, blew smoke in his face.

"Hard to say."

Fen smiled, a wall of yellow stained teeth. "You should be a politician."

The cars would not fit down the narrow *hutong* so they parked and walked. The streets made him feel small, out of place, these streets he had hidden and fought and been chased in all his life. Wong was the skinny little boy always attached to Xiao-Di, but smaller. Thinking back, Lu had never really registered him or felt close. If he was ignoring or tormenting Xiao-Di, how could he not do the same to a boy smaller and younger? Now Wong was gone. Lu read a report stating that Wong and a gang of protesters had assaulted martial law troops with Molotov cocktails and rocks, and had even wrestled away firearms from downed officers. They had killed two PSB officers and injured dozens of PLA soldiers during an entire day's fighting and looting, sneak attacking anyone in uniform. There were official witnesses. He was shot by an armed police officer in self-defense. They needed to speak to his mother to see if she might know where Xiao-Di had gone.

The gate leading inside was open. Lu could hear voices and sobs behind the front door. They knocked. The smell all around reminded him of his own home: the sweet smoke of frying sesame oil, scallions, and ginger. Incense burning, the faded rot of the outhouse. It was a struggle to keep his thoughts straight. They needed answers. It was near nightfall. It had been more than twenty-four hours since Xiao-Di had disappeared. Lu thought, He could be anywhere by now.

A man came to the door. Lu did not recognize him but could see the rage and sadness in his eyes. He looked at Lu squarely.

"What . . . what are you doing here? What else do you want?"

Liang walked up next to Lu and told the man who they were. Lu said, "Let us in." The man tried to reply but the words clogged in his throat. Lu pushed open the door and stepped into a room glowing with candles. There was a small wood table and chairs, a bed in the corner unmade. A thin rug that did not stretch to the corners of the room, bare gray, scratched walls and broken chips of paint. Like his own family's house, but smaller. On top of a high mantel was a black-and-gray picture of Wong, with incense burning, the flickering flame of offering in the glass.

Wong's mother sat in a chair, collapsed, surrounded by two old women. His grandmother was not there. First Wong's mother looked up, sensing the presence of the outside. Her face was wrinkled and puffy, red. When she saw Lu she wailed, recognizing him instantly. Her frail and withered hands clutching the arms of the chair. The women held her down. She screamed and stared.

Liang walked around Lu and the man who had answered the door, who was Lu's age, the look of a scholar with his chubby face and glasses. He stood from his kneeling position, as if to defend the women from attack. Lu grabbed him by his shirt and pushed him down in his chair. The women were looking at all of them as if they were monsters, specters. Lu sat next to Wong's mother. He took her hand. She was bawling silently now, as if her body did not have the breath for such loud cries anymore.

"I'm sorry," he said. Lu asked if his brother had been there. Through her weeping she shook her head. She would not look at him.

Lu said, "We have to find him. If you know where he might be . . . you have to help us."

She said, "Why my little boy? He was a good boy . . . a good, good boy." She said, "They wouldn't let me take him back from the hospital. He's lying there . . . with the rest of them . . . . Why won't they let me take him back?"

"I don't know," said Lu. Liang told her they could help get him back.

"Back?" She turned her head and looked up at him. Her eyes and cheeks were swollen, dribble running from her nose like a child. Lu wondered if the men outside were watching. Wong's mother raised her chin and her features seemed to tighten, solidify. She coughed and spat in Lu's face.

"MURDERER! YOU KILLED MY BOY! YOU KILLED MY LITTLE BOY!" The two women fell on top of her. Lu stood as he wiped the spit from his eyes and face. Mrs. Wong was howling and the two women were muttering fast in her ear to stop, that things would be okay.

"You're a killer! Murderers! Kill me too! Kill old ladies and children!"

The other agents were inside now, guns drawn. Liang told them everything was okay. Mrs. Wong was still wailing, high piercing animal cries.

Wong's mother, the two women, and the man were led out into the *hutong*, into one of the cars and taken away. They searched Wong's mother's home and found nothing. They left the picture of Wong and the candles next to his face burning.

Fen's car phone rang. He picked it up, listened, nodding.

"On the highway, they found a construction truck overturned. They also found a small bag of food and clothes. Belongs to the fugitive."

"What else?" Lu asked. "They didn't find him?"

"No, but he's out there, northwest of the city."

10

Comrade

The doctor told him that he needed to rest, take a break. The stress plus his poor diet and lack of sleep in the last few weeks were affecting his heart. He gave Deng medication and told him to rest. "These will help your blood pressure, and these will help you sleep."

"I don't like medicine," Deng said, thinking of Mao, how he had been such a hypochondriac, always needing medical attention, bombing his system with pills. Deng was proud of his age, his condition, that his mind and senses were still sharp. The doctor left the plastic bottles on the table and left.

That night he took the pills. He dreamed he was holding a picture of Pufang, already in the wheelchair. He stared at it and after a few moments he could not make out the face anymore. But he knew it was Pufang, his son. He looked across the room at Mao.

"It's your fault. You almost killed him."

"But I didn't. He lives. He is still with you."

"But he's . . ." Deng was staring at the picture again. "Look at him."

"Little Soldier, don't you remember? My wife was executed, two of my brothers were killed. I've had my children die before me, some even as infants. I don't even know how some of them died.

"For the revolution lives have to be sacrificed. Your family and children now, they are all alive. You might consider yourself lucky."

"I'm not like you," Deng said.

The ghost said, "You are nothing without me."

He had more dreams, but they were not turbulent. Inconsequential, peaceful dreams. He had not slept so well in so long.

11

Dissident

I listened to the cart driver's bell and the squawk of the chickens as we bounced along the edge of the highway. With each bump in the road I felt a new pain; I suspected at least broken ribs, but I'd never been hurt severely before in my life, at least not the way Lu had been, so how would I know? The worst had been riding a bicycle when I was a boy, me pedaling with Lu on the handlebars of a wreck we had found, brought home, and patched up. The tires were bent and missing some spokes, and the chain and frame were rusty and weak. But we didn't care. It rode well for a bike so beaten up, and free, and only when we pushed our luck too fast around a *hutong* curve did we crash. I remember being airborne, landing awkwardly on one foot, then tumbling and smashing a few more feet along the road. Lu and I sat side by side, examining our wounds. I had a cut on my forearm, and my ankle was swollen to the size of a large onion. Lu gingerly touched his face and leg. He seemed okay. I couldn't walk so Lu carried me back to the house, where Grandfather called us idiots and Grandmother cleaned and wrapped my cut. I thought I might get another whipping, and Lu one for not protecting me, but we didn't. I was glad we did not have to go back to the doctor for stitches, the way we had for Lu.

Grandmother said, "You won't be happy until you're both dead, is that it? You want me to have a heart attack." She pointed at Lu and said, "Look at him—don't you remember?" Lu put his hand up to his face.

I drifted, rocked by the rhythm of the carriage, then woke to someone tugging on my feet. I screamed as I slid free from the bottom of the carriage. It was hot and I could smell myself—chicken shit, the sweat and grime of my body—and I looked at the carriage driver as if for the first time. He was smiling. I could not stand, so I slumped to one knee.

He helped me to a small cabin hut, laid me down on a bench, then left. I heard him talking just outside the door. Inside the cabin it was cool. The smell of dirt, the clean scent of wood. I lay there until two women came in, a burst of sun behind them. One was larger and older, the other small and lithe, a teenager. The woman said, "Be careful," and from behind she put her fat soft hands under my arms and slowly sat me up. The girl took off my shoes and pants, then my shirt. They unwrapped the shirt tied around my head. I could feel strands of hair thick with dried blood snapping like thin branches. After that my head felt light, like it might tip off my shoulders.

The woman said, "Drink this." She spoke *putonghua* with an accent I barely recognized. I sipped when I felt the cup at my lips, a hot spiked tea, pungent and bitter, like a potion boiled from the earth. I was so thirsty, I drank it all. I could feel the girl wiping at my head with a hot wet rag.

I tried to talk but couldn't. The woman said, "Calm down." Her voice was stern and level, much like Grandmother's. "Close your eyes," she said.

* * *

When I woke I was on the ground in a nest of blankets on a bed of straw. I wore clothes that were not mine: a light cotton shirt and pants too baggy and short, nothing on my feet. I did not stink like chicken shit and sweat anymore. I touched my face and arms, felt clean and dry. There was a new dressing on my head. Even the wound on my scalp did not throb and pulse the way it had, though I could still feel a stabbing pain in my chest. My stomach was growling, churning. For a moment I wondered how my grandparents were doing, then knew it was best to keep my mind dark and blank.

They came back a short time later, the woman carrying two small bowls in her big hands and the girl carrying two glasses. All of it was steaming. They pulled up work stools and sat next to me. When I tried to adjust one of the blankets the woman said, "Leave it."

She set one bowl down and stirred a spoon in the other. I could smell the steam coming from the bowls and cups. It made me even hungrier, my stomach roiling, my throat dry and cracked.

"Eat it all," the girl said. Her voice was soft and sweet. She had long hair in pigtails and wore a plain work dress. She was very pretty, her skin gold from the sun.

The woman said, "This will help."

The woman began spooning and I could taste chunks and bits of vegetable and roots, a rough soupy millet sliding coarsely down my throat. Between gulps from the woman's bowl the girl fed me sips of that harsh tea. I could feel my body filling like an empty cup with water. The girl checked the dressing on my head. I looked at the woman feeding me. Her face and hands were dark, her hair slashed with gray and knotted loosely with long pins. I saw the girl watching me. She looked away, quickly feeding me another slurp of tea.

I thought they would ask me questions, but they did not. They fed me until the bowls and cups were empty, and I was stuffed full and warm. I was sweating because of the hot food. What was going on in my body that I didn't even know about?

"Now sleep," the woman said. I felt comfort in the authority of her words. I didn't know what time it was; it felt like it had been so long since I'd left my grandparents and Beijing. The woman said, "Don't touch your blankets. Stay covered up." She motioned to the girl and the girl pulled a small pipe from a pocket in her dress. She lit it. I paused and looked at both of them before the girl put the pipe to my lips. The woman said, "More," as I sucked harder and only when she said, "That's good," did I stop inhaling and blow. My lungs were on fire, my head swimming. It was so hot. She said, "We'll be outside if you need us." The last thing I remembered was the huge swaying backside of the woman and the sticklike figure of the girl, their shadows in the open sunlight of the door flashing white in the midday's haze.

*   *   *

The phase of dreams seemed to keep me awake; I thought I could feel the mending powers of the tea and millet. My brain floated in colors, flashes in a lightning storm. I saw Lu and myself walking the edge of a ditch, skipping stones over shallow water. I saw Wong sitting at the base of the Monument to the People's Heroes, smiling that grand smile, telling me everything would be okay. I dreamed I'd brought Elsie back to Beijing and introduced her to my grandparents and they accepted her, loved her like their own grandchild. Elsie with Grandfather speaking a beautiful, elegant Chinese, holding Grandfather's hand and telling him stories from her childhood, stories she had never even told me. Grandfather appreciated this and Grandmother taught her how to cook. This did not offend Elsie, modern woman that she was.

I saw bullets floating like fat glowing bees just before they hit Wong's body. I thought I could catch them but my feet were cemented, my arms bound to my sides.

Lu in his soldier's uniform standing over me, towering like a cartoon giant, waving angry fists. The skin on his face smooth and clear. He was telling me that I'd been bad.

"But I'm just a boy, how can I be in so much trouble?"

"You have no idea," Big Brother said.

In my dream state I could feel myself sweating and obeying the words of the woman not to touch the blankets, to keep covered up to my neck. I wanted Grandmother to be there to dab the sweat from my forehead, for Grandfather to tell me stories like he used to when I was a child. I saw Xiao-An walking down a ceremonial wedding aisle in a flowing white dress and veil, her short stumpy body not long enough to fill the dress, her thickness stretching the lace. I was hooked through her arm, wearing a tuxedo too large for me because I was just a little boy. Elsie on my other arm in a traditional silk Chinese robe, red and adorned with gold and her white-yellow hair tied conservatively in a bun. The sleek angles of her face, the blue blaze of her eyes.

"You always ask why I love you," she said. "But why do you love *me*?"

When I woke I felt so cold. The blankets were soaked. The smell of the cabin hut and everything inside seemed to permeate my senses all at once. My blood running cool through my muscles and bones—could I feel the areas inside me where I was beginning to heal? What powers and mysterious tricks did these people know? I didn't know if it was night or day, how long I'd been asleep. I slid an arm out from under the covers to touch the dressing on my head. It was soaked with sweat, not blood. I lay there, content to wait for someone to come back.

When I opened my eyes again they were standing before me. The woman said, "Well?" and I said, "Can I have some water?" They laughed and the girl gave me a full cup. I drank it down in one breath. The girl set to changing my head dressing. The old woman had brought new blankets with her. She ripped the old ones from me and set the new layers on top.

"You slept a whole day. That's good," the woman said. "You needed that." She and the girl pulled up work stools and sat.

"So now I'm all better," I said.

"No, not quite."

The girl giggled. I asked them their names.

"That's Xiao-Mei, my baby," the woman said. "You can just call me Ma, like everyone else." She smiled. I knew she was the wife of the man who had driven the carriage and brought me here, and the girl was their daughter.

They did not ask my name and I did not tell it. I thought maybe the man had discussed with them my circumstances, or what he thought they were. It was better that something so simple as a name be left unsaid.

"I feel much better," I said.

"Good," the woman said. "Soon we'll have to put you to work."

*   *   *

I stayed in the cabin two more days. Like the days following the hunger strike, for the most part I slept. The woman and the girl came to feed and clean me. They always came together and I did not see the man, the carriage driver, at all. When I needed to, the woman helped me out behind the hut to relieve myself. She kicked dirt over my refuse and I cleaned myself and went back inside. I did not feel embarrassed.

I ate more of the grainy millet—I could taste mushrooms, corn, garlic, loose roots. I drank lots of the tea, which did not stink so badly anymore. Though it was summer the cabin was cool. I wondered if they had read in the papers or heard on the radio what had happened in the city. What else had happened since I'd made my run? Was there a manhunt going on? Had the student leaders who had been so boisterous in the square fled or been caught? And what did these people up here in the country feel about it all? What else did they know? The man knew, so I thought his family would know. But they said nothing, acting as if I were some distant relative fallen sick. It was their duty to nurse me back to health.

In the evening I lay by myself because the family retired not long after sunset. The woman and girl would come out to feed me and clean me for the last time. Lying in the dark by one candle, listening to the rustle of small animals out behind the hut, the chirping of crickets, subtle movements of night. I thought of my grandparents, missing them terribly. I thought of the hunger strike, my interview with the reporters in the square, then the tanks. How had anything we had done made the situation any better? People were dead and none of it mattered. It had cost Wong his life, so many others. I'd helped make it worse. The soldier's face when he had opened the hatch. Now I was laid up in the countryside, still running. I needed someone to explain it to me, help me make sense out of it all. I blew out the candle and spent hours staring up at the black ceiling, trying to forget, to sleep.

The next morning I woke with some pain in my chest and my head aching lightly, but I felt much stronger. I imagined the hot tea I'd been drinking was like glue sticking my vitals back together. I slowly stretched my arms over my head, rubbed my hands over the places where I had been most severely bruised. The marks were disappearing, especially on my legs and arms. My breathing felt easier, lighter.

The woman and girl came in. They seemed shocked to see me standing. They were wearing clean dresses and their hair shone in the sun reflecting from behind. The girl held an armful of clothes. The woman said, "Let's give you a quick washing first." I sat on a bench. They took off my dirty clothes and the woman wiped me down with a hot towel. The girl washed my hair, lightly rubbing and soaping my head. The woman was scrubbing my skin harder than I remembered her doing before. She snapped at the girl, "Careful of the cut." When they were finished I felt wholly new, my head clean and stinging lightly from the soap that had reached the gash on my head, but it was okay. Gently, the girl combed my wet hair.

The girl turned her face as I dressed. The woman had a pair of old shoes that were a bit too small, cramping my big toes. The girl turned back to me again and her smile told me she approved.

"Now you're ready to go," the woman said.

"Go where?"

"Church," the girl said.

I put on the shirt and pants. The shoes were definitely small but it did not matter. I said, "Are you sure? I mean . . . is it safe?" I looked at them, again probing to see if they truly understood. The woman nodded and smiled.

They helped me out of the cabin hut, the shoes and clothes scratching my raw skin. Outside the old man had hitched a new rear to the cab of his carriage. The woman told me to ride in back with the girl. As we mounted the seats in back I looked around and saw the main house. Beyond that toward the woods was a barn and a small field where I saw on the fringe the chicken coop, a pig pen, another small hutch. We were surrounded by a ring of hills, the backdrop of black mountains huge and clear in the distance. Being so far away from the city, I could taste the freshness of the air. There seemed to be no place to fit another family for miles unless they were tucked away beneath the cover of trees and hills, the way these people were. We sat securely in the carriage and the man pedaled us down a dirt road that led deeper into the woods.

The girl asked me, "How do you feel?"

"Much better," I said, though the bumping of the carriage on the dirt road made my ribs and innards hurt. "Whatever is in that tea and porridge, it's amazing."

"Old family secret." She smiled and looked down between her knees. Her hair was tied tightly back and I looked at her profile, compared her to Xiao-An. Xiao-Mei had big, bright eyes and long lashes, a small chin and wide cheeks. Her skin was clear and smooth. Xiao-An could not compare physically, but there was something about Xiao-Mei that reminded me of her. The way Xiao-Mei spoke in a quiet, subtle voice. How she didn't look me in the eyes for too long, out of respect or tradition, embarrassment, I didn't know. And the air about her, grounded, stable, as if she knew who she was. No rumbling or burning self-conflict inside the way I always sensed inside of Elsie. All these things I started to realize about Xiao-An, only after I'd been away from her for so long, with no hope of going back. I never loved her, and knew I never would have. But could I have gotten to understand her better, realize things about her, by being away? Or was I just going crazy?

We were going to church. I had gone to a church once with Elsie, the first time, because I was curious where everyone rushed off to so early on Sunday mornings. Elsie did not believe in religion. "It's another organ of the government that tries to control your mind, make you behave and think a certain way, make you do things that maybe you really don't want to do."

"Sound like you talk about China," I'd said. But she was very passionate about this. "My parents made me go to an all-girl Catholic school, up to high school when I finally argued my way into a co-ed school. It's bullshit," she said. "I believe in God, but I don't believe a word of this . . . rhetoric." She explained to me briefly the difference between Roman Catholic and Protestant. I didn't understand. We wore our nice clothes and went to a small church that many of the students went to. The sermon wasn't long. I held a small Bible and did not bother trying to recite or mimic everyone else. I was there for the experience. Elsie looked bored the entire time.

Now I looked around at the trees and the road. I wanted to talk more with this girl whose hands were so small, yet dark and hard from work. Instead I listened to the woman and man bicker up front. The sound was comforting.

We traveled a series of back roads, then we came to a small village with groups of old brick buildings and many cabins, huts made of wood. Random people walked the streets. There was an old man in filthy rags with a long white beard down to his chest. Clusters of children chased a dog, shooting it with slingshots and hurling small stones. A group of women headed into one of the brick buildings. The old man stopped the carriage and we stepped off. Xiao-Mei gave me her hand and helped me down. We followed the women in the clean dresses into the building, through the door and up a flight of stairs.

The staircase was old and dusty, creaking. I stepped carefully and Xiao-Mei walked behind me, as if she would catch me if I fell. At the top of the stairs we entered a small room where incense burned and candles glowed. The window was covered with a thin sheen of colored wax paper. Soon the room was full, old women and men, a few young couples, all sitting on stools and chairs. Though everyone seemed to know one another greetings were few. I thought people might look at me because of my bruises or the dressing on my head, but no one did. We sat and waited, Xiao-Mei next to me.

A man entered and was greeted by the room. He began to speak a dialect I did not understand. He wore a clean white shirt and glasses. His hair was dark, he had wrinkles around his eyes and chin, the corners of his mouth. After a short speech, he read from the Bible; I recognized its leather casing and the heft of its value in the man's hands. I wished I understood what he said. I followed the actions of Xiao-Mei and her parents, kept my head bowed slightly. Everyone in the room murmured and kept their hands steepled. They recited together. There was a big cross on the wall hanging just behind the preacher. I understood their need to congregate in closed and hidden surroundings. If the government was attacking Tibetan monks, what would they do to Chinese praying to a Western god? I remembered Elsie and others arguing about the value of religion and worshiping an iconic god. Had they even thought of people like this and the risks they took for their beliefs? I had never.

The ceremony was short, and afterward, in segments, we left the room. Everyone shook the preacher's hand before heading quietly down the steps. Xiao-Mei, her parents, and I were the last. We stepped back out into the street, the sun high and hot, the air dusty, charred. The old man said, "We have to get some things from the store. I'd make you come with us to help me carry, but you're no good like this." He and his wife looked at me and Xiao-Mei. The mother said to her, "Get him something to drink."

They walked down the street and disappeared into a small crowd. Xiao-Mei led me in the opposite direction, past the church. We found an old woman sitting behind a wooden stand on the side of the street. She was tiny and shriveled like a gnome. She peered up at us with a rodent's dark eyes. She said, "What happened to your head?" I looked at Xiao-Mei, then told the old lady I'd fallen from a horse.

"A horse? You look like no horse rider to me."

We bought from the woman two cups of cold tea. Xiao-Mei asked if I felt okay and I told her I was fine. We went back to the carriage and waited for her parents.

"How old are you?" I asked.

"Nineteen."

"You've lived up here your whole life?"

"Yes." She did not look at me as we spoke. "I've read books about the cities and other places, but I love it here. You know, the Great Wall is very close."

"I've never been there."

"But, aren't you from . . ."

"Beijing. But I've never been to the Great Wall. We always thought it was for tourists."

"There are a lot of tourists now," Xiao-Mei said. "Father says another part of the Great Wall is north and to the east, that hangs over the water. It's supposed to be very beautiful. But I've never been that far away." She turned to me and put her hand gently over the dressing on my head, testing it for moisture.

"How long have you all been going to that church?"

"I don't know. For a long time. As long as I can remember."

"But you know, that's not the . . . normal religion for Chinese."

She was looking at me and I could tell she did not see my point. She said, "We've been going for a long time. Father says a man came to our village, before I was born, around the time Mao had beat Chiang Kai-shek. He taught people Christianity. A white man. Then he went away. But there are many of us who practice now. Do you usually go to church?"

"No, not usually. How often do you go?"

"We go different days, different times. Sometimes we don't go for weeks. Father says it's to rest, but I know there are soldiers who don't like our church and want to shut it down."

"Are you Catholic or Protestant?" I asked. I had to test her.

"Protestant," she said.

"Do you know the difference?"

"The difference between what?"

Her parents returned. I was glad; I was beginning to feel nervous about being out in public. As we rode in the carriage I started to feel agitated, even a bit angry, that the parents had taken as long as they did. I held my tongue. We left the village. I knew people would be talking about me. I said to the old man up front, "I should go."

"Go? Where are you going to go?"

"I don't know. But all those people, they saw me. They know."

"Know? They don't know anything."

"But the bandage on my head. And everyone in that room . . ."

The woman said, "No one in that room was paying attention to you." I felt anger at her scolding, as if she did not respect me, know what I had gone through and the things I'd done. I wanted to say, You're a peasant, you're nobody.

I said, "I just don't want . . ." But I didn't finish.

When we got home the women went inside. The old man and I went into my hut. I lay down on the floor and the old man sat on a bench. His skin looked grainy and thick in the half-light inside. He held his head with both hands and sighed.

"I told you, they're not going to catch you. We won't allow it."

"I know, but I'm not sure you understand the circumstances."

"I understand," he said. "You're one of the student protesters. Or are you one of the workers? No, your face is too round, skin too white. You're not a laborer. But I know what you all did. Everyone at the market was talking the day I picked you up. And you're right, you'll have to go soon. But for now, you rest, you stay. My wife really likes you. So does my daughter. They won't ask any questions, so be kind to them."

I said, "Thank you for taking me in. I didn't mean to sound—"

"Forget it, you don't sound like anything. I don't know you from that rock over there, but I like you just as well. The women will be out in a minute with some real food for you. So you don't have to eat that gruel. It tastes like shit, but it works, seems to me. If you can live after eating that, you can survive anything."

12

Soldier

As they made their way toward the accident scene Lu watched the country change. The curve of the land. Flat gray sky, the sun setting behind hanging clouds. It was evening and they had grabbed a sack of steamed pork rolls from a street vendor before leaving the city. He felt drowsy from the hot food and long drive. I'm getting soft, he thought. This is nothing. He compared the last few days, including the fighting in the streets, to all the years of training. How he had been drilled and honed day to day to day. And now this, lolling inside a big car on plush seats, feeling awful and tired. A part of him was ashamed.

He said to Liang, "My grandparents, were they . . . Are they being guarded?"

"They're being taken care of," Liang said. Lu looked back out the window.

They saw police cars on the shoulder. Blue and red lights flashing, officers milling about. Orange cones narrowed the lane, yellow tape sectioning off the scene. He could see the wreck of the truck, piles of wood and metal splashed over the roadside. They parked several yards back then walked into the taped area. Other cars pulled up behind them. It was dark now. With flashlights they moved about the scene. They found a small black bag filled with clothes on the dirt shoulder, snagged beneath two beams of wood. There were two small packs of food wrapped in plastic. Lu half-opened them and poked his finger through: some pickled turnips and sautéed pork. Inside the other pack were cookies and dried black bean cakes, Little Brother's favorites. She always took such good care of him, Lu thought. Shirts and underwear, as if he had planned on being away only for a couple days. Lu held a shirt in his hand, stained now from the accident. He thought he could smell and feel the grit of raw soap his grandmother used to clean their clothes. He let the shirt slip from his fingers, then stood to the side, away from the scene so the feeling could pass.

Fen said, "Any clues?"

"No. Just a few of his things."

"How do you know they're his?"

"The food, some of his favorite desserts."

"But you're supposed to read into it. Tell us what's next."

"It's just food and clothes. That's it." Lu said to one of the policemen, "Did you find the driver?"

"Yes, walking back to the city. He said the fugitive was hiding in back when he fell asleep. Drunk at the wheel."

Lu looked again at the mess of metal and wood, the smashed front of the truck and flipped rear bed.

"The driver told us he went north," the officer said. "Can't be too far gone."

Lu had seen enough. There were more than two dozen Public Security and Armed Police officers who continued to snoop along the side of the highway and at the edges of the wrecked truck. One was taking pictures, another jotting down notes. Many stood around smoking.

After an hour of this they followed a car back to a local police station. There was a large back room with a half-dozen cots. It reminded Lu of the barracks. The officers complained, said they'd been in whorehouses that were cleaner. It did not bother Lu. There was a refrigerator and small kitchen, a small boxy bathroom. They cleaned themselves and ate the leftovers they found. When they finished eating it was past midnight. Liang and the officers left the back room. He said, "We're going to go over evidence, what we know so far." Lu stood to follow. Liang said, "Take a break." Liang looked at Fen.

"Shouldn't I be there to go over things with you?"

"Not right now," Liang said. "We've had some new information come in that I want to review first. I will brief you later." Fen did not seem bothered by this. Liang and the others left. Lu and Fen found a young officer in the hallway. They asked him to bring some drinks. When he came back with the drinks the young officer said, "We have a game room, if you're interested."

They followed the young officer down the hall and through a gray door. Inside were two mah-jongg tables with pieces already set, a pool table, a Ping-Pong table.

"If we had two more," Fen said, "we could play mah-jongg."

Lu said he did not know how to play mah-jongg. Fen looked at him, then broke out laughing.

"How do you not know?"

"I just never learned."

He laughed harder.

They decided to shoot pool. Neither was very good. They both missed simple balls and shot too hard, both concentrating like they were taking scored target practice with rifles out in the field. When he missed, Lu could see Fen getting angry.

"Soldier Lu," Fen said, "you were limping at the accident scene. Is something wrong? Are you hurt?"

"An old injury."

"I know about your face, the scar, but not your leg. Or is it your foot?"

"What do you mean, you know about my face?"

"It's in your file," Fen said. He lit a cigarette and sat on the edge of the pool table, holding the cigarette in one hand, the pool cue in the other. "The report on your brother says that he used to live in America."

"It's your shot."

"He was dating a white girl. Fell in love with her."

"Listen," Lu said. "It's your shot."

Fen took his turn and missed; now he didn't seem to care. Lu sank two balls, then missed an easy shot for the win. He hit his stick against the table.

"No wonder he got himself involved in all this," Fen said. "He thinks he's better than where he came from. I've seen the type."

"You don't know," Lu said, "so shut up."

"Bad temper," Fen said. "Just like the file says."

Liang walked in and said, "What's going on?"

"Nothing," said Fen. "Just chatting with our soldier friend."

Liang asked Lu to go outside with him. He gave Lu a cigarette and they smoked in silence. Lu knew that when he was younger he would have cracked the pool cue across Fen's jaw without warning, tried to stab the tip through his eye—whether he was a ministry agent, platoon captain, or an infantryman. He thought of the old trouble in all the bars and whorehouses since basic training. Fen was nothing, he would have been easy. But it was too much. Who knew how far he would have moved ahead by now if he had had some control?

"Fen has a big mouth," Liang said.

"I can see that."

"Don't let him bother you."

Liang finished his cigarette, stubbed it out with his toe. "Patrols have done some intelligence gathering in the area, but nothing has come up. Someone is probably hiding him up here. We are going to split into teams and do detailed searches." He looked at Lu to make sure he had heard and understood. "We begin tomorrow morning. It's very important to stay focused." He turned and went back in.

Lu decided he liked Liang. He was simple, straightforward. He could understand Liang working for the PSB. Fen he wondered about. His family must have had connections. That could be the only way.

Lu was outside for a few minutes alone. He wondered what Xiao-Di could be doing, thinking at that moment. Was he scared? Did he realize the kind of trouble he was in? And why had he done it at all? That was what Lu could not understand. What could have made him rebel in such ways? To say and do those things. He thought of the video footage he had been shown. He thought more about Wong's mother, his own grandparents, the grief and sadness. But it could not all be blamed on Xiao-Di, or Wong. They did not have to send Xiao-Di to America, where surely he learned all this behavior. Lu felt that through the years he had done his part to discipline his brother, show him the right way. In a sense they all had failed.

The young officer who had shown them the game room peeked his head out. He was smooth-faced, like a middle school boy, and seemed scared to speak. He looked behind him at the door left cracked open. Then he said, "Sir, can I ask you a question? I heard rumors. About Comrade Deng Xiaoping."

"What rumors?"

The young officer sighed. "That he was sick. That he had suffered a heart attack . . . ."

Lu had not heard any of this. He suspected that neither had Liang or Fen, or he would have known.

"They're just rumors. The city . . . is in some disarray, so people are going to make things up. Don't worry."

"You came from Beijing, sir?"

"Yes, we just came from there."

"It's terrible," the young officer said, shaking his head. Lu did not know what to say to him. The young officer said, "I'm glad they're just rumors, sir. I wouldn't know what to do. I remember when Chairman Mao . . . if Comrade Deng, sir . . . I don't know." Lu liked that he called him "sir."

He also remembered when Chairman Mao died, how he and Xiao-Di and his grandparents had huddled in one room. They heard the report on the radio. Then the crying from the streets and houses surrounding the *hutong* began. His grandmother was cooking with her head and shoulders stooped, his grandfather drinking a glass of rice wine. Not drunk, only sipping. Xiao-Di was playing with a wooden doll his grandmother had bought for him at the market earlier that day. The crying outside was loud.

At the moment they heard of Chairman Mao's death, Lu was looking forward to eating. It was only steamed cabbage and rice, some fried eggplant and pickled cucumbers, but he was very hungry. Xiao-Di was on the floor playing, oblivious. His grandfather murmured to himself here and there, but otherwise they were silent. No outcries, no emotion, as if it was just another boring, quiet night.

Over the next few weeks most of the kids wore their Chairman Mao pins in mourning. They continued to carry copies of the Chairman's *Little Red Book*. Lu was embarrassed because his pins were gone, and he had no *Little Red Book*; he had burned them all after his grandfather's incident. But he and Xiao-Di did not get in trouble for disrespecting Chairman Mao. Everyone knew they were poor, knew they'd had trouble in the past. The class wrote essays eulogizing the Great Helmsman. Lu wrote the same things as everyone else.

Soon life without Chairman Mao sunk in. Nothing changed. They were still poor, still not members of the Party. His grandfather was still blind. Lu knew even then that his grandparents were happy Chairman Mao was dead. Though they could never show this on their faces much less say it out loud.

Lu said to the young officer, "How long have you been stationed here?"

"Over two years, sir."

"Are you from these parts originally?"

"No, sir. Originally I'm from the country, near Harbin. Much colder. But I like it here. It's very quiet. The people are good people."

"You know them well?"

"I do. At least I think I do. They remind me of people from home."

Lu said, "I want you to do me a favor. Do you know why we're here?"

"Yes, sir. At least I think I do, sir."

"We are looking for someone. A fugitive, escaped from Beijing."

"Yes, sir. That's what the captain told us."

"We think he's hiding in one of the villages."

"There are so many villages up here, sir."

"I realize that. That's why you have to find some things out for me. Do you understand?"

The young officer looked at Lu. Lu said, "It's important that we find him. It would be a great service if you could assist us with information."

"Yes . . . yes, sir. I'll see what I can come up with." The young officer stood. For a moment he seemed confused, as if he should salute. He did not salute but went back inside.

When he went back in Liang handed Lu his brother's file. "You better look through this. Make sure we are all on the same page." Then Liang went to sleep. All the cots were taken. Lu found a place on the floor against the wall. The file detailed everything—their parents' death, his grandfather's incident. Xiao-Di's grades, the kinds of reports he had written in school. It was okay for him to study abroad. There were reports on what he had studied in America: numerous math courses, theories and applications. Even with their family record, Xiao-Di was not considered a political threat. Until he had returned, and the report by Xiao-An's father was made. A bad situation, all of it, with the ugly girl and her family. What were his grandparents thinking? What could Xiao-An's family really have done for them? If he asked, surely they would say none of it was worth what was happening now.

There were reports on the letters Little Brother had written to his girlfriend after he came back. There was concern over the dissatisfaction he had voiced, over his life in Beijing, his inability to find a job. The potential for political instability, the report said, even though they were just love letters. But there were no actual letters to read in the file. Lu combed through every page like it was a novel, fascinated. Like his little brother was a villain, or a cult hero. A character, make-believe.

He fell asleep wondering about the details in his own file.

*   *   *

At sunrise they cleaned themselves and got dressed. Liang and Fen were now in military fatigues. The young officer brought them breakfast bread and tea. He seemed happy to serve them. Lu wondered how good an officer he could be if he was so happy to please.

They were outside, smoking and feeling the sun before leaving. Lu saw the young officer motioning to him at the side door of the station. He walked over.

The young officer said, "Sir, last night, you were serious about what you said?"

"Of course."

"I will try to find out some things from the villagers."

"You tell me what they say. I'm sure it will be valuable."

They split into search groups. The other teams in their cars started to pull away. They were given sectors to patrol, specific villages to search. Lu walked with Liang to the car where Fen was already behind the wheel. Liang took out the map of the area locating all the villages and obscure farms hidden to the east and west of the highway. Their targets were circled.

"If we can't find him," Fen said, "we take a day and see the Great Wall. It's just twenty minutes away!"

They drove and no one talked. Liang turned down the radio. Then Fen said, "We have this map and know he's headed north, so why do we need him?" He was driving and he turned to look at Lu. The ruts and scabs on Fen's face made Lu feel sick. That arrogant smile.

Liang said, "Just drive." Lu thought he looked like a man who did not often sleep and always wished he was somewhere else.

In the first village they came to Fen parked the car in a clearing. They gathered all the people to explain what they were doing, who they were looking for. Liang showed the pictures of Xiao-Di. He had Xiao-Di's file in his other hand, as if ready to give a talk. He said, "He is one of the fugitives from the recent turmoil in Beijing. He is very dangerous. If you know of his whereabouts or have any clues, you must come forward. You will be rewarded." Dangerous? Lu wondered if this was really true. And had these people up here even seen the graphic details of what had happened in the city? How would they? Did they know what Xiao-Di and all the rebels had done, what it meant? Liang's questions were met with blank stares, like they were out looking for some mythical creature.

Lu thought they would need more than three men to handle the situation, but the villagers cooperated, were docile. He remembered his forays into the provinces to help peasants in the past. They were cowed by the uniforms, the sight of guns. They searched three villages that day. In each village there were no more than fifteen to twenty adobe-and-wood huts, storage sheds, shacks, pens for animals. Their homes were poor and broken, dirty, worse than he could have imagined. He had always believed that he had grown up in a desolate condition, but now he saw that many of the roofs of the adobe huts were blown open with holes, many with no windows to keep out the wind and rain, the bugs and humidity. At least he had always had a decent roof over his head. They always had food and food coupons, his grandmother made sure of this, so even if they ate only a thin porridge or corn glue, they ate. They never went hungry, unlike what the faces of the children and old people told him now. He could sense their sickness, the starvation. They were wondering and scared, some like walking skeletons, and now men with guns had come to their homes.

Liang stayed outside with the people. Fen and Lu kicked open doors, smashed bottles and jars, broke down chairs, flipped over tables. Lu quickly forgot the feelings he was having for the villagers. With his boot knife he cut into mattresses and pillows. With the steel butt of the knife handle he easily cracked the thin walls, as if Xiao-Di might be welded inside. He kicked down outhouses, raided coal and wood storages. He found barrels of grain and rice saved from a large harvest. Otherwise there was nothing.

In the car between villages no one spoke. Lu kept thinking about how easy it was, how the villagers put up no resistance. It must have been this way when the Japanese had attacked generations ago. How most of the nation had lain down and agreed to slaughter. At least Little Brother was putting up a fight, he thought, though for all the wrong reasons. He could not understand. Xiao Di was out there, somewhere. He could sense him now like he used to when they were children playing hide-and-seek. He would be bundled away under a table, lying flat behind a low wall, and he could feel Xiao-Di creeping, hear his footsteps and breathing, sense his nearing without ever seeing him.

They spent the next two days following the map, gathering the villagers in each place, then tearing apart their homes. A handful of times some peasants showed resistance, were offended and angry. They shouted at Lu and the agents, cried out while their houses were being sacked. But Liang would calm them, tell them this was part of a state assignment. It was best if they did not interfere. It worked, the peasants didn't know any better. They picked up small clues—food products or clothes or trinkets with English words, letters. But most had been traded for, and when Lu looked at the clues—old broken toys, shirts that were too small for his brother, a plastic wristwatch that a peasant had been hoarding like a treasure—he knew they had nothing to do with Xiao-Di.

Afterward they went back to the station. The other search teams had come up empty as well. They were not going to find him like this.

Lying on his cot, Lu wondered how different their lives would have turned out if his parents had not died. Both his mother and father had been very tough, tougher than his grandparents. He remembered being spanked by both of them, and being hugged by both of them. He remembered helping his mother carry small buckets of water and grain when he was only four years old. She had called him Xiao-Lu, until his brother was born. After that his brother became Xiao-Di and Lu was just Lu.

When Xiao-Di turned three years old, he started asking questions about his parents. What were they like? What had happened to them? Lu never answered, did not know what to say. He left that to his grandparents. They told Xiao-Di that their mother and father had been called away on a long journey. Xiao-Di asked where. Then his grandmother told Xiao-Di one day what it meant to die, to be dead. She said the body stops being, but the spirit rises to a higher, greater place where it can watch over the people it loves who are still alive. She told Xiao-Di that their parents were still watching over him and Lu, loving them more now than when they were alive.

Afterward, Xiao-Di stopped asking Lu questions. All those years Lu had not forgotten—he had just forced himself not to remember. His parents would not have allowed Xiao-Di to get away with the things he had his entire life. They wouldn't have let him grow up soft, spoiled. They would have hit him more, chastised him more, made him work harder. He would have understood discipline, how to appreciate the blessings he received in life. If his parents hadn't died, then maybe his grandfather would not have been blinded by the Red Guards; maybe he would not have become a soldier. Xiao-Di might not have met Xiao-An and gone away to America. Their lives would not have been their lives. They would have been different people altogether. None of this would be happening.

The second night Lu walked through the station and found the young officer. He smiled when he saw Lu. They went outside where they stood alone.

"I wasn't hearing anything in the station, sir, so I took a drive around. The villagers . . . didn't want to talk to me. But we arrested a prostitute today. I asked her. She said she knows something."

They went back inside. Down a short hallway lined with small cells they found her at the end. The young officer opened the door. The girl was sleeping and the young officer woke her up, led her out of the cell and to a door. Inside the small and dirty room were a table and three chairs. The young officer left them. The girl did not look scared. She had long hair, and after a better look Lu saw she was not that young. She said, "You're not a policeman."

"No."

"A soldier. But you probably want what they want."

She made him uncomfortable, like every whore he had ever been with. She sat with her legs crossed, one elbow on the table, hand supporting her head. Lu said, "We're looking for a fugitive from Beijing. The officer says you know where he is."

She asked him for a cigarette and Lu told her he did not have any. She looked away, then she said, "I might."

Lu stood. She looked up.

"The officer says you know. If he's lying . . . if you're both lying . . ."

She stood so they were facing each other. She was tall for a woman, almost as tall as Lu. She said, "Get me out of here." There were wrinkles around her eyes, the corners of her mouth. "I know your type. Fun first, like the officers. Then business." She smelled of sour perfume, a stale mix. She put her hand on his stomach, slid it down to his belt. "I know," she said. "I can make it easy."

"How? Who told you?"

"The villagers talk. You probably went looking today and no one knew a thing. But they all did."

He felt her working at his belt. She kept her eyes on his face. With her other hand she caressed his good cheek. When the belt was undone she started to work on the button. He thought of the dirty girl from Changsha, how she had helped ruin him. He pushed the prostitute away and she fell back in her chair. He put one hand around her neck, felt her oily skin. "Do not play games with me," he said. He squeezed, felt almost her entire neck in his grip. The prostitute shook her head, grabbed at his wrists. He let go. She kept her eyes down, breathing hard.

"Jade Hill Village," she said.

They put the prostitute back in her cell. The young officer drew a rough map for Lu. "Jade Hill Village isn't even on any of the maps." Lu said he knew this. The officer gave him the map.

"This is helpful, sir?"

"We'll see what we find."

"Is there anything else I can do to help, sir?" His fingers were fidgeting, and he was tapping his foot. "I could have gotten in trouble for letting you talk to the prostitute."

"We're with the Ministry of Public Security. You are assisting in state matters."

"Yes, but . . . that's not the way the captain would have seen it, sir."

"But the captain doesn't know. And I won't tell him." Lu stood to go. "Someday you will be rewarded," Lu said. "If you continue to work hard." He wondered if he had been this gullible when he had first joined the army.

*   *   *

The next morning they set out. On the road Lu said, "Go this way. Jade Hill Village."

"Jade Hill?" Fen said. "That's not on the map. What are you talking about?"

Liang looked back at Lu. He took the map from him, looked it over. He nodded. He said to Fen, "Follow this. Let's go."

They turned off the highway and routed into a web of back roads. They had to drive the car over an old wood bridge. "We are going to die," Fen said, but they made it. There were more back roads. At one point the car bounced and rocked so hard that Lu thought they were breaking ground that had never been trod before. Then they broke out of the brush and trees and onto a slim dirt path. The car barely squeezed by, was getting scratched by branches and rocks. Until they found the village inside it all. There were close to a dozen small buildings and huts. The homes were made of rotted wood and brick, adobe, as if they had just been rescued from war. Liang called out the people. The children with dirty faces, shoeless, clothes filthy, and scratching at their cheeks and hair. The men and women and old people, afraid, unknowing. Even the wandering chickens and pigs looked skinnier, sickly. A place like this called Jade Hill? Nonsense.

Lu thought of what the prostitute had said and it made him angry, thought she had lied. Would villagers like these really risk their lives to hide Xiao-Di? Lu wanted to say that Xiao-Di definitely was not here. They should not waste their time. These people were too depraved to take care of themselves, much less a fugitive. But maybe they were protecting him, like he was somehow one of their own. Had he talked his way into their trust? What lies had he told them? Even up here in the country he benefited from favors.

Lu and Fen started searching, smashing. The villagers did not resist. Lu toppled altars to ancestors and charity plates, broke open any container of dark glass. He stepped on a framed black-and-white photo of an elderly couple that dated back to the beginning of the century, from the cut of the people's hair, the looks on their faces, their clothes. If they were lying, they would regret it. He dug through rooms, banged on walls, rummaged through closets, cellars. All this time his leg did not hurt, the scar did not itch. The people were quiet because they understood how things were. It could have been much worse.

In the last house there was a rustle from a back room. Lu walked down a short hallway, kicked open the door, and saw a body hunched over in a chair. He could not tell if it was a man or a woman. A turn of the head and the long hair splashing down, he caught a glimpse of her face. She did not look at him. "What are you doing in here? You were called outside." She heard him but did not acknowledge. She would not turn toward him. Maybe she had a bomb or gun and it was already too late.

He stuck his gun to her temple, his free hand on her shoulder to turn her toward him. She would not budge, so he pulled. She made no sound. There was a baby in a towel cradled in her arms, the mouth clinging to her bare breast. By her arm he lifted her to her feet. They marched outside. She was still holding and feeding the baby.

"Why were you hiding in there? Don't try to play dumb."

She wasn't responding. She was young, maybe twenty. Her hair was tangled and dirty. She was thin and too bony, her flat breast stuck in the baby's mouth. Lu could not tell if it was a boy or a girl. She plucked the child's mouth from her breast and buttoned her shirt.

They walked up. He could feel the shift in the crowd.

"Why didn't anyone bring her out?" he shouted.

No one answered. The murmuring and crying hushed.

"If you know where the fugitive is, you better tell us." All of them were blank, like they had never seen this woman before. Like he was speaking a different dialect. He thought of what the prostitute had said.

He drew his gun again and pressed the muzzle to the woman's cheek, stared at the crowd. No response. He looked at Liang and Fen, then banged the butt of his gun on top of the woman's head. He felt his hand rise and watched it fall, heard the sound, the feel of the strike in slow motion like it was not him doing it. The woman made a loud grunting sound and her knees buckled, the baby still in her arms. She did not hit the ground because Lu had her by the arm. The baby was wailing. The woman was bleeding from the crest of her forehead. The blood ran in two thin lines down her face and neck and dripped over the towel wrapping the baby. Where was this man who had told the whore what she knew?

An old woman stepped out of the crowd. She held her hands out as if begging for charity or in prayer. Her face was puckered and wrinkled, she was short and small, like a gnome dressed in rags. She said, "Stop, please. She's deaf and dumb. The baby . . . has no father. We all just leave her alone."

Lu thought of the woman from the night they entered Tiananmen, how she had stepped before them, fearless, and lain down in the street. These old decrepit women, so courageous, Lu thought. Like some were probably saying about Xiao-Di. Lu said to the old woman, "What do you know? Did you see him somewhere?" He pulled out the picture they were using but she did not look at it.

"In church," she said. "My son saw him."

"Church? What church? Where?"

"The other village." She pointed beyond the hills. "He was with a family. They live close to here. We trade with them at some of the big markets."

"Where is your son?"

"He's gone," the old woman said. "I don't know where he is."

Liang was talking to the villagers now, trying to keep them calm. Fen was looking back and forth between the crowd and Lu and the old woman. Fen helped the woman with her baby stand and led her away.

The old woman looked up at Lu. Her gnarled wrinkled face, tears in her eyes.

"That's all I know," she said. "I'll even show you where it is. But please, leave us alone."

PART III

I have made this world, and now I am losing this world. I have done this all myself. I have no regrets. I win and lose by my own deeds.

—YANG JIAN, THE EMPEROR WENDI,
FOUNDER OF THE SUI DYNASTY (581-618)

13

Dissident

I helped with yard work, cleaned and fed the animals in their pens, tidied the cabin hut. I was strong enough to walk with only minimal pain; I did not feel dizzy or light-headed anymore. They began feeding me normal food—vegetable dumplings and *doufu,* small portions of sweet potatoes and turnips, cabbage and rice. They were not leftovers. I thought they might invite me to come live and eat with them inside, but the invitation did not come. I did not insinuate. I was grateful, after all, for everything they had done.

In the afternoon Xiao-Mei took me to the river to help her with the laundry. We waded in up to our knees, the water cool and fast. We rubbed the clothes and soap over the smooth clean rocks. Birds chirped and a soft warm wind blew. Though her lithe frame did not reflect it, she was very strong. She carried most of the clothes by herself in a giant balled-up basket because she knew I was no good at lifting. I felt she liked just having me there. I imagined her boredom performing these chores alone.

"Do you always wash clothes here?"

"Only in the summer," she said. "If the weather is bad, we do it inside." She did not look at me, kept her eyes fixed on her work. "More soap," she said. I passed it to her. I watched her scrub the shirts hard against the rocks, then in the water. The day was getting hotter. We kneeled in a spot of sun but she did not sweat. I liked watching her, her hair tied back in a long, thick braid. The skin on her face and hands, though gold and dark from being outside, was still clear and smooth.

"I haven't washed clothes with my hands in a long time."

Xiao-Mei stopped and looked at me. "Then how do they get clean?"

I realized the ridiculousness of what I'd said.

"In college," I said. "Machines washed and dried for us." I tried to sound serious and not too stupid. Xiao-Mei shrugged and went back to work.

When she finished the clothes I helped her hang the wash on lines. Even as we hung each piece a breeze swept up the thin red dust of the farm and speckled the newly cleaned clothes. The mother came out, waddled over to us. She asked me, "How do you feel?"

"Much better."

"Did you help with the wash?"

"He did," the girl said. The mother looked at me, said, "Then you're better than you look."

I spent the rest of the day lying in my hut. Xiao-Mei had disappeared. It was near the end of the week. The days did not matter out here. I'd left Beijing last Sunday evening; we had gone to church a few days later. It struck me how far removed I was from everything that had happened already: I looked at my clothes, my body pulsing with that slight healing ache. I felt like a different person. But I wanted to know how my grandparents were. And I thought about Wong; I missed him.

The mother came in holding a pair of scissors in her hand. She said, "The old man told me to give you a haircut. Take off your shirt and sit on the stool." I did as told. She grabbed a handful of hair and started clipping. I did not say a word. As she cut and the hair fell about my face she said, "So you're getting better."

"I am," I said. "That porridge and tea you gave me, it's amazing. What's in it?"

She laughed and said, "Very simple. Lots of fresh ginger, a bit of ginseng. Extract of mushrooms and mustard seed."

"My grandmother used to make the same when we were kids. She had a potion or recipe for everything. You have all those herbs and extracts up here?"

"Where do you think they come from?" She poked me in the back of the head and laughed. She said, "We have everything we need."

We were silent for several moments as she sheared off the longest locks of hair. Then I could feel her clipping very close to my scalp.

"You've lived in the city your whole life?"

"Yes. Except when I lived in America."

Her hands stopped moving. I could not see her face, though I could feel her massive presence around me. The clippers went back to work.

"What did you do there? Are you rich?"

"No. I went to school. Then I came back."

We were quiet the rest of the time. When she was done with my head she splashed cold water over me to wash away the stray hair. She used a flat razor to scrape away the rough patches. I toweled off and put my hand over my head. It felt cold and prickly, short nubs and spikes, like a melon's grainy hide. She brushed one hand over the front of her dress and said, "Tonight you have dinner with us."

*   *   *

Xiao-Mei came to get me. She wore a plain blue dress that came down past her knees, a trim of white and red flowers lining her cuffs and hem. Her hair was tied tightly back. I followed her across the yard and into the house.

Inside it smelled of heavy burned wood and coal. The front room was small, hardly big enough to fit a table. There were no cabinets on the walls. The floor had a dark rug thrown down but beneath I could see old nailed wood. An iron stove sat in the corner. I compared this to Grandmother's sorry kitchen and thought that even we had it so much better than this. I remembered the kitchen areas we had in the Cornell dorms, the white walls and shiny stove tops. We would try to cook even the simplest of things, noodles or canned soup, and make a terrible mess. But we never had to clean because there were people whose jobs it was to clean up for us. The massive kitchens with the gleaming steamers and ovens and fryers behind swinging doors in the dining hall, where they prepared more food in one day than I had seen cumulatively in my entire life. Not even the People's Liberation Army could be this well fed, I'd thought the first few times. I could not draw a line between what I had seen there and what I lived here and now, and consider either one reality.

I sat at the table with the old man. Xiao-Mei and the woman bustled about, finding plates and cups, still stirring and cutting. The woman put down a big pot of stew—I could smell onions and garlic, spotted bits of diced carrots and celery, other herbs sprinkled on top. Xiao-Mei dished up a plate of fried eggplant and bean curd. I smiled, let out a small laugh.

"What's so funny?" the mother asked. "Is there something funny about my cooking?"

"No," I said. I looked at the table, then back to the mother. "It just . . . reminds me of my grandmother's cooking. It's great."

The old man began to eat even before we were given bowls of rice. I followed his lead. The stew was loaded with shredded chicken in the thick broth. It was good, and it did taste like Grandmother's cooking, I was sure of it. The red chili peppers and herbs, soft onions and chicken, each mouthful seemed to spread through me bite by bite. I felt like I hadn't eaten in months. I thought of the dining hall and my first few months, how the taste was so intense because it was so different. But I cherished this so much more. Anything I had eaten over there would never make me feel the way this meal did, the way Grandmother's care always did.

The old man said, "We should have guests more often. So we can feast." I could see the happiness in the old woman's eyes, the same way Grandmother would glow for a day if Grandfather paid her even the smallest compliment.

We all barely fit at the table. There were no sounds outside, dusk settling. I imagined a peace like this every night. I finished my rice and scooped a second serving of the stew. I drank cup after cup of tea, then water. Not even after the hunger strike had I torn into food like this—maybe because I was too weak, or because my body and mind were not properly adjusted. But I was better now, healing. They all watched me as I ate.

The mother said, "He's lived in America."

The father looked at the woman, then at me, as if waiting for me to validate this statement. I said nothing and continued to eat with my head bowed. Xiao-Mei was not looking at me.

"What did you think of church?" the mother asked. "Do you go to church? Are you a Buddhist?"

Again the father looked at the woman, this time glaring, but she ignored him.

"No, I don't worship . . . but the church was nice. Very interesting."

"We all need God."

"Enough," the father said.

"Enough what? You eat enough."

The father looked down at his plate and sighed.

"I feel much stronger now," I said. "It's all this great food." This lightened the mood slightly. Then Xiao-Mei asked, "When you're better, what are you going to do?"

We were all quiet for a few moments, then I said, "I don't know yet. But I'll be fine, I'm sure."

After the meal Xiao-Mei brought to the table two small cups and a bottle of potato liquor in a gray clay bottle. I remembered Grandfather having similar ones when we were children, before he switched to the new clear-bottled rice wine. Xiao-Mei and the mother began to clean. The old man took out a pack of cigarettes and poured our cups full.

"We usually wait for the new year to celebrate. But this feels like a celebration."

I understood what he meant. We smoked and the old man went through cup after cup in single gulps—*gan bei*—taking only a few minutes in between. I tried to keep up with him but couldn't. I looked around the room. Xiao-Mei and the mother were gone.

The old man said, "When I picked you up I thought you were some wild man out of the forest. I guess you are in a way, aren't you?" He drank more and smoked. We stopped *gan bei*. My stomach felt warm and my head was spinning.

"I don't know if they're going to come all the way up here. I heard most of the searches are by ports and railways."

"You heard this."

"During my trips into town. No one was talking too loudly, of course. But still, there's quite a stir." He lit another cigarette. "They've got a list, everyone they're tracking down."

"I'm not going to stay much longer."

"You stay as long as you have to," the old man said. His eyes were turning red from the drink and smoke. "Are you afraid?"

"Yes. Very much."

He waved his hand at me as he shot down another cup of potato liquor.

"Don't be afraid, son. Let me tell you, there are two kinds of Chinese—fanatics, and the fearful. Fanatics have been killing and raising war since the first Qin emperor. What do you think he was? A fanatic, obsessed. The government today? Still obsessed. The fearful have always lain down, made it easy. They wait for other fanatics to fight for them. So the killing and fighting go on. Fanatics rule until other fanatics kill them. But you're not really afraid, or else you wouldn't be here. Anyone can see that. So what are you?"

"I'm tired. Getting drunk."

The old man laughed. "Good. Maybe that's the best way to be."

"And what about you? Which one are you?"

I heard the challenge in my voice, though I hadn't intended it. I looked at the old man to see if he had taken offense. He was getting drunk, but he was still clear and pensive.

"I'm just a farmer," he said, "a peasant. We all are. I thought the Communists would fight for us, but they didn't. We've been waiting . . . for the next people to fight for us."

"I'm a peasant too," I said.

"Peasants have become emperors. Or maybe those are all myths. Lies . . ."

We were quiet for several moments. We didn't look at each other. Then he said, "So how long were you in America?"

"Three years."

"You studied there?"

"Yes, sir."

"Do you wish you could go back?"

"Right now I do. Yes."

"I'll bet."

I liked the old man very much. I wished I could stay on with him and his family until I grew into their lives and they into mine, if they had not already. Start fresh, become a new person.

"They came looking for the Communists," the old man said. "We hid them underground, nailed up behind boards, in the roof. They never caught anyone, and back then we had to hide them often. Because of the civil war. Chiang Kai-shek, another fanatic, crazy. So this is nothing. And you're not a stupid boy, I can tell.

"Then they came back, the same boys we risked our lives to save. Now they were Red Guards, on our farms, tearing things apart in the name of Chairman Mao. It made me think we should have let Chiang catch them. Or maybe we should have let the Japanese catch all of them. Either way, it would have been hell."

"They blinded my grandfather during the Cultural Revolution," I said. "The Red Guards did it. My brother, he thought he was a Red Guard."

"Your brother was a Red Guard?"

"He thought he was. We were just kids."

"And what does your brother think of you now?"

I looked at the old man and said, "I don't know. He's a soldier." I knew I was drunk.

The old man said, "The city still needs settling before they come looking for the likes of you." He blew smoke into the light. *Gan bei* started again.

I poured myself another cup of potato liquor. The old man called out to his wife and Xiao-Mei. They came back to the kitchen together.

"Sit down," he said. "Celebrate with us." He had his arm around my shoulders. Xiao-Mei and her mother traded wary glances, then sat. Xiao-Mei brought two more cups to the table.

"You're drunk," the mother said.

"So what? He is too. I feel good. I want to celebrate with my family." He leaned over and gave his wife a kiss. He poured all our cups full and the drinking continued. Xiao-Mei coughed after her first cup, and we all laughed. We drank more. I kept looking at Xiao-Mei. She was smiling and her eyes were moving fast. I could tell that she had never sat at the table with her parents, shooting down liquor and laughing like they were at some crazy party. But it wasn't crazy. It felt good. I could not remember being so happy in a long time.

"Here's to our . . . guest," the father said. His eyes were glassy and his words were starting to slur. He raised his cup. "Get better, take care. May the future . . . hold significant fortunes!" We drank and the old man slammed his cup down on the table, breaking it into pieces. He was cackling even as his wife tried to hush him.

He said to me, "My daughter, you think she's beautiful?"

"Yes, sir. She's very pretty."

"Take her! I give her to you."

"Stop it," the mother said. "You're acting stupid!"

"She's old enough for a husband now. And you seem like a good man . . . ."

Later the old man's head was on the table and his wife was pulling him up. She got him to his feet, both of them still laughing. They left the kitchen and Xiao-Mei looked at me, red-faced from drink, embarrassment. She said, "I should make sure they're okay."

* * *

I went back to my hut and lay down in the hay. I was about to fall asleep when I saw the door crack open, a slice of moonlight cutting through the dark. I went stiff and looked around for a pitchfork or stick, anything I could fight with. I held my breath and felt my heart beating fast. The door went wider.

"Are you awake? Hello?"

"Here," I said.

She closed the door. She still wore her clean new dress. She came over to me and I sat up as she pulled up a stool. Even in the dark I could see her round pretty face. I thought of Elsie and Xiao-An, the only two girls I'd ever kissed, and how it felt the first time with each of them, how bad I wanted to kiss Xiao-Mei right now.

I said, "Your father will kill you. Then he'll kill me."

"He's asleep already. Are you drunk?" I told her I was and she laughed. "I am too."

"Go inside," I said. "Where's your mother?"

"She's asleep too. They're both drunk. I've seen Father like that before, but I've never seen my mother. I don't think she's had liquor in years."

"She's the one I'm really afraid of, if she catches you."

"We're not doing anything. I wanted to talk to you."

I slid toward her so we could speak in lower tones. I said, "We shouldn't be talking. Go inside."

"You lived in America?"

"Yes."

"What was it like?"

"It was different. Great . . ."

"I wish I could go," she said, but we both knew she never would.

She took my hand and helped me up. We tiptoed outside and opened the door slowly so it did not creak. We moved fast across the yard, behind the barn and up a hill. I thought the animals would make noise, but they did not, as if the entire farm and countryside had fallen asleep. We walked quickly up a path she seemed to know by heart. We made our way through some light brush and onto a narrow dirt road guarded by small trees. "Where are we going?" I asked, and she said, "Just come on." I could smell things burning off in the distance, ash in the air. When we reached the clearing we were atop a hill, beneath a scattered map of stars. I could see other villages clustered against the small ring of mountains around us.

"There," she said, pointing. "The Great Wall."

I thought she was joking. Then I focused and scanned the dark. My head was spinning but Xiao-Mei was holding my arm. I saw a bump in the landscape first, then slowly the length of it, how it stretched like the mountains and hills themselves, the wall rising like the blade-scale back of a dragon, curling to the bend of the earth.

* * *

In the morning I did not hear her father or mother outside my hut as I had the previous days. Xiao-Mei opened the door and said, "Come on, we're going."

The horse was hitched to the carriage. In back were baskets of fruits and vegetables covered by a web of straw. I thought I would see her parents outside to wave us off, but there was no one else. We sat in front and she snapped the reins. The horse started down the red dirt path.

"Where are we going?"

"To the market. My parents don't feel well," she said, smiling. "My father's blaming you for drinking too much. So you're helping me today."

Xiao-Mei gave me two cold pork buns for breakfast. When we reached the highway she handed me a straw hat like the one she wore.

She said, "We're not going to the usual market."

"Then where are we going?"

She pointed north up the highway and said, "The wall."

I remembered the night before, how she had pointed it out in the shadows. She snapped the reins and alongside the highway the horse and carriage rattled and clopped as cars passed us.

"Where are you going to sell your things?"

"Down by the parked cars."

We rode for over thirty minutes, but soon I felt nervous being out in open daylight on the highway. What if police or soldiers should see me out here? What if there were roadblocks set up along the way? I said this to Xiao-Mei and she said, "We're almost there. Don't worry. You look just like my father." I felt better with my hat pulled down tight over my new-shaved head. The sun was hot, hotter I thought up here in the countryside, closer to the mountains, than in the city where things were so choked and clogged. I breathed in the fresh heat and air.

Xiao-Mei said, "I asked Father if you were in trouble. He told me to mind my own business."

I didn't say anything, didn't look at her.

"I saw you that first day, being dragged out of the bottom of Father's cart, the condition you were in. Father thinks I'm a little girl, stupid. He doesn't talk to me about these things. But I know what happened in the city. Everyone in the countryside knows. If you're in trouble, we'll help you. We can find a way, everyone around here. No one will ever find you."

"Xiao-Mei . . . it's not that simple."

We had turned off the highway, down a steep road and into a lot of parked cars. A parking attendant shouted at Xiao-Mei to pull her cart farther to the side. She steered toward the vendors lined up to the rear and left of the lot. The other attendants glared. Xiao-Mei stepped off the carriage and untied the horse. She led it farther back to where other horses stood tied to poles. Then she approached the old woman selling baseball caps and wooden Buddhas, other trinkets made of plastic painted to look like jade or gold. She asked the woman to watch our things just for a little while. The woman kindly nodded and told us that was fine.

There were buses coming in now, schoolchildren dressed in uniforms of blue-and-red with white shoes trooping off. The lead child carried a white flag with the school's name emblazoned in red characters. They marched in unison and some of them were singing. The teachers paid them little mind. We walked beside the students heading toward the ticket gate. Xiao-Mei's hair was still neatly plaited from the night before. Anyone looking at us would have thought we were cousins or maybe even siblings, she the more sophisticated and I the lowly farmhand. We stood on line and Xiao-Mei bought us two tickets. Then we marched up the stone stairs.

All my life I'd heard stories and read the history of the wall but had never actually stood on it. My grandparents remembered it as a symbol of imperialism and repression. They talked about how many millions had died over the centuries to build it, some rumored to have been buried where they fell into the earth and brick. But that was centuries before Mao had come to power and used the wall as a symbol of strength and unity for the Chinese people. Maybe that was why all the world's leaders, when they came to visit, always went to the Great Wall: to show they supported that unity and strength.

The sky was clear, the sun rising. We stopped to look out over the wall at the vast spread of country and sky. I breathed deeply and felt Xiao-Mei close by my side. You could see the whole stretch of earth like one great plain taking you from end to end. Even though it was summer and hot, there was a hard, cutting wind. No trees or buildings or foreign elements to stop it. I imagined the wild Mongols, their bloodthirsty cries, the centuries and lives it took to build this spectacle. I took my hat off and breathed, felt dust on my tongue. Xiao-Mei took my hand in hers and I squeezed it once, then let go. We walked up higher. The schoolchildren were catching up to us.

As we climbed, the steps became steeper and less level. We held the rails and each other. I looked out over the wall at the twisting snakelike body. It spread for miles. Xiao-Mei said, "So beautiful," and I nodded as we climbed higher and moved on. At points there were cubed and roofed areas with small windows carved out, lookout posts in the stone. We hid there for a few moments. I had never felt so astounded, this quiet awe, like I was a part of something so great and yet I was so small. The closest thing was the first time I'd stepped onto Cornell's campus and had seen the eminent buildings and sprawling, lush lawns, all adorned by tailored foliage. This sense that I had reached a new and greater place, that my life was going to change. But it was not the same, could not compare to this. The university and my life was just a speck in the shadow of all this.

There were no big crowds, as I had expected. A young Chinese couple asked us to take a picture of them. I snapped the picture and the couple moved on. There were some foreign tourists in big white hats, older white men in blazers and khaki pants, women in high heels. I tried not to look at them, did not want to draw attention to myself or seem suspicious. My ears began to hurt from being so high up, so we started back down. We were headed toward the schoolkids, who all looked so happy. They were small and agile and moved with great confidence from step to step. The teachers snapped at them to be careful and to stop squirming. The kids laughed.

Then the soldiers were behind them, tall in their hard green uniforms. They were right behind the schoolkids, ready to pass through.

I yanked Xiao-Mei over to the side of the wall and leaned over so it seemed we were looking at something down below. She said something I didn't hear. We stood up straight again, lest we look peculiar hanging off the ledge of the wall. The soldiers were showing the schoolchildren pictures. There were only four soldiers, and I scanned their faces. They smiled at the kids and the kids smiled back. They shouted, "Yes, sir!" and saluted. The soldiers showed the pictures to the teachers. The teachers nodded and smiled as well.

I grabbed Xiao-Mei by the arms so her back was to the wall and she was facing me. I brought her in close and hugged her so my face rested on her shoulder. She put her arms around my waist. I listened to the clop of the army boots, like I'd heard that night escaping Beijing, the sound of the soldiers walking around the truck. I lifted Xiao-Mei's face, could feel the soldiers hovering in our area as my lips touched hers. The soldiers were looking at us—at me—and I pressed my mouth harder against Xiao-Mei's, felt nothing in return.

Someone slapped me on my back. I forced myself to turn slowly. A soldier grinning at me, his skin dark like red clay.

"Enough of that, eh? Have some decency!" He and the other soldiers laughed. He was younger than me and very skinny, looked more like a middle school punk than a soldier.

"Yes," I said. "Of course."

The soldier stared at me for a moment, as if he might recognize me. One of the other men was holding the pictures. The soldier said, "A peasant like you with a girl like this. You are very lucky." The soldiers laughed again. He gave me a smack on the arm and turned to join the others. We watched them move on until they were showing the pictures to another group along the wall.

"Come on," I said. We walked more quickly going down than we did going up. The children and teachers were preoccupied with the evenness of their steps. I was holding Xiao-Mei's hand and could feel my palm sweating inside hers. Xiao-Mei said, "Stop, you're going too fast." I slowed as we neared the bottom of the wall. We walked out into the parking lot, sauntering like tourists.

* * *

When the day ended she had sold most of the fruits and vegetables. What was left she gave to children who begged on the street. Their dirty hair was lice-infested, clothes torn like rags; they had round faces and giant heads on skinny bodies. Some had bloated bellies, as if drawn for cartoons. Xiao-Mei said, "Orphans, all of them." They were mostly young girls.

She counted the money and told me to hold on to it. I knew it was not very much. I wondered how much pressure I had put on this family, with the money they made and the life they lived. I thought of the money I had made at the fitness center, then about Elsie and her family. How she probably made more in one month than these people made in two years.

I had to leave soon. I realized through most of the day, even while climbing the wall, that I'd experienced very little pain. I wanted to thank Xiao-Mei for taking me there, but I didn't think she wanted to talk.

On the way home I said, "I'm sorry. About before."

"Don't be sorry." She did not look at me. We were both sweating from the high sun and dirty from the dusty highway.

"The soldiers, you saw them there."

"I know."

"They were looking . . ."

"I know."

As we neared the house she said, "Did you do something very bad?"

"It's complicated, Xiao-Mei."

"Don't talk to me like I'm a child."

I wanted to explain the feeling of holding Wong's body as he lay dying in the street, describe the electric pulses shooting through me as I stood in front of those tanks. I wanted to tell Xiao-Mei about all of it but I could not. I was glad we were home.

I did not eat in the house that night. I told the mother I did not feel well. When it was she who brought me a bowl of rice and cabbage and not Xiao-Mei, I was disappointed. The solitude that night felt sad and awful, so I thought about Xiao-Mei and our day together, the strange beauty of our kiss.

*   *   *

I dreamt of Elsie. We were studying for finals. I was lying on her bed, and she was sitting in a chair on the other side of the room. We were both very quiet so as not to distract the other. Then she came across the room and lay down next to me. I could smell her hair falling around me, the light sweetness of her perfume and shampoo. Thumping music played through the walls.

In my dream she slipped her tongue in my mouth as I lay there, eyes wide open. And even in my dream, as I did true to life, I pictured Xiao-An. I thought of all the times we'd kissed and tried to be romantic; I'd never done more than touch her small breasts, run my hand over her stomach and back. Once she put her hand over my crotch and left it lying there. But Elsie kissed me all over my mouth and face and down my neck. When she moved down to my chest her kisses became bites and I pulled her by her hair. I saw Xiao-An, her moon face. She was bald, crying, with blood dripping from the corners of her mouth. "I wish you were dead," she said. In English, Elsie's voice, Xiao-An's face and tears and eyes.

I woke up startled. After a few moments I went out back to relieve myself. I came back in and lay down feeling slightly scared. I thought of my next move, which would be what? There was only so much longer that my luck would last: How many more gracious families could I run to? Where else could I go?

I heard footsteps, knew they were Xiao-Mei's. The door creaked slowly open. I was glad to be awake, watching her enter from the night.

"You're up," she said.

She sat next to me. She looked very tired and I was not sure what time it was. I put my hand to her cheek. Her eyes were sad, her face sullen and collapsed. Still she looked beautiful, as far as I could make out her features in the dark. She lay down next to me. In my half-conscious state it was like having her slide into my dream. I put my arm around her and she curled her body. My nose in her hair, I could smell the dust and oil from the day's work.

"You're almost better. Mother says you've gained back some weight."

"It's all her good cooking. Tell her that."

"Didn't anyone cook for you before? You were very skinny when you came."

"I used to be fatter."

"When you lived in America? Tell me stories about America," she said. "Tell me anything about anywhere, except here."

I told her about the rolling green hills of Cornell's campus, how it was laid out for miles like some perfectly sculpted fantasy. Huge, muscled athletes in their numbered jerseys, and skinny girls wearing blue jeans and Greek sorority colors and symbols. Blacks and whites and every shade in between, their eyes, clothes, hair, the myriad shapes of their bodies and faces. The eccentricity of some professors who led their classes with total and liberal autonomy, who encouraged open discussion, even conflict. Unlike the teachers I'd grown up with who stuck so close to the Party line. Cornell's student paper was filled with articles and editorials attacking the university's administration, the U.S. government, down to local businesses who would not give students discounts. You stood up and fought for what you believed in; it was almost expected of you. Any opinion or problem you could talk about, whenever and wherever you liked.

Xiao-Mei stared at me. She did not understand.

"No fear," I told her. "In China it's like we live inside a cage and the bars are electrified. This is not the way it's supposed to be."

"Father says we're lucky we live up here, where city officials can't sneak in on us." Then she asked, "Why didn't you stay?"

"I had to come back, for my family." I told her about my grandparents in Beijing, about Lu, the soldier. I did not mention Wong or Xiao-An. I told her while at college I had been with an American girl.

"Did she love you?"

"I thought so. I don't know anymore."

"What was her name?"

I said in English, "Elsie."

Xiao-Mei made a face, looked away. "That's a dumb name." She pressed herself closer. "Was she pretty? Did you love her?"

"I did," I said.

"Because she was white?"

"What?"

"Father says that some Chinese move to different countries and marry white people. Even black people. Because it makes them feel better about leaving their homeland. It makes them more acceptable wherever they are. Like they are trying to forget that they are really Chinese."

She was waiting for a response. I could tell by the look on her face that she was not trying to challenge me. We were just talking. I didn't know what to say.

"Your father's very smart. But that . . . that wasn't the case."

"Then why did you love her? When I get married, I want a good, honest man like my father. Who works hard and treats his family right. He doesn't have to have money, or be very good-looking. But he has to have a good, strong heart."

We were quiet for a few moments. I could feel her caressing my chest, her head on my shoulder. Then I said, "What if someone was married to a white man or woman up here in the village? How would you treat them?"

"Don't be ridiculous," she said.

I didn't know how to put all my feelings together so that she would understand. It started to make me sad and angry thinking about the past, the choices I had made. If I hadn't met Elsie, or been with her, or told my grandparents about her, as she had not told her parents about me; if I hadn't broken my promise to Xiao-An, her father, my grandparents. If only I had been stronger, or had I really made any choices? I wanted to believe that everything had happened for a reason, in this set sequence, because it was all part of some greater progression. But that wasn't true. Everything anyone in my life had ever said or done or even thought had affected me somehow, as everything I had ever done would affect them. So I kept talking, told Xiao-Mei as much as I could, as if going through a catharsis. I knew at some point I would never see Xiao-Mei again. I didn't want her to forget me.

She looked up and kissed me, her lips dry and flaked, her skin not soft and smooth the way I remembered Elsie's, or even Xiao-An's. I thought that if her parents came through the door now they would cut me up with kitchen knives and feed me to the animals in the barn.

"Xiao-Mei." I pulled away from her. "Wait."

"For what," she said.

I could feel her sweating. She slipped her nightdress over her head, folded it neatly, laid it on the seat of the stool. She sat there, watching me watch her. I made out the curves of her body in the darkness, used my hand to slowly guide me. Her breasts were small, her waist narrow, hips swelling out. Her arms were lean and hard. She was kissing me on the face and the side of my neck.

"I'm scared," she said.

I put my hands to her face, felt her tears sliding through my fingers.
"I'm going to be okay."
She said, "I'm not worried about you."

* * *

Later we lay in the straw holding each other, feeling the sweat dry on our bodies, our smells mixed with the straw and dust. She stood and said, "I have to go back in." She put on her clothes and I watched her, my eyes long adjusted to the dark. She kissed me once more, then she was through the front door. I listened to her footsteps as she made her way back to the house. How was it that she could move around in the evenings so freely and never be caught? Then I thought her mother would know—the smell of straw and man all over her daughter. I fell asleep with this.

In the morning I heard the commotion, first the sound of a horse riding up fast and coming to a stop, then the mother's voice. I pulled on my clothes and as I did I could hear her shouting outside, loud and urgent, the father calling back. When the door swung open I was ready. I thought she would have that pitchfork or kitchen knife in her hands, but she had nothing. The mother's face was red and sweating. I could feel the heat blowing in through the open door. I heard the horse clopping away.

Xiao-Mei was behind her mother, looking very scared. I held my breath.

"Get up!" the mother said. She was on the verge of tears. She looked more sad and anguished than outraged. The father's face was sullen and flat, like the loser of some meaningless game.

I kept my eyes on all of them. It was very obvious I'd never truly belonged, that I'd been fooling myself. Again. I deserved this.

"What . . . what's happening? What's wrong? What did I do?"

"Soldiers, some kind of search party," the father said. "In the village next to us."

I looked at Xiao-Mei, her eyes wet, her hands knotted up by her chin, covering her mouth.

"A lot of them?" I asked.

"No," the father said. "Just a few."

The mother, crying, said, "Come on, son, there's not much time. You have to go."

14

Soldier

They parked in the middle of the main street. There were two columns of wood and adobe homes. Children were playing in the dirt, kicking at some tiny animal darting around inside a circle. An old man pushed a wheelbarrow to and fro between a small patch being prepared for planting and a giant pile of dung. No one came out to meet them.

They walked over to the children in the circle.

"Where does the preacher live?" Lu asked.

They stared up with blank eyes.

"Where is the church?" The children looked at one another. One of the boys pointed at a building isolated in the center of the street. The kids looked at the boy as if he were a traitor.

"Good. Go home." The children scattered. The soldiers walked toward the small building the boy had pointed to. The man and his wheelbarrow had disappeared.

Liang knocked on the door. Lu could feel the eyes of the village all around them, as he could feel the city invisibly watching back in Beijing. A man and a woman came out. They were small, middle-aged, with plain features. The man wore glasses. They could have been from any other village the three of them had been to so far. Lu saw a calmness in the man's face, no fear like there had been in all the others. He wore a faded black coat and a white shirt, the woman in a drab brown dress. They did not extend their hands in greeting or smile.

Liang said, "We've been informed that a fugitive from the rebel incident in Beijing has been seen here."

The man said, "A fugitive?" He looked at the woman.

"Is this the church?" Lu asked. "Are you a priest?"

"I'm the pastor," the man said.

They stepped inside. The pastor said, "We're hiding no fugitive. Look around. We're a small village. We would do no such thing."

"Show us," Lu said.

The pastor led them upstairs into a small room filled with chairs. There was a cross on the wall and candles. The air was dusty, like an old closet. The man and woman stared at them as they looked about the room. Fen kicked a few chairs around. Lu went through the drawers of the desk at the front of the room. They stomped over the floor, testing. Where there were bumps in the floor Fen knelt and pulled at the raised wood and tile, found nothing. Liang stood guard, looking back and forth between the room and the front door downstairs.

"You're lying," Lu said. "You have the guts to lie to us?"

"We're not," the pastor said. Still Lu did not sense that the pastor was afraid. They surrounded the pastor, the woman behind them.

Lu said to Liang, "Take her downstairs."

"What?"

"She's in the way."

Liang said, "No one is going anywhere."

"I know what I'm doing," Lu said. "They know where he is." He looked at the pastor and motioned to the woman. No one else moved.

"We don't know anything," the pastor said. But he knew, Lu could sense it. As if the pastor wanted him to know this, testing to see what he would do.

The room was very hot. Lu tried to open the window but it was stuck. They were all sweating.

"Preaching a reactionary religion with crosses and Bibles," Lu said. "We can take you away just for that."

The look on the pastor's face grew less brave. "We hurt no one out here," the pastor said. "We're spreading the word of God."

Lu pulled the pastor's head back by his hair and struck him across the jaw with the bottom of his fist. The pastor hit the floor. Lu kicked him in the side, again in the stomach. The pastor curled himself into a ball. His wife was screaming. Liang grabbed her by her arms and shuffled her down the stairs. Fen stood behind Lu as he squatted over the pastor and hit him. His head bounced off the floor. The pastor covered his head with his arms. Lu aimed his shots. He knew he was hurting him. He wanted him to talk.

Fen grabbed Lu around the shoulders and pulled him up. Lu turned and shoved Fen into a row of chairs. He thought Fen might rush him but he did not. Lu could hear Liang still struggling with the woman downstairs.

Fen said, "Enough! He can't talk if you kill him!"

Lu looked out the window across the street. In other houses he could see faces in the windows, but no one came out. Their presence made every place a ghost town. Liang was now standing by the car alone.

The pastor was bleeding from the nose and mouth, his forehead. Still he had that solemn expression on his face. Maybe the village would come to save him. But the pastor made no noise. Lu wanted to hit him more because he would not talk, because he knew things and was not listening.

Fen said, "That's it. He doesn't know. He's not going to talk." He was standing by the door, looking nervous, shaking. Lu went to the front of the room and pulled the cross from the wall. It was made of wood, beautifully carved, heavy. He did not know where the village would have gotten something like this.

"Come on," Fen said. "You're not going to find anything out like this."

"Is this too much, Agent Fen? I thought you'd be able to take more."

"You're crazy."

"If you can't help, go downstairs."

"Who gave you the cross?" Lu said to the pastor. "An American? A Westerner? Who taught you to worship like this?"

Fen left the room. The pastor was trying to get to his feet. He was on both knees, breathing hard, his hands holding his ribs and stomach. Lu held the cross with both hands, feeling its heft. When the pastor saw Lu holding the cross, he stopped trying to get up. On his knees he sighed, then clasped his hands in front of him, closed his eyes. Lu picked the cross up over his head and swung down, smashing it against the pastor's shoulder. The thud of wood against the pastor's flesh; he tipped over like a statue and lay on his side. His hands were still clasped, eyes still closed. The cross did not break. Lu hit him across the back twice then threw the cross on the ground, kicked him in the ribs. He listened to the pastor's wheezing breaths. He was still mumbling, praying. Lu could feel himself shaking, his arms and legs, something inside his chest. A bubble grew in his throat.

"I'll kill every peasant in this hole."

He picked the cross up off the ground and started smashing it on the wall. He did this over and over and the cross would not break. The pastor lay at his feet, silent.

* * *

First came the smell of smoke, then the crackle of the flames building. They were outside, behind the car. People were coming out of their houses crying and screaming. Liang and Fen drew their guns, the pastor at Lu's side barely standing. The smoke funneled through the cracks in the wood, windows filling black. Through the blood on his face Lu could see the pastor's tears.

People stood at the mouths of their homes. The building was engulfed. Some were crying loudly. The pastor was still mumbling. Lu pointed his gun at the pastor's head.

A woman came out running, shouting into the street. It was the pastor's wife, the one Liang had dragged outside. She was crying and stammering as she stumbled toward them. When she was close enough they put down their guns. They knew she was not armed. Lu let the pastor slump to the dirt. The woman tried to go to him but Lu grabbed her and pulled her off to the side.

"Talk."

"Let me help him first!" She tried to go around him but his grip was firm on her wrist.

"Please," she said. "Don't hurt him anymore."

Lu showed her the pictures. She nodded, said she had seen him in church with a family who lived nearby. But he had shaved his head and looked beaten up. She said she knew where the family lived.

Her family had come out of their house, a young boy, a small girl. When she saw them Lu let her go. She ran to them and hugged them. Lu walked over to her and her kids.

"How do I know you're not trying to trick us?"

"No, I'd never," the woman said. "I'll show you. Please, just . . . no more."

The pastor had been taken away by a small crowd. Liang and Fen had not said a word. Lu wrapped a rag around his hand and wiped his face of sweat, drips of the pastor's blood. The church was still burning. No one moved to put out the fire.

"Your boy," Lu said. "He will take us."

"Him? But he's . . . he's so young. And he's slow . . ."

Lu stared at the woman. She said, "Please don't hurt him. Not him."

It was late in the afternoon. They listened to the crackle and rush of flames. The summer and dry season, the old and broken wood, people stood outside their homes to watch. Lu thought of Xiao-Di, being children, lighting small fires of sticks and brush. Sitting around in the *hutong* telling ghost stories on summer nights. How simple and easy things had been. He listened now to the crackle and blaze as the small house crumbled and cut itself in half.

*   *   *

That night they went back to the police station. The other units had not returned. The only talk was Liang and Fen exchanging quiet words. They made a call back to headquarters, spoke in low tones, but Lu could hear them. They reported their whereabouts and plans for the next day. They said they had a lead, that they were close. They said nothing about Lu.

Liang hung up and said, "Soldier Lu, we need to talk." Liang and Fen turned to face Lu. They all sat. Fen would not look at Lu. He was very nervous, not his usual cocky self.

"We just spoke with the ministry office. We want to go over what will happen when the mission is complete."

"We have to catch him first, don't we?"

"Not necessarily. The office says we have another two days. After that, we will hand this over to the Central Military Commission, and they will lead the investigation."

"Why? I don't understand. We're close, I can feel it. That boy tomorrow, he's going to take us to the family."

"We have made good progress," Liang said. "But your tactics have not brought us to this point."

"They won't cooperate if we're not tough. They are all lying to us! Can't you see that?"

"Your actions today were a liability," Liang said. "And hitting that mute woman. You cannot take those kinds of risks without warning us first. It endangers the mission. We cannot let our emotions hinder our objectives. If you mistreat the peasants too much, you can cause a greater disturbance and they will all turn on us. They appear weak and stupid, but they are not. So far they have been cooperative. We need to keep it this way. Do you understand?"

"No, I don't. We wouldn't be this far without me."

"Don't question," Fen said.

Lu looked back at Liang, his face big and white. He was angry, eyes fixed on Lu. He thought Liang might come at him, but he knew Liang was exasperated, too tired.

Liang said, "I also want to let you know what will happen if we do capture your brother. I will suggest in my report that you be promoted to the rank of sergeant, and lead your own platoon in a different group army, different division. You will be transferred, destination to be determined at a later date."

Lu did not know what to say. Sergeant? He should have become a sergeant years ago. And a transfer? He did not want to be transferred. What if they sent him north to Harbin, or even west to Xining, south to Kunming? The different dialects, customs, patterns, the physical area. Regardless of rank, it would be like starting over again.

"What about . . . you said Comrade Deng, and Party Central. Will I receive any kind of honors? This is not what we agreed to."

"An official commendation from the Central Military Commission is possible. But that remains to be seen. Nothing was ever promised, Soldier Lu."

"Remember the words of Mao," Fen said, "'the People's Army does not hurt the people.'" Fen smiled, his eyes narrow.

"This is not about the people," Lu said.

Liang and Fen left the room, went outside to smoke. He told himself that they could not trick him, lie to him like all the others. But he would deal with that later, when they had caught Xiao-Di. Lu wanted to follow them out, had more things to say. But he couldn't get up. His leg hurt so bad, he could not move.

*   *   *

In the morning they went back to the village. The boy, short and skinny, waited for them in the street. He had a big head. He wore a dirty long-sleeve shirt and shorts. Lu thought there was a chance the mother and the boy might have run away, but they were still there. Lu knew in the countryside it was very much the same—the work, the people, the circumstances. He had seen it all before; one place was no better than the other. There was nowhere else to go.

They drove up to the burned down house church, looked at its charred remains. A pile of black ash and rubble. Soot collected finely around it in the dust as if someone had swept it into a neat perimeter.

They sat the boy in back with Fen. Liang was driving and Lu sat up front. Liang turned the air conditioner on high. "You like that?" he asked the boy. "Ever feel something like that?" In the rearview mirror Lu could see the boy looking around the car, shocked, amazed. "No," the boy said. "Never." They drove away from the village. The boy continued to gaze about, feeling the upholstery of the car, plastic handles, smooth clean glass.

When they reached the highway the boy said, "Are you going to take my father away?"

Liang looked back at the boy, then turned his eyes back to the road.

"What do you mean?" Liang said.

"Yesterday, you beat him . . . . Why did you beat him like that?"

The boy was maybe seven or eight years old, wide-eyed, not scared. Like his mother said, dumb and slow.

Liang said, "Show us where the family lives. Then everything will be okay."

They turned off the highway at the boy's direction. But the boy shook his head, said this was not it. They did not bother to get out of the car, turned back and went to the highway. Twenty minutes later they did the same thing again, going off the highway, to the wrong village. The boy kept staring, looking for a symbol to recognize.

"You better know where you're going," Lu said. "Stop playing games."

"Whose idea was this," said Fen, "to follow a little boy?"

Liang put up his hand. "Both of you shut up." He turned to the boy. "Are you sure of the direction we're headed, young comrade? This is very important. We can't afford to waste time."

"I know where . . . the highway, it's confusing."

At the next exit they pulled off and made their way onto a dirt road. After a minute the boy said, "Yes, here." They drove over a narrow path cut for mules and horses, wagons and carriages. They came to a clearing. It was not a village but a farm. An adobe hut stood to the left of the main house. Behind that was a barn and a field with pens of animals. Grass and woods beyond. The boy said, "This is it." They got out of the car.

They told the boy to wait in the car. He sat inside with the windows open. Then they approached the house and no one came out. At the front door Lu knocked until an old man opened it.

"Sir, please come outside," Liang said. The man stepped out. He was wiry, as if his body had been whittled from sticks. His hair was silver gray, his skin red like the dirt surrounding.

Lu said, "We need to search your home. Your property."

"But . . . I've done nothing." The man sounded but did not look confused or scared.

"We have reason to believe you are harboring a fugitive," Lu said.

The old man scratched the side of his face with one bony hand.

"Young soldiers, I mean no disrespect, but I think you're mistaken. We haven't seen anyone on this farm in a long time. Who's not related to us, at least."

The old man told them to search the house, his entire property. Like yesterday's pastor, Lu thought he did not look scared or guilty. He called his wife out to the yard—a heavyset woman in an old housedress. He told them to search whatever they needed, do what they had to do.

Fen and Lu went in. Liang stayed outside with the couple and the boy in the car. Lu did not like the look and feel of any of this. The old man's complete confidence that they would find nothing. They are all lying, Lu thought. Fen flipped up the rug and turned over the beaten straw mattresses. It was the oldest and filthiest place they had been to so far. Lu wondered what the old man outside thought now, listening to the carnage inside his home.

From the house they went to the hut outside. They stabbed pitchforks into stacks of hay, broke into every corner and stall. They searched up near the ceiling where Xiao-Di might wedge himself, which Lu knew he could. But there was nothing, no one.

Fen said that was it, that they should go.

"The boy's lying," Lu said.

"Lying or not, he's not here."

"Out back. The woods."

"If you want to search the whole forest, go ahead."

They went back to the car. Liang was showing the picture to the old couple and talking quietly. He saw Fen and Lu returning, and put the picture away. "Nothing," Fen said. The old couple was silent. They started walking back toward the house.

Lu opened the back door and pulled the boy out by his shirt.

Liang said, "Let him go."

The boy said, "This is the place. The old people, I've seen them."

"No one is in there," Lu said. He felt stupid and hot, being led around by an idiot. Liang and Fen were next to him. He did not understand why they cared if he threatened the boy.

The boy said, "Did you talk to the girl? The pretty one. She'll tell you."

They looked back toward the house. The old couple was about to enter. Liang told them to stop. If they had been younger they might have tried to run. But they were not. They stood by the door, waiting.

*   *   *

They found her in the woods kneeling by a stream, washing clothes. When she saw them her face was steady, like she knew that people would be coming. She was pretty and had gold skin, long braided hair. Lu told her to come back to the house with them. She stood, said nothing. She carried the big basket of clothes with her.

In the house the old man said, "He was here, but we didn't know. A straggler. We gave him some food, let him sleep in the barn, that's all." The woman was crying. The girl sat next to her, silent.

"Where is he now?" Lu asked.

"Gone," the old man said. "He left days ago. Please, I swear." The woman was weeping, could not speak. She kept looking back and forth between them all. Then she put her head down and cried loudly.

"Which way is he headed?" Lu asked.

"We don't know," the old man said. "He just . . . left. We didn't ask."

"Why didn't you tell us about her?" Liang said, pointing to the daughter. "Were you hiding her? What does she know?"

The girl looked at Liang, then at Lu. "Father told you already, we don't know where he went." She was completely calm. Like the prostitute at the station; Lu wanted to slap her in the face. Fen took the old woman outside. Her crying was breaking their concentration.

"Please," the father said, "he didn't tell us anything."

"Old man," Lu said, "shut up." His babbling was making him sick.

Lu looked around the kitchen: earthenware pots, shards of broken plates and cups scattered over the small counter and across the wood boards. Fen had broken all the windows in the process. The old man knew they would tear his home apart but still he had lied. Xiao-Di had swayed them somehow, convinced them he was someone else. Or else they would not have risked their own lives. The old man looked tired, scared. His eyes were half shut and Lu could see his chest rising and falling, as if his breath were failing him. This gave Lu some satisfaction. Fen and the old woman came back in. She was sobbing now, quietly. Liang lit a cigarette.

Lu went through the basket of clothes the girl had brought in. Half was dirty, half had been cleaned and was still wet. The father was going on again, that they knew nothing, that they had done nothing wrong. They let him talk. Then Lu saw the shirt, wet and gray with crimson letters across the chest. He could not read English but he recognized the characters. There were dark stains which the girl had not been able to wash out.

"She knows," he said. He had the shirt in his hand. He told her to stand.

"Soldier Lu, what are you doing?"

"Finishing this."

He walked over to the girl and pulled her up by her arm. They all saw the shirt. The girl looked to her parents, waiting for a sign what to do. Liang stood and said, "Let go of her." He drew his gun but did not point it. "Sit down."

Lu let go of the girl's arm and she sat back down. He returned to his seat next to Liang. Liang reholstered his sidearm, and Lu slammed his elbow up into the side of Liang's head. He stood over Liang, had his gun drawn. Liang lay at his feet, holding his head even though he was out.

Fen had his hands half up in the air.

"Give me your gun."

Fen looked back and forth between Lu and Liang lying on the floor. He handed over his gun. Lu wedged it inside the front of his pants. He told Fen to find some twine, to tie up the parents and girl.

"Make sure the boy outside is there. Tell him we'll be finished soon, to just wait. If you try anything, I'll shoot him." Fen looked down at Liang, then went outside. He came back quickly with some rope from the hut.

In their chairs Fen tied the family's hands behind their backs. Fen was moving too slowly and Lu told him to hurry up. He kept his eye on Liang, who was still unconscious on the floor. The mother and father were both crying now. Lu separated them so the parents sat together on one side with Fen guarding, Lu and the girl on the other side facing them.

"Please stop," the old man said. "We don't even know his name!"

Lu looked down at the daughter. Her face had lost its color. He admired her long hair and big pretty eyes. She was much prettier than Xiao-An. If it had been so easy to find Xiao-An for Little Brother, why did they never bother for him? He was the oldest son. He was entitled. His parents would have helped him marry first. They would have found him a pretty girl like this one, from the country. He could feel how easy and pure she was. How it would have been a pleasure for her to come to the city and be with a young man away from this farm.

He ripped down the front of her shirt. Her breasts fell out. They were small and white compared to the gold of her face. The mother was crying uncontrollably. The father was screaming, pleading. Lu thought of the prostitute from the police station, the dirty girl from Changsha. They were all the same.

He grabbed the girl by her hair, held her face close to his. "You're not saving anyone."

She tried to bite him. He smacked her in the mouth, then held her by her chin as she struggled to turn her face. He holstered his gun and pulled out his boot knife. Her skin in his hands was very soft. With a snap of the wrist he sliced a thin red line down the side of her face. The cut was long, deeper than he had wanted to go. The blood ran thin and fast down her face and over his fingers.

The old man was screaming. The girl was silent, in shock. Lu wiped the knife on his thigh and sheathed it. He drew his gun again. He told the old man to stand. The woman next to him had gone limp, like she had suffered some kind of attack. He tore down the old man's pants and shoved him back in his chair. The girl was screaming now. There was a tingle in his leg, but it did not hurt.

"Talk," he said. He looked at Fen, who was standing to the side of the old woman with his eyes down. Liang was still motionless on the floor. Lu grabbed the girl by the back of her neck. Blood dripped steadily from her face onto the floor.

Lu lifted her from her chair, pushed her to her knees in front of her father. He pointed the gun at her father's face, felt the strength of the girl's scrawny neck as he tried to push her head into the old man's lap. The old man was weeping like he had gone mad. The girl wouldn't budge, her body tight like a thin piece of metal. Her eyes were closed. Lu looked at the old man's limpness, how his legs shook.

"I fuck your mother," the old man said. He was looking up at Lu. "I fuck your grandmother, all your ancestors. I fuck their dirty cunts!"

Lu thought the girl was going to pass out, fall over. "He told me," the girl said. Her eyes were closed, her voice low. "He's going home."

Lu was looking at the girl and didn't see Fen jump. He had his arm around Lu's neck; could feel Fen's punches bouncing off him; he was grabbing for Lu's gun. Lu drove his knee between Fen's legs and sent him flying off. His gun was on the ground somewhere. He rushed Fen, took him by his neck, and drove him into the wall. He had his thumb pressing into Fen's right eye, was reaching for his knife with the other hand. Then he heard the pop, felt the liquid heat screaming through his leg. He felt empty very fast, his whole body. He tried to stand but could not. He couldn't breathe. He let go of Fen's neck and face and fell back. On the ground he lay level with Liang, whose eyes were open, gun in hand. His left leg, the one Xiao-Di had broken when they were boys, was smashed and bleeding again.

15

Dissident

On the highway I waved at every car that passed but no one would pick me up. I had nothing with me: no food, no extra clothes. I still looked like a farmhand, a beggar. I walked for a long time, kept my eyes open for military trucks or police vehicles, but there were none. If they came after me, what would I do? I wouldn't run, I knew this. That time was over.

Eventually I heard the loud sputtering of a truck. With the sun behind it I saw the silhouettes of men standing in the cab. I turned and waved with both hands. The truck came to a stop on the side of the road. I ran to catch up. The men in back were young and old, all different. I could tell from their clothes and the looks on their dark faces that they were from the country. They helped me up and asked where I was headed.

"The city," I said. "Looking for work."

"Just like us," one of them said.

"Where are you from?" another asked me.

"From the village."

"The village? Which village? Jade Hill? Red Sun Village? There are hundreds of villages."

I ignored him, leaned back and closed my eyes.

"You had better improve your attitude," the man said, "if you're going to find a job in Beijing."

We rode for over an hour. The men chattered, smoked. Some spoke dialects or had accents I couldn't understand. The wind of the highway did not bother them. Obviously they had all done this before. When we neared Beijing I could smell the city like I had never before, as if my senses had been cleansed up on the farm. Oily restaurant food, exhaust and fumes, smoke and dirt, garbage and refuse hidden down alleys. My home. When I'd returned from Cornell I'd had a similar shock, this feeling of loss like a soul trapped in the wrong body, a crossed dimension. But it was different now, worse.

In the streets I looked for signs of the military—trucks and APCs, packs of soldiers roving—but I saw only the occasional soldier or policeman coupled with a partner. I did not recognize the area where we stopped. A part of me was happy to be back in Beijing, the hugeness of the city engulfing. But there was still danger, for the things that had happened and what I'd done. I wanted to see my grandparents, make sure they were okay. I tried to detect any kind of tension in the air, but I felt nothing. It was like there had never been a movement in the square, like the city had not been infected and swept with change. Didn't they remember? The television cameras and reporters swarming? That buzz in the streets because the students were standing up? The hunger strike? Grandmother was right. We had risked our lives for the people—lost our lives. For what?

The streets were flooded with traffic. People sauntered the sidewalks and rode their bicycles casually. The gang-mix of their voices, but it was all different. I remembered the stony faces of all the men and women, young and old, well-off and poor. I didn't know any more, did not feel I could trust my perceptions. All that was clear was how the frenzy of the city controlled all our lives.

We came off the main road and pulled up to the gates of a factory. I thought we might be in the northwest sector where some of the big factories were. We got off the truck, and the driver told us to stand outside the gate. It was near evening, the sun glimmering in the pink haze. We stood and waited. A few of the men smoked and offered me cigarettes. I wanted nothing to do with these workers. I had heard of the men who came from the countryside to find private factory jobs, who walked the streets like vagrants. Now I was one of them? I just wanted to go home.

I told the man next to me that I had to go to the bathroom. He did not look at me or say anything back. I walked away and no one noticed. I turned a corner and kept walking.

The warmth of the air, I breathed in deep and tasted its metal thickness compared to the cleanness of the farm. It had only been a few days, but it felt much longer. As I walked I tried to recognize exactly where in the city I was. I felt like a stranger, unknowing, dropped in a new land. Not until I saw signs for the Temple of Earth and the Lama Temple, popular tourist attractions, did I realize I was directly north of Chang'an Avenue by two or three miles. I was so tired, and hungry. Even the greasy smell of food from the food stands and nearby restaurants was making my stomach roil. I would have done anything for that rough porridge the family had fed me those first few days, or even the slightest scrap of Grandmother's oldest leftover soup.

As I walked I realized I didn't know what day it was. From the number of people on the streets I thought it was a weekend. Couples were out strolling, mothers and fathers with their small children walking between them, in and out of restaurants and shopping plazas. I thought they might stare because I was dressed like a farmhand, but no one cared. When I'd first come back, everywhere I went people looked at me like I was different; now I had fallen below the fault line and did not exist. An old man sat on the side of the road fixing bicycles. He had bristly short gray hair and was missing his two front teeth. He looked up and said, "Need a ride? I'll sell you a bike. In ten minutes." I kept walking, heard him laughing behind me.

I meandered into the swimming crowd of people. On the sidewalk I stopped and looked into the stores. I contemplated groveling for a cup of dumpling soup or fried noodles, a piece of candy or cake. But I didn't. I thought of the woman at the food stand when Wong had offered to buy and I'd refused. I recalled all the food I'd thrown away at Cornell; I had habitually overordered and could never finish the hamburgers and french fries, pizza, soda, fried chicken. It made me sick to remember. I knew if I wasn't careful I could be accused of being a pickpocket or stealing from a street stand.

I found a newspaper and tucked it under my arm. I stood on the side of the road for a moment regaining my direction. I started walking. I looked on the street for lost change, hoping to scavenge enough to buy just one bite. In the storefront windows I saw my reflection. I stopped to touch my face and see myself. There were dark pockets under my eyes, the bones of my face sharp, my chin pointy, forehead too large. My face was stubbly, my head covered with nicks and nubs. I looked so skinny, sick, some deranged refugee, starving again.

I reached the *hutong* that night. I could feel my bones shaking with each step, my legs and feet stiff and sore, swollen from all the walking. I thought the *hutong* might be sealed off because of me, what I'd done, but it was clear. I could smell the communal bathroom. A few houses down I heard the welcome chatter of my neighbors in their homes, the air redolent of cooking: chicken and fish in frying oil; I thought I could pick out the sugar and garlic in the air, the light sweet spices. As I approached my door I stopped and listened, heard nothing. I could feel my grandparents' absence, not sure if this scared me or gave me greater relief.

The kitchen had been ransacked. Broken glass littered the counter and floor. The refrigerator had been overturned and its contents lay spilled and rotten, the awful wrenching stink. I knelt and ran my fingers through—I could not eat it. Pots, pans, and cups were scattered all about. They had cut open the padding of Grandfather's favorite chair. In the bedroom the mattresses were sliced, torn through as if bandits had raided it for hidden gold. What could they have been looking for? In my room it was the same, torn casings and clothes, relics and mementos I'd collected over the years strewn about.

In the corner on the floor was my old photo album ripped into pieces. All the pictures were gone. I remembered the photos I'd taken of Elsie, her gold hair and white straight teeth. That smile. I wished I'd been able to take one of Xiao-Mei and her family, so I could remember them. I wondered who had done this, if they had taken my pictures for some sick kind of keepsake or evidence against me. But that was not important anymore.

In my grandparents' room there was junk piled on the ground. Their photos had been raided as well, but some remained scattered. I kneeled and sifted through. They were mostly pictures of me and Lu and a few of my grandparents. I found pictures of my parents when they were very young. I'd never seen them before. They stood together, holding hands, smiling. They were in a courtyard standing before a school. This was not the village where we had been born. They did not look like peasants. The parents I never knew, who I loved in the sickest hurting way.

I found one of myself and Lu and my grandparents. Grandmother is sitting with me on her lap. Lu stands to her right, and Grandfather stands behind us. We are all dressed in our finest clothes: Lu and I in dark pants and white shirts, shoes that shine. I don't remember ever having such nice shoes. Grandmother and Grandfather wear clean, pressed tunics. I am no more than four years old. Lu looks so much bigger than me. The skin on his face is clear. Lu and I are smiling. My grandparents are smiling. I didn't know for what occasion this was taken, nor did I remember posing for it. Lu is holding my hand. Grandfather's eyes are clear, staring with strength and confidence. Grandmother is smiling with her arms wrapped around my waist.

I went back to the kitchen and sat in the middle of the mess. I had the picture in my hands, pressed it to my face. I was crying, trying to hold in the sounds pouring out. I could not. I wanted to be a boy again and live with Lu and my grandparents and be happy. So that none of this would have happened. So we could be together.

I was so tired, I didn't know what to do. I could go nowhere else. I felt empty and light, raw, like something had torn out my insides.

Later I picked up the paper and looked at the date. I was still not sure if it was today's paper or yesterday's. I wanted to read to take my mind away. There was news about thieves who had been raiding a cemetery and stealing flowers left for the dead, to resell on the sides of roads. A notorious prostitute was publicly executed. There had been a significant rise in Japanese investors in Chinese land development and business over the last year. Nothing about the demonstrations, the students, the square.

Until I reached the back page and saw their faces in print, their names and the accusations. Over twenty of them, mostly students, some young workers, were listed in three long rows. Their pictures, in black-and-white, seemed copied out of a police book of criminals, all sullen and gray. No one was smiling. These were the leaders Wong and I had seen in the square, exhorting and challenging, giving speeches and moving testimonies as to why we needed to do what we were doing. Where were they now? What had happened to them, their families? The young men and women who had risked their own lives and so many others. I glanced through the names and captions and felt things twisting inside me. I read the fabricated stories of their evil intentions to establish a new counterrevolutionary hierarchy. Some were foreign spies. They were all conspirators planning to overthrow the government.

I came to the bottom of the page. My name and face were nowhere to be found.

* * *

When they came for me I did not struggle. It was the middle of the night. I was sleeping on my bed, on top of all the rubble. I was dreaming that Lu was next to me, nearly crowding me to the floor. I was about to fall. Then I opened my eyes and saw the soldiers and men. There were close to a dozen of them. They came in pushing and grabbing, had guns drawn. They were screaming at me not to move.

Outside there were two cars and an armored truck. People were out in the *hutong*, watching. My hands were cuffed behind my back, my feet shackled. I looked at all of the people, my neighbors, who had known me since I was a boy. I tried to meet each one's eyes even though it was dark. I wanted them to see me one last time, and remember. Lu was not there. I had thought he would be here when it happened, but I was wrong.

They kept me in a cell, but not in a jail. When they beat me and I screamed no one seemed to care. Twice a day they gave me a ground, soupy millet and a glass of filmy water. It made my stomach hurt and turn. I called out to the guard, but no one came. I shit on the floor. When the guard returned he hit me twice in the face and knocked me to the bed. "Pig," he said. People came to clean it, but I did not look up. Afterward my stomach felt knotted and bloated at the same time. I wondered if I had contracted some kind of disease, either out in the countryside or by eating the gruel, an infection they had purposely delivered into my system. They forced me to eat it, even when my mouth was too swollen and my jaw was nearly locked shut. I knew they would not kill me, would not let me die. It made me more afraid.

When I was alone in the cell my hands were not bound, but when the interrogators came a guard always tied my wrists tightly before marching me through the white halls. Once inside the questioning room they tied my hands behind the back of the chair with rope or wire. The main interrogator was a short, stubby man with very white skin and black eyes. His head was shaved to the scalp. His partner, an older, fatter man, sat off to the side.

"You're working for American intelligence. You were planted by the American government to start the student uprising."

"No."

"You didn't study in America? No one from their government ever contacted you or paid you for information?"

"I went to school there, but I studied math."

The interrogator smashed me with a backhand across the face. At this point I felt the thud but no pain.

"Who did you plot with at Beijing Normal University? You were spotted on campus several times. Who were the leaders of your gang?"

"Wong . . . He's dead. You killed him already."

The interrogator looked at his partner sitting across the room. The sitting man wrote something down on a pad. The interrogator looked back at me and slammed me again in the head.

When this team finished another came in and started all over again. I started recognizing patterns in their technique. The first team was always violent and quick to punch and kick. Other teams liked to yell, their stinking mouths inches from my face. I thought, What can you do to me? They would not let me bathe. I could smell myself, and yet the odor of the interrogators—their rotten teeth and cigarette breath—I picked out like an animal sensing danger. They came in waves, two by two, for much of the day. They asked the same questions in different ways. They were trying to wear me down, make me sign the confession they laid out before me. It was several pages thick. I would not even read the first words.

The team I hated most was two skinny men. They never touched me, never berated or threatened. They usually came last in the order. Instead of one walking and one standing, both sat close to me and just talked. They had smooth calm voices like my Cornell professors delivering lectures. They said I could walk out and be a free man if I just gave up the right names, said the right words.

"You'll be out in two years, maybe three. Culpability is important in being a good-standing citizen of the people. You know this. I know you do." They said this over and over again. They wouldn't hurt me anymore if I cooperated. They offered me tea and better food. At times they sat quietly humming and singing. "What's your favorite music?" they asked. They would try to harmonize and could not. They laughed at themselves when they heard how bad they were. They said they would bring me to my grandparents within twenty-four hours if I just told them everything. "Your grandparents are fine," they said. "And your brother. They're waiting for you. You want to see them, don't you? Look at all the trouble you've caused. You don't want to cause any more, do you? Think of them. Let it end here. Sign the paper."

I told them again that I was not a spy. I had come back from America, had no job; my ex-girlfriend's father was screwing me. My grandparents were old and sick. I was angry, frustrated, like all of us were. But we were not trying to overthrow the government. We wanted to exercise some freedom, make our point, have our voices heard. Because we had been silent so long, the whole nation conditioned like zombies. The student movement was democratic, judicious. Our right to demonstrate was stated in China's constitution. We were practicing our rights.

"We have the tape of you denouncing the Party, the socialist state," the interrogator said. "Even Comrade Deng Xiaoping by name! And that trick, standing in front of the tanks. You expect us to believe you don't have political affiliations? That you're some random boy with a lot of guts? You must think we're idiots."

"You are," I said. I thought they would hit me, but they did not. I did not have to look up to see the disappointment in the interrogators' faces.

They took me back to my cell. With my arms still bound they gave me shots out of a long needle, and even this did not hurt or scare me anymore. After the shots, two a day, I'd feel drowsy, the heavy wave pulsing through my limbs and head and chest. Was this some kind of truth serum? I was telling the truth.

They came in to feed me once more, and I spat the gruel back in the guard's hands. The guard railed me with a fist to the head and I lay back laughing because this time I felt the pain. I tasted my blood dripping from the reopened wound on my head, felt it sliding in a warm thin line down my face.

*   *   *

They had to restitch my head. Had the guard who had struck me been punished for what had happened? I did not feel hate or wish for vengeance upon any of them. None of them had faces anymore. Where was Big Brother Lu now? He was a soldier, it was his job to protect me. The People's Army protected the people. Big Brother protects Little Brother. So where was Lu? I wanted to know.

The next day the interrogation continued. I had lost count of the days. It could have been two or five, maybe less or more. It was one long, black dream. The questions: Who are you working with? Who are your contacts in America? Taiwan? What was your secret plan behind the student movement? What other dissidents do you know who are hiding? Give them up and we will be lenient with your sentence.

"Sign the confession," they said. "Just sign." As if they were getting tired of this game as well.

I did not incite the guards by spitting food at them anymore. I said, "I've told you already." They didn't hit me anymore. No one was getting anywhere. I told them the same things over and over because there was nothing left to tell. Until the day they realized I was telling the truth, or the day they got tired and angry enough to kill me. If it was Lu asking the questions, maybe I would have budged, made up a lie just to give Big Brother something to go back to the authorities with. It would make him look good in the eyes of the people. He'd be a hero, a savior of some kind. But I never saw Lu in those rooms, and to these people I had no allegiance, nor any kind of truth to bestow.

The interrogators did not come in for a day. A guard came instead. He said, "You stink like a dead mule." They let me shower. I saw how bruised and wrecked I was. I could see the outline of my ribs, the pointed corners of my hips. My old Americanized body, tough and hard with muscle, was a memory. I was skeletal now, had never looked this way in my life, not even at our poorest when I was a child. It hurt to move my arms across my body, to bend at the waist to wash my legs. My joints felt locked as if by some magic or rot of flesh.

When I got back to my cell there were two slim packs on the floor by my bed, tied together by string. In one pack were envelopes of varying shapes and sizes, white and pink and parchment. The handwriting was in different colors—red, blue, black, green. My grandparents' address was written in English. In the lower right corner she had printed my name and address in Chinese.

The other was a pack of my letters to her. The handwriting was stiff, black ink on white paper. All the envelopes were cut neatly open across the top.

16

Comrade

Beijing, 1969

They took him and his wife away early in the morning as the sun was rising, the sounds of birds waking and calling in the distance. They were led to a car by three men Deng had seen before, though he did not know their names. Maybe part of Mao's personal squad of bodyguards, men who had protected them in the past; now they were Deng's jailers and keepers. Indeed this was important then, for Mao to sacrifice his own protection, at least for this day.

It was October and turning chilly. Zhuo-Lin held his arm and pressed against his side. She was crying. They took between the two of them only one suitcase filled with clothes. They had no pictures, no mementos. He patted her arm and whispered that things would be okay. Even if he did not believe it, this was what he had to portray.

"Where are we going?" Deng asked.

"Quiet," the driver said.

"All I'm asking—"

"Nanchang. It's a long time on the road. Don't make this hard."

He could see the driver's eyes in the rearview mirror, the quiet trouble in the young man's face. None of the other guards spoke, not even among themselves.

It took them three days to get to Nanchang. When they arrived they were met by a provincial army officer. Deng could tell by his uniform, reading the rank on the soldier's sleeve. He was tall and lanky, but with a fat head and bloated red face. The guards who had driven them down stood behind Deng and Zhuo-Lin. The officer said, "You are under military arrest. As criminals of the state, you are allowed no contact with anyone, no communications. You are subject to the confines and regulations of all state criminals. Is this understood?"

The officer's voice was shaky. Deng nodded and took Zhuo-Lin by the arm. They were marched into a small building and to a room on the first floor. There was an old dirty bed on a rickety frame, cement floors and walls covered with mold and dust. No windows. A sink and a small toilet. No mirror. The door was shut behind them. Zhuo-Lin lay down on the bed, ignoring the stink and dirt. They had driven very far and eaten little, slept at military outposts in barracks guarded by dozens of men. They did not know where their children were, what was happening to them. Who knew what Mao would declare next, to perpetuate the revolution. It was unstoppable. Deng sat down next to his wife and held her hand, stroked her hair, and told her he would take care of them, that in the end all this would straighten itself out and everything would make sense.

* * *

Days later two guards came to take them. Not the same guards who had driven them down to Nanchang, but new men he had never seen. One of the older soldiers said, "Come on, we're going," and ordered them into the car. The other soldier who accompanied them was young with a smooth face. Deng saw the soldier looking at him and Zhuo-Lin as if staring at a pair of apparitions, heroes or villains unsure.

They were taken to an old school just outside the city that had been shut down since the launch of dongluan, chaos. The grounds of the campus were grown up in weeds. There were random broken windows along the sides of the main building, like a plague had driven off or destroyed the student body. Behind the main building was a small compound. The car stopped and they were told to get out. Guards stood at the compound gates. They saluted the two soldiers, who walked up in front of Deng and Zhuo-Lin. Then the guards led them through the gates, and the soldiers did not salute nor did they meet Deng's eyes.

It was a two-story bamboo house with a balcony overlooking a large courtyard. A high metal fence surrounded it. The rooms were large and Deng was grateful that they had been taken out of that awful cell. They had the whole house to themselves, and it felt eerie and cold. Outside the high fence were the compound guards' quarters. He looked at Zhuo-Lin. She did not cry anymore now that she had had time to adjust to the situation. But he still sensed that guarded sadness, as if she were afraid to show her weakness, even to the only person in the world right now who understood.

That night guards gave them two bowls of corn glue, some dried pork fried with leeks, and two packs of cigarettes. Zhuo-Lin took it and Deng said to the guards, "My children. I want to know where they are. What's happening."

The guards traded glances, then turned and started walking. He called out to them, pleaded to their backs, but the guards kept walking and did not turn or say a word.

*   *   *

In the mornings he went to the backyard and chopped wood and shoveled coal for their needs. He was sixty-five years old and doing manual labor and it did not bother him. He had accomplished and endured far greater challenges—as had Zhuo-Lin—and this would be just another test to overcome. He tried not to think of why Mao had banished him, why he was not allowed contact with his children. But then he could not help it; he wondered if he had done the right thing. He could have supported the Chairman's urge to create this new revolution, to rile the masses once again, as they had in order to defeat the Nationalists twenty years ago. "We should be the most powerful nation in the world," Mao said. "But the people are getting lazy, weak. We need to raise them to action." But it was the wrong thing—there was no defined point, or purpose. He had already begun to wonder about Mao's sanity, his paranoia. Deng opposed the idea of the Cultural Revolution and said so. So now this. He accepted it all as fact. It was the only way to move forward. To waste his mental energy wondering would do him and Zhuo-Lin no good.

During the days they went to work at a tractor-repair factory. The factory was not far away and they were escorted each morning and evening, there and back, by guards from the compound. They did not learn any of the guards' names, but soon Deng was sharing cigarettes with the young guards and they opened up to him only so much. They knew him, what he had done, the old soldier and revolutionary forever. In their expressions and body language, though they tried to hide it, Deng could feel their respect. He felt traces of his past standing side by side with young fighting men.

At the factory no one spoke to him. They showed him the work he was responsible for on the line and that was all. He worked with men and women, all ages, all kinds. He thought he could pick out the schoolteacher who had spoken too liberally in class, accused of spreading capitalist rhetoric; the factory chief corrupt and loose with his rules; the relatives of landlords and rightists, guilty by association. His crime: not showing Mao his full support. That was enough, that slight trace of doubt. Zhuo-Lin's crime: being his wife. All the same. All in need of reeducation.

When it was mealtime he and Zhuo-Lin ate together and people did not bother them. They did their work as best they could, did not complain or try to get easier tasks farther up or down the line. Zhuo-Lin cleaned coils of wire. Deng chipped rust and dead metal from wheels and engine frames. They worked hard and the other workers appreciated this and let them be. Deng joked with his wife, "I worked in factories when I was sixteen in France. I think I'm regressing." Zhuo-Lin laughed but said nothing in return.

Some mornings they were not escorted to the factory but instead were taken from the compound and walked farther down the road to a clearing where dozens of soldiers and guards and peasants all met. Here Deng and Zhuo-Lin wore the wood placards draped around their necks, CAPITALIST PIG or RIGHTIST COUNTERREVOLUTIONARY. They gave speeches of self-criticism, and when that wasn't enough they were made to do the airplane—a wood plank strapped across their shoulders, behind their necks, tied to their elbows and wrists—as they were spat upon and kicked and beaten, a cacophony of mad voices surrounding. They witnessed the trials and beatings of many others and learned to live with this. Deng wrote self-criticisms and letters and asked the guards to give them to their superior, who would hopefully mail them to Beijing. He wanted to show Mao he was repentant, wanted to prove he still believed. He did not know if the letters were ever mailed or received.

They still knew nothing about Zhifang or Mao-Mao or Pufang. As if they had all fallen off separate ends of the earth.

*   *   *

Winter passed with him reading whatever books he could get his hands on and playing solitaire in the study because he had no partners for bridge. Then the spring came and Deng and Zhuo-Lin gardened in a small patch in the courtyard. They planted cabbage, beans, chilies, and squash. They raised chickens for eggs and meat. They became self-sufficient and they went through their daily routine to kill the worry about their children. It had been months now since they had heard any news. Their children were alive, that was all anyone would tell them.

Until one of the guards came to get him in the courtyard. He'd developed the habit of walking the perimeter of the courtyard to think and rest. He had finished his chores and completed his work at the factory. Zhuo-Lin was inside preparing dinner. A knock came at the door and Deng kept walking, did not break his usual routine. It normally took him over an hour to complete this, and if he broke his concentration he'd lose track of how many steps he had taken, where he was.

A soldier came into the courtyard with Zhuo-Lin. He said to Deng, "The commander would like to see you." Deng stopped walking, kicked his feet lightly against the fence to knock away the dust. He followed the soldier out front where another soldier and a car waited. Zhuo-Lin trailed them and the soldiers told her she could not come.

"Why? Where are you taking him?"

Deng looked at her and raised his hand. "I'll be right back."

It was a short trip to a huge house flanked by the flat spread of fields and trees. The soldiers walked Deng through the front door. Inside the housekeeper stared at Deng, awestruck. They walked by the housekeeper and into a large living room with a big sofa and ornate paintings on the walls, a glass table upon which sat a tea set. A man in a crisp navy tunic sat on the sofa with his legs crossed, sipping a cup of tea. He had black-and-gray hair combed back, smooth with oil, thin wrinkles in his forehead and in the corners of his mouth. He reminded Deng of a young Zhou Enlai, handsome and well kept. Deng had never seen him before, knew he was only a district commander. He did not stand to greet Deng and did not welcome him or say anything except, "I have information about your children."

The soldiers left. Deng was still standing. The commander also stood.

"Your daughter and younger boy are in Shaanxi, in the countryside. They are in good health and are being treated well. Their reeducation is proceeding nicely."

"Good," said Deng. "That's very good."

"Your older boy, Deng Pufang," the commander said, "is in Beijing Hospital." He sipped his tea. He did not look at Deng. From another room Deng could hear children playing, a woman calling out in the background.

"What . . . what happened? What's wrong?"

The man put down his teacup. He walked around as Deng stood still in the center of the room. The man sighed.

"He fell out of a window and broke his back." He turned to look at Deng. "It was an accident," he said.

"Accident."

"He started a brawl with a Red Guard faction. That's all I can tell you. He's lucky to be alive."

The soldiers came to take him away. They looked somber and worried, as if they had heard and understood. It was dark now as they drove home over the crumbled concrete and dirt roads. Through the open window the cold wind blew on his face. He had not eaten in hours but he was not hungry. Dinner would be cold. He thought of Mao-Mao and Zhifang living in the countryside, a place they had never known. Who knew what was happening to them, what kind of ridiculous torture and pain they were sustaining because they were born of his blood. The transplanting and test of their lives. It had happened to him before, and though he had conditioned and convinced himself that this was the price of the life he had chosen, it hurt him to think his wife and children were suffering for choices he had made. He wished he had never chosen the revolutionary life. Not because he had been banished and punished for what he believed, and not because of what was happening to Mao-Mao and Zhifang. They had never been pampered growing up; they would not break. He could accept all this: it made a certain strategic sense he could live with, deal with pragmatically. It was the thought of telling his wife that Pufang was in a hospital, their son's spine broken in two, that made him not want to live.

*   *   *

He had rested for a few days, taken the doctor's pills, slept well, recuperated. He had needed it, felt fresh again. He read the Public and State Security reports on rumors about his own assassination, or that he had had a heart attack, explaining why he had made no public appearances, no attempts to personally calm the situation or speak to the people. He should have expected this, from the public political differences that had been on display between Zhao Ziyang and Li Peng, the rest of them. It had been like this in the days of Mao as well. When things were not perfect and right, people would talk, instigators trying to take advantage. Now he would show them that they were all wrong. He felt better than he had in months. The nation was coming to peace again. The chaos and turmoil were over. He, and the Party, were still in control.

He could hear the hall filling up outside as he sat in back with a handful of advisors and guards. All of them were nervously smoking. President Yang Shangkun and Premier Li Peng had taken their seats outside. They had recently come to the decision to replace Zhao Ziyang with Shanghai Party secretary Jiang Zemin, a conservative who would help win public support. He was in his early sixties, a hard-line straight talker with enough political experience to be able to look forward without treading on the past. A more likable, flexible man than Li Peng, but not loose or unpredictable. Li Peng wanted to be general secretary, Deng knew this. But the public hated Li Peng, had criticized him too much. He stirred their bad blood. They could afford no more turmoil inside the Party, no more public splits in ideology. Jiang Zemin was in, and their position was solidified.

Deng went through the files of official incidents, kills, and deaths: dozens of soldiers dead, hundreds wounded. There was no official count yet on student and civilian casualties. The exaggerated numbers touted by the international press and floating from the lips of the people were not important to Deng. They were unofficial. He was talking today to officers at the corps level and above from the martial law enforcement troops—the Public Security Bureau, the Armed Police, the PLA. He leafed through intelligence and press photos of troops that had been mauled, nearly dismembered by angry crowds; bodies naked and burned; soldiers and police being attacked with clubs and sticks, punched and kicked by mobs. Bloated corpses bursting their green uniforms. It brought back the memories of all the fighting he had lived through and endured his entire life. Deng wanted the troops to know and feel his appreciation and pain, knew that they needed it. Without it much of their cause would be lost.

He was led out to the stage. He strode up to the podium. There were bright hot lights on him. He could not see past the glare, but he could feel the crowd gathered, several hundred men in the auditorium, hear the shuffle of chairs and the roar of applause when he appeared. They did not stop clapping until he raised his hand. He could feel everyone watching him. He laid his notes on the podium, adjusted the microphone, and looked past the glare into the dark sea of faces.

"You comrades have been working hard!"

His voice echoed through the sound system, huge and booming. There was a rush of applause. He did not smile. He had to look harder and tougher for his men. He imagined himself twenty or thirty years ago, when his vigor flowed at a level he could no longer match.

"To begin I would like to express my profound condolences to the officers and soldiers of the People's Liberation Army, the People's Armed Police, and public security officers and police who died heroic deaths in this struggle! And to all those who were injured defending the state and the people! I propose that we all rise and stand in silent tribute to those martyrs."

Everyone stood. He counted thirty ticks in his head. There was no sound. He could feel the room gelling, the nervous rustling edge melting. This was what he wanted. He looked up and adjusted the microphone again, cleared his throat.

"This disturbance would have come anyway. It was destined to come and an outbreak of this kind is independent of man's will. It was just a question of happening sooner or later, and of how serious the aftermath would be. It is to our advantage that there still exists in the Party a large group of veteran revolutionaries who have experienced many disturbances and understand how to weigh the advantages and disadvantages of affairs. They support resolute actions against rebellion. Some comrades do not understand that right now, but they will eventually support the decision of the Party Central leadership.

"It all became clear once the incident broke out. The rebels had two key slogans: to overthrow the Communist Party, and to topple the socialist system. Their aim was to establish a bourgeois republic totally dependent on the West.

"In putting down the rebellion, many of our comrades were injured or even killed. It was a severe political test for our army to handle this incident. Practice shows that our People's Liberation Army has passed the test. Using the tanks to run over the demonstrators would have brought about confusion in the entire country regarding right and wrong. Therefore, I must thank the PLA officers and men for their attitude in handling the incident of the rebellion. It showed everyone what type of people the PLA soldiers really are, whether there was a bloodbath in the square, and who really shed blood."

As he spoke he could feel them absorbing the words. He talked about the rebels and how their purpose was to give rebirth to *dongluan*—chaos. He kept bringing up the bravery of the young soldiers who died defending the Party's cause. He criticized the United States for remarks made about the incident when they themselves unleashed troops regularly to brutalize protesters with far less sinister causes.

He talked about the power of the state, how they had hardly begun to harness and master the potential that could make China the giant of the world. They needed to put ills such as this behind them and look to an unlimited future. He needed to turn this from negatives into positives. They had to leave this room believing in who they were and what they did or else the cracks and dents in the armor would rust and rot the entire fabric of what they had constructed. This could not be allowed. It was why all this had happened: the sacrifice of a few lives to save those of the majority. Mao had preached this, too, as long as he could remember. So Deng spoke and the men believed.

" . . . and conscientiously sum up our experience and carry on what is right, correct what is wrong, and make efforts to improve what is unsatisfactory. In a word, we must sum up the present and look forward to the future."

He tipped his head slightly to signify that he was done. The agents in the front row rushed out on the stage as if to intercept invisible enemies. Bodyguards on the side of the stage walked out and escorted Deng off. Behind him was the racing roar of applause.

*　　*　　*

Later that night he waited in the screening room. The screen was blank. Months ago he had set up a satellite dish and now they had channels and shows transmitting from Hong Kong, Taiwan, Japan, other places halfway around the globe. Deng could spend hours clicking through the foreign lips and faces like a puppet show. Besides himself, only Pufang could go in the screening room and watch whatever, whenever he wished. But no one had watched much of anything recently. He especially had not. Every channel he clicked to, everywhere in the world it seemed, showed footage and broadcast stories on Tiananmen Square.

The door opened. It was Pufang. He saw his father and paused, as if deciding if he should enter or exit. He wheeled himself in. Deng saw the look on his son's face, haggard, frustrated, as if it had been his personal cause that had been silenced by the military. He knew Pufang was upset by the recent happenings, but they had not talked about any of it together. There was no need. Pufang wheeled himself into the aisle, next to his father, a two-foot gap between them.

"Nothing to watch?" Pufang said. He had in his lap a notepad, two thick paperback books. The covers were wrinkled and worn. More research for his foundation, Deng thought. The boy worked very hard.

"No, just . . . resting. Thinking."

Pufang leafed through one of his books, looked down at his pad. He said to his father, "Are you feeling okay? You should get more rest."

"I've been resting too much," Deng said. "That is the problem."

His son looked at him, said, "It's over now, Ba. It's finished. You don't have to worry anymore."

"You don't know what I worry about, Pufang. You never have. You will never have to."

They traded stares. He could not tell if his son was upset with him, testing him, or if they were both just tired. Or was he being supportive? He didn't know how to read his son, how much Pufang understood of the situation, what had happened with Zhao Ziyang, with Gorbachev, all the rebels and student leaders they were after now. Pufang knew things through his own network of connections—liberal connections, no less—but Deng did not pry any deeper. Pufang was his own man, and he would let him think his own thoughts. He was his own son, after all, and he understood loyalty.

"This whole thing," Pufang said. "I don't want you to get sick, Ba."

"Dreams," Deng said. "I've been having bad dreams. It's that medicine the doctor gave me." He lit a cigarette and said, "If you don't mind, Pufang, could you read in the study? There are some things I still want to finish here." His son nodded, then turned and wheeled himself up to the door. Deng looked at Pufang's wide thick shoulders pushing himself in the chair, felt proud. After all these years, he had adjusted and overcome the handicap, made himself his own man, with his own interests and determination. Pufang reached back and closed the door behind him.

He remembered those first days having Pufang back with them, seeing Pufang in his chair for the first time. He had expected the boy to stand up and walk, then the realization struck that he never would, would never see his boy tall and upright again. It made his heart cold and sick. They helped the boy to the bathroom, helped him bathe. He could do nothing by himself. They rubbed his back and legs, gave him massages, cooked for and fed him, treated him like a newborn. Pufang's depression made them more determined to be positive. It was possible—new medical advancements could not be underestimated. You just had to do your best and see. Thinking back now, he had never felt so close to his son as he did those days taking care of him in the wheelchair, tending to his every need. Closer than they had been when Pufang was a child. But Deng had been fighting a revolution back then.

He wanted to wash his brain out, clear himself so he could rest. His heart was pounding, his breath short. He did not understand why the prisoner would not confess, would not cooperate. He knew they were going to torture him, or worse, if he didn't. And yet he continued to defy. He didn't understand it.

He needed a drink but was too tired to call for tea. He turned on the big screen with the remote. The screen flashed and the volume was very loud. He turned the volume down. He flipped channels, found CCTV news. The pretty newscaster was talking about the national soccer team and its newest rising star, who was only seventeen years old. They had sent the boy to play in South America to prepare for the upcoming world games. He lived in a special facility just outside Shanghai with the rest of the team, where coaches had been hired to work only with him. He was a special boy who would bring honor and glory to his country and the people through his skills and talents. He could bring joy to the world by playing a harmless, juvenile game.

The prisoner could have done the same, brought pride and happiness to his family, his country. All the student protesters had that chance. If they only recognized what could and could not be done. So young, they did not see the world the way it needed to be seen, by the facts, not through the lens of unrealistic ideology. He blamed himself. He had given them the right to be selfish. The prisoner, all of them, would confess, or . . . he didn't want to think about it anymore. Deng wondered which one was worse: the brother who had turned on his nation, or the brother who had betrayed his own blood to serve it. If it was Deng who had been ordered to find his own brother, or his own son, he would have refused, or he would have tricked and lied his way out of it. He would never have been able to see through such a mission in his heart.

But it didn't matter because Deng had not been asked to. The soldier had, and he had done his job. It was over now.

*   *   *

He was with Mao, just the two of them. They were on a mountainside overlooking the diving ledges and spearing tips that reached up into the sky. It was cold. Both he and Mao wore gray tunics and wool pants, slippers. They were old men, both of them. They had no weapons, no maps or binoculars or tools they had carried with them in battle and on the Long March all those years. They sat together, smoking. Deng was reading to Mao the dissident's letters.

Mao said, "Little Soldier, you have repressed the revolution instead of supporting it. This is a mistake."

"No, it was counterrevolutionary. They were rebels, instigators. They were trying to overthrow the Party. All that we've created, built for them."

"Could children overthrow the Party, Xiaoping? We were men in our forties and fifties before we had really changed the world. Look at these letters you were so worried about—love letters. They're just children. Harmless."

Deng was getting angry. "We were part of the revolution since we were sixteen, seventeen years old. They called us children then, too. Look at what those children did during the Cultural Revolution—they nearly destroyed the country." He stared at Mao, knew he was challenging him. He was dreaming, so it did not matter. Mao could not hurt him, or any of them, anymore. Deng rolled the letters up like a baton.

"Those children," Mao said. "Their hearts were in the right places. I wanted to . . . to help them. All of us. The people were not happy. We had to make changes for the good of the people."

"No good was established for the people," Deng said.

"Things will always be like this, Xiaoping. They will never be fully settled, steady. We carry our customs, traditions, with us for thousands of years. But the people, what we do with our lives, it will never remain the same. The people will always change. They must change. There will always be conflict. We must always be in a state of chaos, emergency, to move forward."

"It's not true," Deng said. "I bring them peace. I bring them stability. It's what they want, what they need."

"How do we ever know what the people really need?" the ghost said.

The dissident had joined them, walked up from behind and sat next to Mao, away from Deng. His hair had grown back, was no longer shaved. His body was thicker, stronger now, like an athlete.

"This is the one," Mao said. Deng nodded.

"You caused quite a stir," Mao said to the dissident. "No one would ever have dared to talk to me like that. Do those kinds of things in my presence. Would you have?" Mao smiled at the dissident like they were friends, as if the dissident had gained Mao's respect. It made Deng angry to see this.

"We did nothing wrong," the dissident said. His voice in Chinese was different from what Deng had expected. He had heard it in the footage, but it had been dubbed over by the translator. Now it was steady and clear, as if he wielded a certain amount of legitimate authority.

Deng grabbed at his belt for a knife, his pistol, but he was bare. He wanted to lunge at the dissident, but Deng could not get up, could not feel his legs anymore, could not move. The dissident was staring at him, disdainful. He wanted to cut the dissident's throat, shoot him in the head, end it for good by himself. There was nothing he could do.

"I read your letters, saw all your pictures," Deng said, waving the cluster of paper in the dissident's face. "Your file, every word. You're no spy. That's why I don't understand why you did these things. How you could have done them yourself? I give you, all the people, a good life. And you turn on me because it's not good enough for you. You don't know how hard I've worked!"

"Chairman Mao," the dissident said. "You were a true Son of Heaven. But he is an imposter." He pointed at Deng. "We don't need him anymore."

The dissident stood, looked at Deng, then at Mao. Then he walked off the lip of the ledge, disappeared into the mist drifting through the mountains. Deng could stand now. He went to the edge and threw the handful of letters into the air, watched them spiral down into nothingness. The dissident was gone.

"We shouldn't be talking like this," Mao said. "Go home. This time is over." Mao stood and walked off the ledge, diving with his arms spread like swan's wings, vaporizing in the abyss.

He went home to his family. Pufang was a little boy, five years old. He had a bicycle, toys scattered. Deng was a young father, chasing the boy about. The boy was laughing, pedaling fast as his father chased him, riding circles around the small yard. Bugs flew about the blooming flowers. He caught his son and lifted him off the bicycle, and the boy shrieked, clapped his hands playfully, kicked his legs as if he were trying to run through the air. Deng held him close and kissed him on his forehead and face. He sat down with Pufang in his lap and played with the boy's feet. His little legs kept bouncing, as if he couldn't control them. Then he got up and ran. They played tag, chased each other. They kept laughing and running until they were both tired and out of breath.

Later Deng sat in a chair and the boy slept in Deng's lap, his tiny body collapsed. He kept stroking the length of Pufang's legs, imagining the power and strength of his son's body when he would someday grow to be a man, already knowing what kind of man he would be. He wished they could stay like this forever.

EPILOGUE

Her handwriting was loopy, swirling. The letters were arranged in chronological order. Who had done this? he thought. He saw notes in the margins, in Chinese, translations of what she had written. Nothing new or different or special that might tell him who had been reading. The paper was wrinkled, curled at the ends, as if the letters had been handled many times.

The first was dated February 1:

> *I miss you so much. I hate it here. I hate my life. I hate my parents. They are the same unreasonable snobs they have always been—closed-minded, shallow, unthinking, heartless. They don't care about me, they only care about themselves and their image. It's amazing to me that I come from their blood. Maybe I am adopted.*
>
> *I started working for the producer. It's rotten—all I do is answer his phone. And he flirts with me, stupid fat old man. There was a parade in Chinatown for Chinese New Year, with dragons and firecrackers, these girls dressed in pretty red dresses dancing. I thought of you, and the stories you used to tell me.*

February 22, she said,

> *I understand if you're angry with me, if you don't want to write back. I should have told you about James, but I didn't think there was anything to tell. Would you really have stayed here to be with me? You would have. It makes my heart hurt to know that.*
>
> *James and I aren't together and we never will be. I told him this. My parents are so mad at me. Those last weeks at Cornell, I thought that in the end I would be strong enough to make a decision for myself and not because of my parents. But I was wrong. I wish I could have been strong, like you. I see now how hard it must have been for you to*

come over here and do the things you did. And you did great. I'm so proud of you. I want to call you but the number will show up on the phone bill, and my parents will freak out. I told them about you. I haven't spoken to either of them in almost a week. At least I saved you from them.

March 15, a short letter with a picture. She was kneeling on the sidewalk with a fluffy gray dog. He had never seen such a dog; he wondered if it was hers or some stranger's. Who was she with? Who had taken the picture? She was smiling. She looked happy. Was her hair shorter? Was she wearing more, or less, makeup? Had she gained weight? She had changed, but he could not say exactly how.

April 8, she said,

> *I'll be in a store or in the car and I'll just start talking like you're there. But you're not, and it's at that point I realize how stupid I was. How this is all my fault. I have no one to argue with, no one to tell me stories, show me new things. I have no friends. I don't belong here. For no reason I feel like I want to cry.*
>
> *I've called you three times. But I keep getting your grandmother. I tried telling her who I was, but we couldn't understand each other. Did you get any of my messages? Your grandmother sounded like she was yelling at me. Then she just hung up. I just wanted to talk to you for a minute. I just wanted to hear your voice.*

He read all the letters slowly, carefully, word by word. He had some trouble with her handwriting, the translation. He kept seeing the mystery editor's notes every few pages. When he finished, he skimmed them all again.

He did not reread the letters he had written to her. She had never heard his complaints or read his tirades, understood what he felt and thought. She would never know how they had existed, for these past brief months, on the same plain. He wanted to be angry with his grandmother, but he did not have the energy. At this point he believed he almost understood how his grandmother thought and felt. How would any of this have changed him, if he'd had the chance to communicate with Elsie, to keep that long line open, even from such a distance? Would it have made things better or worse? Too much had happened. He could not say. He wiped his eyes and face with the palm of his hand. He kept all the letters bundled up close to him.

Her last letter, May 14. She said,

> *I'm sorry I haven't written in a little while. Then again, you haven't written me at all. I hope you are getting these. I hope you are reading them and understanding what I'm saying, why I'm saying these things. You must be very angry with me still. I know I hurt you.*

And I'm sorry. But this is the way things have gone, and we both have to deal with it. I guess this is how you are dealing with it.

I've been watching all the news reports on Beijing and the student protests, the hunger strike that just started. I keep thinking about you. I have this strange feeling that you are out there, somewhere, in the middle of all those people. I have never seen so many people before! Tiananmen Square and Beijing look as beautiful as you said it was. I look for your face in the crowds.

From what I understand it's a very powerful thing that's happening over there. Maybe all those stories you told me about having no freedom and democracy will not always be true. These students are so courageous; watching them makes me feel selfish and weak. It's all over the news here. Everyone is talking about it.

I just want you to know that I still miss you and love you very much. I hope you are being careful with all the excitement that is going on. I hope you are not out there starving yourself. You like to eat too much, so I am not worried. I'm going to write again, but I want to tell you now that no matter what has happened, or happens in the future, I'm always going to remember you. You helped me grow, taught me things. You let me be and loved me for who and what I am, and I want to thank you for that. I hope you can feel and say the same about me. You will always be a part of me, somehow, my best friend.

Two guards came to get him. He grabbed all the letters, stuffed each pack in a front pocket. He thought the guards would cuff him and chain his feet, but they did not. They led him out front to a car. Where were they going? Maybe now was the execution, the end. He expected this, but he had no idea. The thought did not fill him with dread. He did not want to die but he was no longer afraid. He did not feel the need to struggle anymore.

It was a short drive to a building he thought was almost identical to the one they had just left. But there were many buildings like that in Beijing, short, gray, blocky. Walled in. Military or government buildings, he could tell from the barbed wire and soldiers with rifles posted at the gates. When the drivers pulled up to the gates they gave a quick wave to the soldiers out front. The soldiers, without nodding or acknowledging, opened the gates and let them through.

They took him inside the building. On the first floor they made him wait in a small room by himself. The walls were blank, the windows barred. He looked at the dusty gray floors. Where are my grandparents? he wondered. He thought about Xiao-An. He kept his hands pressed over the letters in his pockets.

The soldiers came back and told him to stand, move out. They led him back to the car.

Before he slumped in he saw his big brother, the soldier, sitting in back. He had blotchy bruises on his forehead and under his eyes. The left side of his face was swollen, as if stuffed full with cotton, the black scar riding down the right side of his face. The soldier was wearing gray pants, a loose white shirt similar to the prisoner's own. His hands and feet were not chained. The soldier's left leg was in splints, wrapped with bandages spotted brown and red. It looked crooked, limp, did not look right. The prisoner looked at the soldier's eyes. They were red, glassy.

The soldier looked up. They were both frozen, staring. The prisoner felt tears in his eyes, so tired and relieved and sad to see his big brother. He wanted to hug the soldier, be hugged. He wanted the soldier to tell him that the ride was over and everything would soon be safe.

"Xiao-Di," the soldier said. "We found you." The soldier leaned back and adjusted himself in his seat to make room for the prisoner.

"Lu, where have you . . . What happened to you? Lu . . . you need to get to a hospital. Your leg . . ."

"No, I'm fine. I can't feel it. It doesn't hurt anymore."

They looked away, then stared at each other again. They were frightened, embarrassed, happy. The prisoner leaned close to put his hand on the soldier's arm.

"No," the soldier said, "don't . . . don't touch me." He told the prisoner he thought his ribs had been broken, his collarbone, maybe some bones in his face. It hurt to breathe, to think, to move. Except his leg, which was dead, numb. If he could not see that it was still connected to his body, he would have thought it had been cut off.

The car was moving fast now. They did not look out the windows to see in which direction they were going.

"Lu, they called the army into Tiananmen Square."

"I know."

"How . . . how do you know? Where were you? Were you there?"

"We were looking for you, Xiao-Di. We were given orders." He looked away, sighed. He did not want to see the prisoner's face, even though he was so happy to be with his little brother again. The soldier did not know how to express this. He could not feel the muscles in his face, felt he had no control over his eyes. He could not tell the prisoner what had happened, what he had done. Maybe he would later, when things were peaceful and right and they could just sit and talk without repercussions. But how would he ever be able to explain what he had done to the preacher and the church, and to that family in the end? Were these his little brother's friends? Ultimately the soldier did not know what had happened to them. He had lost consciousness, saw from a different angle the girl's bleeding face. When he next awoke he was in a detention cell.

"They lied to me, Xiao-Di. I know that now. They lied to all of us."

"Lu, you're really hurt. We need to get you to a hospital."

The prisoner banged on the plastic divider that separated them from the two guards up front. He shouted at them to stop, to find a hospital and get help. They ignored him. The prisoner kept banging, then he stopped. The guards were unfazed, as if they were deaf, as if the prisoner did not have a voice.

"Xiao-Di, you don't look so good yourself."

"Grandma and Grandpa, have you seen them? Are they okay?"

"I saw them . . . about a week ago."

"Do you know where they are? Someone tore apart the house. Everything was wrecked. Grandma and Grandpa weren't there."

"Is that where they found you? In the house?"

The prisoner nodded, looked down at the floor, clasped his hands together between his knees. "I couldn't run anymore, Lu. I just wanted to come home."

"Okay," the soldier said. "It's going to be okay."

"Lu, who did this to you? Were you in the square? Did the students do this to you?"

"No," the soldier said. He wished he could say who exactly had done this to him, but he couldn't remember if it was the PSB agents or the guards in his cell. When his leg hurt so badly and he knew something was wrong he had screamed for help until his throat was hoarse and his lungs burned. Then he could not scream anymore. No one came. The leg stopped hurting. It didn't matter. They had all lied, were all the same.

"Xiao-Di," the soldier said. "They showed me these tapes of you. In the square, talking to reporters. You said things about Deng Xiaoping. And the tanks, on Chang'an Avenue." He paused, looked out his window, took a breath. "That's why we were looking for you."

The soldier watched the prisoner's face go stiff, then break down. The soldier knew already, but he wanted to hear it from the prisoner's own mouth, either absolve himself or confirm. The prisoner didn't know what to say, how to tell the soldier anything. He just wanted to hug the soldier, but he was afraid to touch him. Who could have beat his big brother so badly? Why?

"I can't explain, Lu. Not right now. I'm sorry."

"Don't be sorry. They lied. They all lied." The soldier was tired, the pain having absorbed all his energy. He wanted to close his eyes and sleep.

"Lu," the prisoner said. "Where are they taking us? Where are we going?"

The soldier had already closed his eyes, could not see the prisoner's face but could hear his voice drifting like he was dreaming.

"We're going to Grandma and Grandpa, that's where they're taking us. It's going to be fine. Everything's going to be fine."

The soldier could feel the prisoner's hand on his knee. Then he felt the prisoner pulling lightly on his shoulder, guiding him as he lay down across the backseat so he could rest his head on the prisoner's leg. He kept his feet down on the floor so they did not move his hurt leg. It felt good to lie down, to rest with his eyes closed. He had not seen his little brother in so long. He could feel the prisoner's leg quivering, shaking.

The prisoner looked down at the soldier's body. Who had done this to him, and why? His big brother's leg was ruined. The prisoner knew from the raggedy bandages and cracked splints that no one would be able to fix it. Someone had made sure of that. The prisoner gently touched the soldier's face, his hair. He let his hands rest on the soldier's shoulder. The soldier seemed to have fallen asleep, or was just resting well. The prisoner did not want to bother him. It was better this way. For now they had run out of things to say. They had never really known what to say. It was easier to be silent and together, so they were. The prisoner gazed out his window at the empty road.